Arthur Wollaston Hutton

The Vaccination Question

being the second issue of a letter addressed by permission in the autumn of 1894

to the Right Hon. H.H. Asquith

Arthur Wollaston Hutton

The Vaccination Question
being the second issue of a letter addressed by permission in the autumn of 1894 to the Right Hon. H.H. Asquith

ISBN/EAN: 9783337368302

Printed in Europe, USA, Canada, Australia, Japan

Cover: Foto ©Andreas Hilbeck / pixelio.de

More available books at **www.hansebooks.com**

THE
VACCINATION QUESTION

BEING THE SECOND ISSUE OF A LETTER ADDRESSED BY PERMISSION
IN THE AUTUMN OF 1894 TO THE

RIGHT HON. H. H. ASQUITH, Q.C., M.P.
At that time Home Secretary

TOGETHER WITH A LETTER ADDRESSED BY PERMISSION
IN THE AUTUMN OF 1895 TO THE

RIGHT HON. ARTHUR JAMES BALFOUR, M.P.
First Lord of the Treasury

BY

ARTHUR WOLLASTON HUTTON, M.A.
Formerly Scholar of Exeter College, Oxford
Librarian of the National Liberal Club

WITH NOTES AND CORRECTIONS TO THE LETTER TO MR ASQUITH

AND AN INDEX

Si quid novisti rectius istis,
Candidus imperti ; si non, his utere mecum
HOR. EP. I., vi. 67.

METHUEN & CO.
36 ESSEX STREET, W.C.
LONDON
1895

PREFACE.

THE exigencies of stereotype printing, coupled with a due regard to economy, have prevented me from making corrections and additions to the actual text of this second issue of my letter to Mr Asquith, which thus appears here (pp. 1-128) precisely as it did when first published in November 1894. But new matter will be found in the supplementary letter to Mr Balfour, as well as in the notes ; and the index enables me to call attention to the few points where correction had to be made.

I have reason to be satisfied with the reception given to my first issue. The subject is one that provokes feeling, perhaps even bitterness, on both sides. Anyone who adopts the cause of the "anti-vaccinators" is, *ipso facto*, reckoned by a vast number of people—who on any other subject would judge fairly and patiently—a crank, a faddist, and a fool. And, with that singular logic, characteristic of all controversies in which orthodoxy denounces heresy, the mere fact of his having lapsed into unorthodoxy deprives of all weight the arguments he may use ; and he has to console himself with the reflection that the heresy of to-day is often the orthodoxy of to-morrow. And, apart from the vehemence of the professional advocates of the accepted doctrine, he has also to reckon with the indifference of the great majority, whose mental lethargy resents the intrusion of criticism into what they had always understood to be a settled question.

It is to this indifference that I ascribe the fact that, with two or three exceptions, all the London daily papers, morning

v

and evening, ignored the publication of the book altogether. The *Times*, indeed, did not ignore me, but it thought it enough, with a lofty air of contempt, to use a correction on an unimportant point which I had myself privately communicated to the editor—the error itself being ultimately due to an uncorrected misprint in the *Times*—as a basis for a general charge of inaccuracy, a charge that it would have been impossible to sustain. There is no meaner method in controversy—though there is, I fear, none more common—than thus to ignore entirely the main line of the argument, and, with an affectation of being surprised and shocked, to kick up a dust over the discovery of some trifling inaccuracy of detail. In treating a subject-matter of this kind some inaccuracies are inevitable, however careful the writer may be. The question to consider is, whether the argument as a whole is not sound.

But the silence of the other papers is, to my thinking, less intelligible than the unfairness of the *Times*. Here is a question which even the *Lancet* admits to be "difficult and momentous." There have always been medical men disbelieving in vaccination, and their number to-day is rapidly increasing all the world over. This fact by itself renders grave the political side of the question—for a political question, not of course in the partisan sense, vaccination becomes when it is enforced by the State under penalties. And it is a burning question. The persons, otherwise blameless and intelligent citizens, who have been punished under our Vaccination Acts, are to be counted by thousands ; and in some cases penalties for resistance have been enforced that would be reckoned severe even for grave crimes. The Royal Commission has already reported unanimously against the rigour of the existing law ; and its final Report, awaited with much anxiety, many people anticipate will be adverse to compulsion altogether. The controversy is, moreover, a burning one all the world over, wherever vaccination is or has been enforced. And in Switzerland, as well as in some of our colonies, the victory is slowly but surely being won by those who oppose compulsion. Even where the law remains unrepealed, as in large districts in our midland counties, it has proved unworkable in practice, and any attempt to re-enforce it would almost certainly provoke riot and disorder. Such a question as this surely needs full and free discussion in the public press; yet our judicious editors can find no space even to mention a publication that might fairly claim to be a handy, readable and moderate statement of the case for repeal, appearing at a time when, so far as I know, no other such statement of the case as a whole was in existence.

A word of explanation, perhaps of apology, is due to those critics who complain of my language about medical men. Certainly I do not believe in their infallibility, nor does any sane man. They are very frequently mistaken, and they are far too apt to follow mere routine. But on p. 112 I give them a good word which is no more than their due; and, if elsewhere I make little account of the untested evidence they are so ready to be satisfied with in favour of vaccination, that is not because I think them careless or dis-honest, but because, through my acceptance of the Creighton-Crookshank doctrine, I am sure they are mistaken; and I only endeavour to point out how natural it is under the circumstances that they should quite honestly fall into a mistake. I do not pose as an independent medical critic of vaccination. If I did, it would have been my duty to offer myself as a witness before the Royal Commission. I am merely an item of the great British public, driven by circumstances to study the vaccination question, and thus led to accept that account of it given by medical men against whose learning and competence no one had a word to say until their studies in that question had landed them on the unorthodox side.

One word more by way of preface. A critic has complained that the section I have devoted to the practice of small-pox inoculation is "superfluous." This I cannot admit. There is no other method but the historical method that enables one to understand how a doctrine has come to be believed. To accept the belief in vaccination as established, and then to point out how experience confirms that belief, is not a scientific method of procedure. You must first show, historically, how the doctrine itself came to be believed; and if in so doing you are able to lay your finger on mistakes or misconceptions which led to that belief, you are then justified in scrutinising contemporary evidence keenly, for you may fairly anticipate that it is the belief which creates the alleged confirmatory experience, and not the experience that demands the belief. The parallel case of sundry theological doctrines aptly illustrates this view. High churchmen believe in baptismal regeneration, and find a confirmation of their belief in the virtues of baptised children. Catholics believe in transubstantiation, and find a similar confirmation in the saintly lives of those who receive the transubstantiated food. But is the evidence convincing? Surely only to those who were convinced already. A modern critic, using the historical method, gives a very different account in each case. He can trace the growth of these doctrines from their first beginnings, and can show how they were reached through exaggerations, misunderstandings, and interpolations in the text. That being done, the confirmatory evidence needs no refutation. Even those who take the other side must admit that it is neither so uniform nor so unique as to be by itself convincing. I need not point out how these beliefs correspond with the belief in vaccination ; what I am maintaining is the sole efficacy of the historical method in explaining and, therefore, in refuting an erroneous belief. To study critically the history of a dogma is practically to reject it, unless it be sound and true. And it is not only the origin and history of vaccination that needs to be looked into, if the question I am discussing is to be fairly considered. The history of epidemic diseases, how they move in cycles, how one prevails in one century and another in another, how they ebb and flow, and how, ultimately, they may disappear altogether,—all this must at least be noted and pondered over; else the student is liable to accept the fallacy which the late Dr Guy, judging solely by statistics, accepted—viz., that since small-pox has to a great extent died out in the course of this century—since 1780 would be more accurate—while scarlet-fever and measles have done so less markedly, or have even shown a growing tendency to prevail, *therefore* there must have been during this century some special power at work antagonistic to small-pox; and what is that power if it be not vaccination? The argument is plausible, and to believers convincing; but a student of the history of epidemic diseases, with a wider horizon open to his view, will see that the premises do not involve the conclusion.

THE VACCINATION QUESTION.

Dear Mr Asquith,—At a select social club in the
West-end of London vaccination is, I am told, one of four
subjects (the other three being politics, religion, and Wagner)
which members are forbidden to discuss, on the ground that
such discussion leads nowhere, and only ends in irritation.
Nevertheless, although this question is a vexed one, and in
some aspects a disagreeable one, I am disposed to hope
that the present moment is favourable for calling attention
to it, and that some few people at any rate may be willing
to reconsider their judgment concerning it, especially since,
as I think I shall be able to make clear, the question itself has
had much fresh light thrown upon it during the last ten
years, and the authority of great names can no longer be
quoted wholly on one side. I shall make no attempt to
conceal the facts that my convictions are on the side of
those who doubt and distrust vaccination, and that consequently I advocate the total and immediate repeal of the
compulsory laws ; and, as it would, I suppose, lie with you,
Sir, to introduce such a measure, should the Government
decide to adopt that policy, I wish to express first of all my
indebtedness to you for permitting me to address you on
the subject, though I have no reason to suppose that you
have at present any sympathy with the view that I take.
But I am not without hopes that, if you will give a fair

consideration to the points which I urge, you will be prepared to admit that the compulsory law, as it stands, is indefensible, and ought to be repealed without delay.

The Question not one that Medical Specialists alone are Qualified to Discuss.

At the outset I anticipate the objection that a layman has no business to discuss the vaccination question at all; that it is one on which professional men should lay down the law, which the rest of us have only to hear and obey. To that objection there is more than one sufficient answer. I will not content myself with the rhetorical reply—obvious as that is—that where doctors disagree the decision must lie elsewhere. Nor shall it be enough to point out that the question, as it now stands, is by no means a purely medical one; that, even though it were admitted on all hands that vaccination is a harmless operation affording permanent protection against small-pox, the question whether it should be enforced by law is a further and a political one, involving the consideration of a number of points that have nothing to do with medical science at all. And, even beyond this, supposing the right of the State established to enforce a medical dogma or a particular form of medical treatment, there would remain the question of the wisdom and the policy of compulsion; or, further, of its necessity at any given period. But I maintain that even in its purely medical aspect the value of vaccination is a point which any educated layman can easily qualify himself to discuss; and that to think otherwise is, either to attribute to medical men, as such, some mysterious esoteric wisdom, which they do not and cannot reasonably claim to possess, or else to confuse between what is and what is not within the reach of the intelligent outside observer. No doubt, in so far as medicine is an art, it belongs wholly to professional men, and a layman necessarily lacks that experience which alone can guarantee an accurate diagnosis—the one thing of first-rate importance in the physician's art. And in the art of surgery experience belongs even more exclusively to professional men. But, in so far as medicine is a science, what is there to prevent any educated man from learning all that is known about physiology, pathology, and pharmacy? Indeed, if he devotes his attention to any one special field of enquiry, he may easily be better informed in regard to it than a professional man, whose five years of technical training afforded him no special facilities for that particular study, and whose duties since he began to practice have left him little or no leisure for scientific studies at all. This is especially true of the vaccination question. I am informed on the best authority that medical students are taught nothing about the supposed scientific basis of the practice, and nothing about its origin and history. They are taught how to do it—and a child can do it—and how to watch, and, if necessary, alleviate its immediate effects. But its pathology is left out of account, and its prophylactic power is taken for granted, as if it were as indisputable as the purgative power of castor oil. Nor does subsequent experience do much to remove this ignorance; for that experience in the majority of cases, and in the case of nearly all medical men who have begun to practice since 1872, is of necessity extremely limited.* For, although the country is

* How little familiar some medical men are now with small-pox is seen in the fact that, during the slight epidemic of small-pox in London in 1892, out of 299 cases sent to the small-pox hospitals of the Metropolitan Asylums Board, 23, or nearly 8 per cent., proved on arrival to be not suffering from small-pox at all. These figures are taken from the Report for 1892 of the London County Council's Medical Officer of Health. The Metropolitan Asylums Board Report for 1893 shows some improvement, only 81 cases out of 2441 being sent in error to the

now less thorougly vaccinated than it was at the date just named, the vaccinated are still probably some 90 per cent. of the population; and this proportion, while there is so little small-pox about, gives medical men very few opportunities for studying the alleged susceptibility of the unvaccinated as compared with the alleged immunity of the vaccinated. This of course does not apply to those who have the care of patients in small-pox hospitals; and the evidence of these doctors consequently deserves the closest attention. My only point at present is this, that there is no occasion to defer to the opinion of the average medical man on this question of vaccination; for, so far from being an expert, he may know, of his own experience, little or nothing about the matter; while the sources from which he can obtain information at second-hand are equally open to laymen. No doubt, if a medical man, with his mind as free as possible from bias, makes a searching study of this question, scrutinising its history and pathology with all the apparatus that libraries and laboratories afford, his judgment should be treated as of corresponding weight, and should be preferred to that of a non-professional man working with less technical training in the same field. It is in fact on the judgment of such men that my own has been based, so far as the purely medical aspect of the subject is concerned. The great majority of the profession are, I know, on the other side; but it is not in the vote of the majority that scientific truth and progress are to be sought.

The point is an important one, and I may be pardoned if I pursue it a little further. A doctor may " successfully

small-pox hospital ships. The diseases mistaken for small-pox were mostly chicken-pox and syphilis; but fifteen other diseases were represented by nineteen cases in all; and four patients were sent who showed no symptom of any disease at all ! This does not promise well for the advocates of compulsory removal.

vaccinate" hundreds and thousands of children, and yet
never have any real evidence in any single case that the
operation has averted or modified an attack of small-pox.
People are perhaps misled in this matter by the use of the
word "successful." When a doctor certifies that he has
"successfully" vaccinated a child, he does not mean that
he has succeeded in protecting it against small-pox, though
it may be his opinion that he has done so; he merely means
that he has "succeeded," by the subcutaneous insertion
of the cow-pox virus, in raising the small bladder-like
structure known as the vaccine vesicle, which contains a
further supply of the virus, or "lymph," that may be used in
subsequent operations. That is all he knows about it at
the time, and, in the vast majority of cases, all he ever does
know about it. Occasionally a family doctor, who has his
eye on his patients from infancy to mature age, has the
opportunity for inferring more, should a small-pox epidemic
happen to invade his district. But even then, since
immunity from small-pox was known before vaccination
had been invented, and since, moreover, contact with the
infection cannot be taken for granted without proof, his
inference would fall far short of a demonstration of the
value of vaccination, unless he could adduce a variety of
cases in which, amidst other differing circumstances,
vaccination was the condition of escaping and non-vaccination the condition of catching the disease. Such evidence,
it need hardly be said, may be sought for in vain.

The question is, in fact, far less easily disposed of than
people are ready to imagine, if it is treated as a scientific
one, and not as one settled long ago in the affirmative by
authority. The critic's first difficulty is to establish the
proposition that there is any question at all; so prone are
the majority to treat vaccination as a simple subject,
perhaps of no great importance, but anyhow one on which

no one even pretends to have any doubt, save a few *mauvais sujets*, who will never accept anything on the authority of duly qualified men, and who, as individualists, are always making a fuss about their personal liberty being interfered with by the State. If this were all that could be urged against the practice, I should certainly not be writing to you, Sir, as I am now; for though, as an old-fashioned Liberal, I have misgivings about some of the doctrines of the new school, I still hold that, if the grounds on which compulsion was originally established were true, viz: that vaccination is the only generally available security against small-pox, that its performance involves no appreciable risk, and that a single vaccination in infancy secures life-long immunity, a strong case on behalf of compulsion would have been made out. But, as I hope shortly to show in detail, every one of these propositions is now questioned, even the warmest advocates of the practice admitting that the protection afforded by vaccination extends only for a period variously reckoned at from one to ten years, an admission which is of course fatal to the *raison d'être* of a law which enforces the vaccination of infants only.

On the other hand, it is fair to admit that, when once the question has been entrusted to the scientific crucible, the critic's task is an easier one than the advocate's. It is impossible rigidly to prove in any individual case that immunity from small-pox is due to vaccination; whereas in every case of the failure of vaccination to secure immunity we have a distinct contradiction of the theory of its prophylactic virtue. And, what is true of single cases is no less true of communities. If a well-vaccinated country enjoys for a long period immunity from small-pox, you cannot prove that vaccination was the cause of that immunity, unless you can show that there can have been no other cause. *Post hoc, ergo propter hoc* is a familiar fallacy which, I believe, has never been so fruitful of error as in this particular controversy. Whereas, unless, in a well-vaccinated country, small-pox invariably selects the un-vaccinated minority for its victims, the argument against the value of vaccination is a sound one. Vaccination, I do not deny, stands firmly established by law, by custom, by interest, and by the sincere belief of hundreds and thousands of persons; but for its establishment scientific-ally something very different is needed. A sound theory, verified habitually, and under circumstances so varied as to leave no reasonable opening for doubt—this would amply meet the case; but that these conditions are very far from being fulfilled is what I think I shall be able to show.

Apparent Strength of the Case as usually stated in favour of Vaccination.

I have been anxious to make these preliminary observa-tions, because it is only when people see that, in regard to scientific proof, the question, so far from being settled long ago in the affirmative, is almost of necessity an open one, that they are likely to be willing to give a fair consider-ation to a statement of the case which contradicts their pre-possessions. For myself, I will frankly confess that up to about 1887 I shared those prepossessions as fully as any one, and shrank from the anti-vaccinists as "faddists." Indeed, the case in favour of vaccination, as usually stated, seems at first sight almost unanswerable. It is not only to the com-paratively steady prevalence of small-pox in the last century and to our ordinary freedom from it now that you can point. The conversion by Jenner of the medical profession (with but few exceptions) within five years of his announcement of the virtues of cow-pox inoculation, is a most remarkable fact; but not more remarkable than the acceptance of the new doctrine, in spite of national jealousies, by the mass of medical men throughout the world. It is difficult to believe that so intensely conservative a profession could so rapidly have been converted to a delusion ; but it is even more difficult to believe that nearly a century should have been needed for the detection of the delusion. Then we have the extraordinary phenomenon of State after State, beginning with Bavaria in 1807 and ending with Italy in 1892, being so impressed with the immense value of the operation, that, although medical treatment had never before been thought a fit subject for legislative enforcement, they have insisted on vaccination by the imposition of penalties, which in our own country have gradually been made more severe. Surely, if ever there was a case in which the judgment of the civilised world might be reckoned as certain and secure, this would be the one. Such, at any rate, is the opinion one is apt to form after a superficial view of the circumstances of the case. What, in criticism of this view, I shall endeavour to point out in detail is, that the practice originated in what can now be clearly recognised as a mistake ; that there were reasons at the time for this mistake being honestly accepted with enthusiasm ; and that fashion, authority, custom, and interest are responsible for the establishment of the practice, and not the sober judgment of medical science. The key to the whole controversy will, I believe, be found if we strictly bear in mind that the history of vaccination corresponds rather to that of a religious dogma than to that of a scientific discovery ; and that the imposing terms in which its virtues are asserted are imposing in more senses than one, and no more prove the medical doctrine of cow-pox prophylaxy than the silver trumpets at St Peter's prove the theological doctrine of transubstantiation. A selection from official statistics is, no doubt, enough to satisfy those who have already made up their minds to be satisfied ; but, so far as I know, no one who has studied the history and pathology of vaccination has retained his faith in its alleged power.

SMALL-POX IN ENGLAND BEFORE THE USE OF INOCULATION.

The popular notion that in old times small-pox was a veritable plague, against which there was no protection, until in the eighteenth century the practice of inoculation afforded some relief, while the later discovery of vaccination provided an infallible defence against it, has little or no foundation in fact. It is only during the last two or three centuries that the disease has been thought of much account ; and it would almost seem that the special prominence given to it now is due to the interested advocacy of prophylactics against it, in respect to which it holds an unique position in the history of medicine. It is apparently of foreign origin, and has doubtless existed in India and in the East generally from a remote period. Probably it reached England, either through the medium of the Saracens at the time of the Crusades, or else through the Moors in Spain. John of Gaddesden, priest and physician, who died in 1361, wrote on it, and advocated its treatment by the use of red cloth. He asserted that by this method he had cured a son of Edward I. of the disease, which left no marks behind (*sine vestigio variolarum*)*.

* This red cloth treatment was doubtless oriental in its origin, as well as the disease itself; and it had at the first a religious significance, though later a therapeutic power, in bringing the disease to the surface, was attributed to it. The patient was wrapped in red cloth, and bed and window curtains of the same colour were used. The practice had not died out within the memory of persons still living ; and it has quite recently been revived by a Norwegian physician, Dr Svendsen of Bergen, who claims to have cured in this way four unvaccinated patients. See *British Medical Journal* for February 17, 1894. If it again becomes fashionable it will prove a formidable rival to vaccination.

Little, however, is said about it before the seventeenth century; indeed, until the time of Sydenham (died 1689) small-pox, measles, and scarlet-fever were frequently confused together. Two things, however, are clear, one being that the epidemics varied in old times, much as they do now, in severity as well as in extent; and that, under ordinary circumstances the disease was recognised as being by no means extraordinarily fatal, though that character is ascribed to the "flox," which was probably small-pox in its confluent form. Thus, Dr Plot, writing of an epidemic in Oxfordshire in 1677, says that it was "so favourable and kind, that, were the nurse but tolerably good, the patient seldom miscarried."* And immunity of those who attended to the sick was also not unknown in pre-vaccination days; we are told, for example, that, during an epidemic in New England in 1633, which was fatal to whole settlements of the native Indians, "only two families of the English who ministered to them took the infection."†

In the eighteenth century, however, both in this country and on the Continent, small-pox was recognised as a generally prevalent and very serious scourge,‡ and it was especially and very naturally dreaded by ladies, on account of its disfiguring effects. Yet it does not appear to have been more fatal than it ordinarily is now; the proportion of

* Creighton's "History of Epidemics in Great Britain," Vol. I., p. 467.

† Creighton, *ubi sup.*, Vol. I., p. 613. This incident is clearly parallel with a similar experience during Stanley's last African expedition, evidence concerning which was given by the late Surgeon Parke before the Royal Commission.

‡ The prevalence was not, however, universal. Thus it is recorded that at Boston, America, the disease died out in the early part of the eighteenth century, and that there was not a single case of it for nineteen years.

deaths to cases being then, as now, according to a variety
of authorities from 18 to 19 per cent., or less than one in
five. But it was undoubtedly more constant in its presence
than it has been in our own century; insomuch that it came
to be regarded as one of those things that must be gone
through—just as measles are still regarded in many old-
fashioned families—and everyone's anxiety was consequently
to get through it as easily as possible and to escape disfigure-
ment. Probably better nursing and more rational treatment
would in most cases have secured exemption from "pitting";
but it was difficult to escape contact with the disease altogether when the sanitary conditions, under which even
Royalty in those days lived, encouraged the prevalence ot
the infection. Anyhow, the state of mind which regarded
small-pox as almost inevitable was favourable to the reception of an operation which promised alleviation where
exemption was impossible. Only in this way can we understand how the practice of inoculation, or of grafting the
disease on to a healthy person, a practice in itself so revolt-
ing and so contrary to our natural instincts, which bid us
keep scrupulously clear of the foul matter which a zymotic
disease produces, obtained rapidly a wide acceptance, and
so paved the way for vaccination.

SMALL-POX INOCULATION.

It is a singular and a suggestive fact that the practice of
small-pox inoculation, the parent of vaccination, and the
grand-parent of the modern theories of Pasteur and of
Koch, was not the outcome of any scientific investigation,
though for years it enjoyed the almost unanimous approval
of medical men.

Superstition invented it, and fashion insisted on it : the
doctors merely bowed to the fashion, and then found

reasons for defending it. Its origin in India in about the sixth century was undoubtedly religious. It was a way of worshipping Matah, the goddess of small-pox, the devotees trusting that, by thus submitting themselves to her will, they would get off with a mild attack, as no doubt they frequently did. Presumably the origin of the practice in other parts of the world, as among the poor in Wales and Scotland, where it had been known from time immemorial when it first became fashionable in England about the year 1720, was also religious; but no records appear to exist. The superstition spread westwards in a Christianised form; and an interesting account of the contemporary practice in Georgia is given in the *Gentleman's Magazine* for October, 1755, in a letter from Mr Porter, then English Ambassador at Constantinople. He says :—

" With regard to the practice of inoculation in Georgia, a physician of that country, who, though mighty ignorant, picks up a handsome living by his practice here, asserts that among the professors of the true Georgian worship [an earlier correspondent had denied that inoculation was practiced among the Catholics in Georgia] the operation is common, but that its rise is owing to mere superstition. He says it is the tradition and a religious opinion of the inhabitants of the country that a certain angel presides over this disease. That it is to evince their confidence and to bespeak his favour that the Georgians take a small portion of the variolous matter, and, by means of a scarification, introduce it between the thumb and the forefinger of a sound person. The operation never misses its effect, and the patient always recovers. To secure beyond all uncertainty the good-will of the angel, they hang up scarlet cloths about the bed, that being the favourite colour of this celestial inhabitant. Our physician has himself assisted at the operation, and avers it to be a common practice. If so, it is perhaps the only good effect that the monster superstition has ever produced. "

It was from Adrianople, in 1717, that Lady Mary Wortley Montague wrote the famous letter in which she declared that of thousands who were there inoculated year by year not a single one died of the disease. She had her son inoculated, and she took much pains to introduce the practice on her return to England. The physician of the Embassy, Mr Maitland, inoculated under her patronage; and, as soon as two children of the Princess of Wales had been operated on, inoculation became the rage; and, as early as 1724, Steele congratulated Lady Mary on her "godlike delight" in saving "many thousand British lives" every year. Voltaire was in England at the time, and caught the inoculation-fever; and, touching his countrymen in a very susceptible place, he explained that the charms of the ladies of Circassia were due to the practice, and that thousands of English girls had learned in this way to preserve their health and beauty. It is true that the number he gave exceeded the total number of persons who had been inoculated when he wrote; but the student of medical nostrums soon becomes accustomed to statistics of that kind.

The history of inoculation in this country is well worth a study, on account of the singularly exact parallels it furnishes with the history of vaccination. With few exceptions the medical men of the day warmly encouraged the practice. They made light of its risks, and insisted on the security which it afforded. They pointed out that, whereas of those who took small-pox in the natural way 18 per cent. died, of the inoculated only 1 in 91 died; and similar statistics, issued or approved by medical men, could be quoted at great length. Small-pox inoculation was never compulsory, nor was it during the eighteenth century

commonly practised among the poor; but it was authorised by fashion among the upper classes, and, in a sense,
it was enforced by the frown of Mrs Grundy. It is often
said that the domestic literature—the memoirs and correspondence—of the eighteenth century is darkened by the
dread of small-pox which it so frequently records. This
is true; but it is also true that it contains nothing more
pathetic than the agonising cries of doubt which arose from
those who dreaded the introduction by inoculation of a
horrible disease into their households, and who did from
time to time lose a loved child by their rash procedure;
contrasted with the confident and cruel assertions of those to
whom they appealed, to the effect that such was their duty,
and that it could be done without perceptible risk.*

In the early years of the present century, when medical
men, with almost complete unanimity, were seeking to
replace the variolous inoculation by the vaccine inoculation,
they confessed, or rather urged, that the earlier practice had
destroyed more lives than it had saved. And this was
undoubtedly true. For not only did the practice inflict the
disease on the person inoculated, but that person became a
new centre of infection, from which small-pox could be and
was occasionally "caught" in the natural way; and the
advocates of inoculation had no right to assume that anyone must, sooner or later, suffer from small-pox or from any
similar disease; for he might be naturally insusceptible of
it, or, in the ordinary course of things, the infection might
never reach him. No one, in fact, now denies that the
prevalence of small-pox in the eighteenth century was to
some extent due to the practice of inoculation; indeed this
was partly recognised thirty years before the comparatively

* See, for example, the letter of "A Country Gentleman" in the
Gentleman's Magazine for 1752, vol. 52, p. 126; and the death recorded
in Boswell's "Life of Johnson," Vol. IV., p. 293, ed. G. Birkbeck Hill.

safe vaccination came to the relief of the doctors, providing
them with a colourable substitute which at any rate was not
infectious.   In 1764 the Suttonian system considerably
reduced the risk of the operation ; as did also the system
of later inoculators, who used virus taken at such an early
stage of the disease that it often did not communicate
small-pox at all.   We talk of small-pox inoculation, as if it
were an uniform practice ; whereas it really varied as much
as vaccination does now.   It might communicate the
disease in its most deadly form, or it might do just nothing
at all, beyond making a slight sore, which proved, if tested,
no defence against subsequent exposure to the infection of
small-pox.   Disastrous, however, as the practice was—and
so clearly is that now recognised that for the last fifty years
the practice has been penal—it may be admitted that there
was "something in it," and that, in the special cases of
medical men and of nurses, it might still be resorted to
with advantage, if performed in isolation hospitals.   For
although some constitutions are so susceptible of small-pox
(as others are of other fevers) that one attack does not afford
security against a second or even a third, the general rule
is that one attack does confer subsequent immunity ; and
a person inoculated when in good health, and when there
is no severe epidemic about, might conceivably pass through
the ordeal with less risk than if a natural attack of the disease
had been waited for and incurred.   On the other hand,
there seems no good ground for concluding that, in the case
of a person constitutionally liable to a severe attack, a slight
attack only would result from inoculation, or that, if a slight
attack did result, it would afford immunity from a subsequent attack.   It might be hoped, but it certainly could not
be proved, that the less would prevent the greater.   And
so, amidst so much uncertainty, it is doubtless well that the
practice of small-pox inoculation should have been dropped ;

nor would it have been necessary to refer to it here, were it not that, without the preparation which it had effected in the public mind, the practice of vaccination could never have been introduced.

JENNER AND THE INTRODUCTION OF VACCINATION.

The popular notion that a learned and acute physician, after careful experiments, extending over a long period of years, discovered and proved that the disease popularly known as "cow-pox," if inoculated on to the human subject, was a specific defence against a subsequent attack of small-pox, has been so completely disposed of by the historical researches of Dr Creighton and Professor Crookshank that it will not be necessary here to do more than to state such facts as really do underlie the Jenner myth.* Whatever Jenner's merits may have been, he was certainly not a specially learned man, nor was he a patient, nor for that matter even an honest observer. He was an amiable and attractive man, with a faculty for writing verses and also for making fast friends; he had, moreover, a taste for natural history, and he was very anxious to push his way in the world. Undoubtedly he was the first medical man who had the courage to commit himself to a theory—perhaps we should say a "fad"—that had for some years been in the air, to the effect that the diseases of animals might prove of service as prophylactics against the diseases of man. But his professional acquirements were but slender; his medical degree was the outcome of no examination or scientific

* See "Jenner and Vaccination, a Strange Chapter of Medical History," by Charles Creighton, M.D., London, 1889; and "The History and Pathology of Vaccination," by Edgar M. Crookshank, Professor of Bacteriology in King's College, London. 2 vols. 1889. Cheaper issue, 1894.

work, but merely of a fee of fifteen guineas paid to the University of St Andrews; while his other and more important distinction, his Fellowship in the Royal Society, was obtained by what even Dr Norman Moore, his latest biographer and apologist, is constrained to admit was little else than a fraud.* But presumably, if Jenner had not thus been able to publish his "Inquiry into the Causes and Effects of the *Variolæ Vaccinæ*," with the authority that belongs to a Fellow of the Royal Society, the matter might never have gone further. And, as to the claim made for that paper that it was the fruit of twenty years of observation and experiment, it is worth noting that Jenner's first cow-pox inoculation was made in 1796, and that the paper was written the same year, though not printed (in an amended form) until 1798; and that the application to Parliament for a monetary grant to the "discoverer" was made in 1802; so that a period of only six years elapsed between Jenner's first operation and the application for State recognition of his services.† Such a period was far too short to test the permanent value of the operation; and the State subsidy, which of course practically settled the question, so far as the official world was concerned, in favour of vaccination, was altogether premature.

So far from having had cow-pox inoculation before him steadily for some twenty years, Jenner, as recently as 1792,

* See the notice of Jenner in the *Dictionary of National Biography*, and compare what is there said about his alleged observations on the cuckoo with Jenner's own assertions in the *Philosophical Transactions*, Vol. LXXVIII. The paper was read in March, 1788. The whole story is well summarised in a tract entitled "*The Bird that laid the Vaccination Egg*," by J. H. Levy, published by P. S. King & Son.

† It was on May 14, 1796, that James Phipps, a boy of eight, was vaccinated; and on July 1, the same year, he was inoculated with small-pox without effect. This was Jenner's original proof.

had inoculated his own eldest child with swine-pox, which operation was reckoned as protective as any of the subsequent ones with cow-pox. And it was merely due to Jenner's recognition of the fact that swine-pox had associations too disgusting to allow of its ever securing popular approval, that he did not advocate "porcination" instead of "vaccination." This shrewdness in recommending the new inoculation to the public is very apparent to anyone who will compare (and Professor Crookshank's edition renders the comparison very easy) the first draught of his paper on cow-pox with the later issues. In the original statement, the manuscript of which was discovered by Crookshank in the Library of the Royal College of Surgeons, the account of the disease is more frank and vastly more offensive than it is in the printed editions; and a comparison of the various modifications of Jenner's statements may be recommended as an interesting study, both of inconsequent reasoning and of shiftiness for the sake of plausibility. The second edition, it should be noted, as showing how this "scientific discovery" was on its way to gain acceptance, was dedicated to the king, whose "gracious patronage" was solicited in his behalf.*

It is, moreover, inaccurate to describe Jenner as the "discoverer" of vaccination. That persons—mainly of course milkers—who had had the cow-pox, were afterwards insusceptible of small-pox, or, more correctly, did not "take" small-pox inoculation, was one of those bits of farm-yard medical gossip, affirmed by some and denied by others, which, whether true or not, certainly rest on no scientific

---

* While Jenner was engaged in writing up this unfortunate delusion, the "candid and accurate" John Haygarth (1740-1827) was engaged on a truly scientific "Letter to Dr Percival on the Prevention of Infectious Fevers" (1801), in which, as his biographer justly remarks, "he embodied the principles of isolation, ventilation, and cleanliness, which can never go out of date."

basis.   Years before Jenner took the matter up (in 1774)
a Dorsetshire farmer named Jesty inoculated his wife and
his two sons with the cow-pox, in the belief that they would
thus obtain protection.   And, when Jenner referred to the
alleged protection at a local meeting of medical men, they
all professed to have heard of it, but denied the fact from
their own experience.   Jenner's own contribution consisted
in an attempt to establish a scientific theory of vaccination ;
and this attempt of his is the really important matter ; for
it gives the key to the whole controversy.   Unlike some
modern advocates of vaccination, who are satisfied if the
practice holds its ground by law, custom, and authority,
without any scientific basis at all, Jenner saw that, if vaccination was to become, as he hoped, a regular incident of
medical practice, it must have a scientific foundation ; and
that is what, by the title of his paper, " *Variolæ Vaccinæ*,"
he mainly attempted to establish ; and with marked success,
for the time.

THE NATURE OF COW-POX.

Jenner saw that if one disease is to be accredited as a
specific prophylactic against another, there must be some
pathological relation between the two.   In this he was of
course perfectly right.   Where we can now see that he went
astray was in assuming this relationship on the slenderest
evidence, instead of establishing it, if he could, by a series
of scientific observations and experiments.   His theory was
that the disease of the horse's hoof, known as "horse-grease,"
was the source of human small-pox and also of cow-pox ;
and in this way the relationship was established to his own
satisfaction.   Neither proposition is true ; nor indeed did
Jenner care to maintain the truth of either proposition when
the merits of vaccination had once become established in

people's minds; but the theory justified or seemed to justify
him in describing cow-pox as *variolæ vaccinæ* or "small-
pox of the cow"; and it is really this theory which has mis-
directed pretty nearly all the observations that have been
made on vaccination right down to the present day. Sir
John Simon, a living authority on the subject, explains
that persons vaccinated cannot take the small-pox, because
they have had it already; and this belief is still shared by
hundreds and thousands of people.

But what is in truth the nature of cow-pox? It is an
ailment, not of cattle, but of the cow, as its name implies,
exclusively, and of the cow only when she is in milk; and
it is further a disease of civilisation. It does not occur
when a cow suckles her own calf; nor, for that matter, does
it occur where cow-stables are kept decently clean. Jenner
observed that it did not occur when the milkers were
women only; and hence his theory that the disease originated in "horse-grease"; his assertion being (first stated
as an hypothesis, and then, a little lower down, as a thing
which "commonly happens") that the disease was communicated to the cow's teats by a man-milker who had
just dressed the diseased horse's heels. Other observers
also professed to have noted that the disease only occurred
where there were both men and women milkers; but they
drew another inference as to its origin, for which they found
confirmation in the disease's popular name. Apparently
it is in some way due to the friction of the teats by the
milker's hands; it occurs spontaneously (*i.e.*, apart from
inoculation) only where cows are milked; and its name
had reference not to small-pox but to great-pox, with which
its analogy was popularly and correctly discerned. Presumably it is a consequence of its partly human origin that
it is so easily (and ordinarily without danger) inoculable
on man, which other diseases of animals are not. That,

however, is mere conjecture; what is now certainly established beyond all reasonable doubt is that cow-pox bears no pathological relation to small-pox. The similarity in name is the only connection; for, though there is a superficial resemblance between the vaccine vesicle and the variolous pock, the two diseases are really quite distinct.* The definite establishment of this fact, which of course upsets the whole alleged scientific basis of vaccination, is due to the labours in recent years of Dr Creighton and Professor Crookshank, though the real character of cow-pox had long ago been suspected.

Omitting brief and incidental remarks of earlier writers, the conclusions of Dr Auzias-Turenne, communicated in 1865 to the *Académie de Médecine*, are deserving of attention. Unfortunately his investigations did not include any examination of the prophylactic virtue of vaccination. That he took for granted, although he admitted that he preferred "equination" (still much practised in France) to vaccination, properly so called. So that, after drawing out with much elaboration the specific differences between cow-pox and small-pox, he drew the somewhat lame conclusion that other animal diseases might be found preventive of other human diseases, since no specific identity but only an analogy or a superficial resemblance is all that seems necessary. He came, however, very near to laying his finger on the crucial point when he went on to say :—
" Between syphilis and cow-pox the analogy may be a long way followed up, . . . but, happily for the vaccinated, cow-pox passes through a rapid evolution, and does not

---

* Jenner's doctrine was however still maintained before the Royal Commission by Sir John Simon, who asserted that "small-pox and cow-pox are variations of the same disease." But he could give no pathological evidence in favour of this view.

leave virulent remains for so long a time or so frequently as syphilis." *

Dr Creighton, in his work on "Cow-pox and Vaccinal Syphilis," published in 1887, was the first in this country to call attention to Jenner's fundamental mistake, and to its immense importance in the vaccination controversy. The object of his enquiry was to find some explanation for the complaints so frequently made as to the communication of syphilis by vaccination. In his judgment such communication of two diseases by one and the same act was most improbable; and yet the evidence in case after case was overwhelming.† His conclusion was,—and it is now pretty generally accepted, though little is said about it,—that these syphilitic symptoms are a part and parcel of the cow-pox itself, which is bound thus to indicate its presence if it is inoculated in, or if it reverts to, its natural strength, and is not (as is so often the case with vaccination) a mere formality.

In the year that this book was published (1887) Professor Crookshank undertook, on behalf of the Agricultural Department of the Privy Council, an investigation into the micro-pathology of a cow-disease in Wiltshire, which it was thought might bear some relation to scarlet-fever in man. This investigation led him also to enquire into the nature and origin of cow-pox, with the result that his independent researches fully confirmed all Dr Creighton's conclusions. In fact, the syphilitic nature of cow-pox is the theory which now holds the field ; and it is hardly contested

---

* The analogy between, if not the identity of, the two diseases was first definitely pointed out by a Belgian physician, Dr Hubert Boëns-Boissau, in his work, *La Vaccine au point de vue historique et scientifique.* Charleroi, 1882.

† Dr W. J. Collins, in his able pamphlet entitled "Sir Lyon Playfair's Logic" (1883), mentions 478 cases of "vaccino-syphilis," details of which have been published by various medical men, English and foreign.

by the advocates of vaccination, who are content to rely solely on the evidence of statistics. But anyone who at all appreciates the immensely important part which theory plays in scientific investigations will see that this final refutation of Jenner's theory, which held the ground so long, puts the whole question in quite a new light. As Dr Bridges well says :— " To observe without a theory, avowed or implicit, to connect the observations, is all but impossible ; and yet, if the accepted theory be false, the observation will be warped." *

So long as a theory held the field, in accordance with which vaccinated persons *ought* not to have the small-pox, because they had already had it, statistics collected under that belief would naturally confirm that belief, while instances to the contrary would be denied, ignored, or explained away. Events that follow purely as a matter of chronology will, when a theory that connects them is in possession, assuredly be in danger of being reckoned as related by way of cause and effect. Hence, it is important, if the view of disbelievers in vaccination is to be given a fair hearing at all, to insist on the fact of Jenner's pathological error, before proceeding to a sketch of the history of the adoption of the practice of vaccination ; for it was certainly the most important factor in the process which led to the extraordinary triumph of the new system of inoculation.

Vaccination Generally Accepted.

Other circumstances, besides the fact that a medical man, who was a Fellow of the Royal Society, had announced the discovery that cow-pox was " small-pox of the cow," were

* Article on Hippocrates, in the " New Calendar of Great Men," p. 131.

favourable to the acceptance of vaccination. To many who had long advocated and practised the older form of inoculation it came as a welcome relief. The risks of that practice were already pretty generally recognised ; but, such is the tyranny that custom has, and that not least in the medical world, that it was impossible for the practice to be dropped, except by the substitution of some other practice, which could be recommended as an improvement. And, if Jenner's account of vaccination were correct, it was undoubtedly an improvement ; for the disease communicated was ordinarily less severe, while the risk of infection was *nil*. And, as there was at the time a decline in the prevalence of small-pox, it was natural to attribute this to vaccination. The decline, such as it was, needed no such explanation ; for, when the figures are examined, it will be seen that, while the concurrent disuse of small-pox inoculation might account for part of it, the disease being no longer spread so widely by the artificial diffusion of the infection, the natural dying out of a foreign disease, checked by revival in epidemics at irregular intervals, is a more obvious explanation of the decline ; and this indeed is true of the whole history of small-pox throughout the nineteenth century. The abatement was most marked for some years before vaccination was practised. Whether it be ascribed to sanitation, or to improvements in diet, or to what one may call an exhaustion of the soil, there is no doubt whatever about the fact. We have, unfortunately, no statistics for the country as a whole at this date ; but from the London Bills of Mortality we learn that, whereas from 1760 to 1779 the annual number of deaths from small-pox in the metropolis had averaged 2323, from 1780 to 1799 they averaged 1740, or nearly 600 less in each year. The decline continued after vaccination had been introduced, but, as it happened, it was less marked, the average from 1800 to 1810 being

1358, or nearly 400 less per annum than it had been in the previous period.

In a brief statement of the case, such as that on which I am now engaged, it is not of course possible to present statistics with that fulness which is necessary for an exhaustive examination; and, as the mortality varied very considerably from year to year, one must be on one's guard against the arbitrary selection of a few figures which do not bear out the conclusion indicated by the whole series. Thus, for example, it has been pointed out by Baron, Jenner's enthusiastic biographer, that in 1798, the year in which Jenner published his paper, the deaths from small-pox in London were as many as 2237, whereas in 1804, the year after that in which Parliament had voted him £10,000, they had fallen to 622. This is perfectly true; but we can see how rash it would be to infer from these figures any conclusion as to the value of vaccination, when we find that in 1805 they had again risen to 1685, whereas in 1797 they had been as low as 522. I shall have something more to say later as to the precariousness of the argument from statistics.

The series of experiments made by Jenner and others, who followed up vaccination by small-pox inoculation, or by other forms of exposure to small-pox infection, with the uniform result, as they claimed it, that in no case did susceptibility to the disease remain, certainly cannot readily be made to square with that theory of the nature of vaccination which I am now advocating. If the experiments had been made by Jenner only there would have been less difficulty; but they were made also by Woodville, Pearson, and others; and apparently with uniform results. The matter has been looked into by Dr Creighton and by Professor Crookshank, so far as its pathological aspect is concerned; and the conclusion towards which we are

pointed is this, that while vaccination is not, and from the
nature of the case cannot be, a specific prophylactic against
small-pox, yet a severe attack of cow-pox, or, in other words,
vaccination followed by considerable constitutional disturbance, is likely to prove, while the febrile symptoms still
last, antagonistic to the small-pox infection, and, so far,
affords a temporary protection against it. Probably the same
is true of any other disease that produces constitutional
disturbance with febrile symptoms. We must, moreover,
bear in mind that many persons, apart from vaccination,
had been known to show constitutional insusceptibility to
the variolous inoculation, and that that inoculation itself
was often enough a mere formality, producing no results;
and this was extremely likely to be the case when the
operators were anxious that no results should be produced.
Add to this the enthusiasm for the cause, which, unless
Jenner and his fellow-workers had been more than human,
would lead them, without conscious dishonesty, to make no
record of experiments that failed, and we have perhaps a
fair explanation of the whole business; but it is not altogether
a satisfactory one ; and it is difficult not to regret that similar
experiments cannot be repeated now under conditions involving publicity, as that would really settle the whole controversy.

Certainly the times were not favourable for a calm and scientific investigation ; and official sanction was given to vaccination before there had been anything like time enough for a
careful observer to form a judgment on the permanent value of
the operation. It was early, in 1802, within four years of the
great "discovery," for Jenner to petition Parliament for money
on the strength of it, because, as he claimed, vaccination
rendered people " secure *through life* from the infection of
small-pox." Yet a Select Committee of the House of Commons, composed of persons mostly favourable to his claim

was promptly appointed, and reported in his favour in 1803; and in this way, after a very easy-going and unscientific enquiry, and before the new doctrine was eight years old, the whole official world was, by the action of Parliament, committed to its value ; and there began at once the building up of that great vaccination establishment, supported out of public funds, which, by creating interests of one kind or another, has all along formed the main support of the belief in the operation.*

There was much aptness in the motto from Terence : " *Ego amplius considerandum censeo ; res magna est,*" which a Bath physician, who wrote anonymously in 1800, prefixed to a thoughtful but ill-written pamphlet, entitled "A Conscious View of Circumstances and Proceedings respecting Vaccine Inoculation."† He perceived that fashion was setting strongly in favour of the new operation, and he decided to preserve his anonymity so as to escape the personalities he dreaded from the "bigots" devoted to the "present rage." But, to the permanent injury of the reputation of the medical profession for scientific judgment, he and all the other critics of vaccination were shouted down ; and, for a long while after official sanction had confirmed the conclusion arrived at so rapidly by enthusiasm and fashion, their voices were no more heard in the land.‡

* The essential baselessness of the current belief in vaccination, as it appears if historically examined, aptly illustrates a sentence of Bacon's : —"It often falls out that somewhat is produced of nothing ; for lies are sufficient to breed opinion, and opinion brings on substance." Substitute "mistakes" for "lies," and it is the history of the origin and growth of the practice of vaccination in a nutshell.

† Reprinted in Crookshank's "History and Pathology of Vaccination," Vol. II., p. 203.

‡ Among those who uttered a protest against the unscientific use of a zoogenous disease as a prophylactic was the venerable Immanuel Kant, whose eminence as a physiologist and an observer of natural phenomena has been overshadowed by his eminence as a philosopher. See the

That I am not exaggerating the temper in which vaccination was advocated in the early years of this century, is clear from an article in the *Edinburgh Review* for October 1806, written by Jeffrey, the editor, who was himself a convert to the new faith. This is how he characterises the discussion: "In the whole course of our censorial labours we have never had occasion to contemplate a scene so disgusting and humiliating as is presented by the greater part of the controversy; nor do we believe that the virulence of political animosity, or personal rivalry, or revenge, ever gave rise among the lowest and most prostituted scribblers to so much coarseness, illiberality, violence, and absurdity as is here exhibited by gentlemen of sense and education discussing a point of professional science with a view to the good of mankind." *

Meanwhile, in spite of occasional injuries and deaths resulting from the inoculation of the cow-pox virus, and in spite of cases of small-pox following vaccination, the operation itself, enjoying the sunshine of Royal favour, seemed already in a fair way to become compulsory. But compulsion, though it is a legitimate corollary to State endowment, was slow to gain a footing in this country. Germany was, as might have been expected, far more prompt than England in legislating about vaccination. The practice was made compulsory in Bavaria in 1807; and in 1835 the re-vaccination of children attending the public schools became obligatory in Prussia. Possibly the

reference in Buckle's "Miscellaneous and Posthumous Works," ed. H. Taylor, Vol. III., pp. 425-6. Kant died in 1804.

* A second article on the subject, in the *Edinburgh* for Jan. 1810, is also interesting as showing how extravagant were the hopes entertained at that time. The question of compulsion was even discussed; but the writer concluded that it would not do :— "An official body of vaccinators would never be tolerated, either by the public or by the profession, and would soon degenerate into a scene of jobbery and intrigue."

Germanising wave, which was a result of the Queen's marriage, had something to do with vaccination first being made compulsory in this country in 1853; and the provisions were made more stringent in 1867, 1871, and 1874.

But as early as 1810 the enthusiastic writer in the *Edinburgh Review*, already referred to, had declared that, by vaccination, small-pox had been "entirely banished from the higher and middling classes of society," and that the operation had "achieved its total extinction in whole countries." Even in the East Indies he declared its success had been "astonishing," and in the settlements of Bombay the disease had been "altogether exterminated." We can smile at this extravagant language now; but it is worth quoting, as an illustration of one form of the delusion under which compulsory vaccination was advocated. A soberer judgment, made in recent days, on the value of vaccination in India, will be quoted later on (p. 72); and, as to small-pox having been nearly banished from England as early as 1810, we have imperfect records of severe epidemics (notably that of 1825) since that date, and accurate records of others which have occurred since 1837, namely in 1852, 1858, 1863-4-5, 1871-2 (very severe), 1877, and 1881.

Compulsion was thus first advocated because of the great decline in small-pox in the early years of this century; it has since been urged because of the recurrence of epidemics; indeed it has been in the panic of these epidemics that compulsion has become the law, or that the law has been made more stringent. The history of the growth of compulsion in this country is important and instructive, and deserves more detailed consideration.

VACCINATION COMPULSORY.

The passing of the first coercive measure in 1853 is certainly remarkable, because there were at the time

circumstances which pointed rather towards the abandon-
ment of the practice of vaccination than towards its
enforcement under penalties. The great decline in small-
pox which had marked the first years of the present century
(and was, as we have seen, a continuation of the decline
which had marked the last twenty years of the eighteenth
century) had not been maintained; and cases of the
disease following vaccination were reported from all
sides; as, indeed, they had been from the first, though
not in such numbers. A minority of disbelievers in the
efficacy of the operation there had always been; but,
about the time of the Queen's accession, the faith even of
the majority was growing weak; and, as it was of course
impossible to admit that the medical profession had
committed itself to the advocacy of a delusion, the cry
went forth that vaccination was losing its power because
of its repeated transference through human subjects; and
"back to the cow" was the policy recommended. Thus,
Ceeley and Badcock procured a fresh supply of the precious
"lymph" by passing small-pox virus through the cow—a
practice which is now strictly prohibited, as being in fact
nothing less than a revival of the old and dangerous small-
pox inoculation; and, writing, in 1842, "Further Observations on the *Variolæ Vaccinæ*," Ceeley confessed that
the knowledge of the subject was at that time imperfect,
and that its difficulty demanded "the continuance of
vigilant, patient, and diligent inquiry." These modest
statements contrast strikingly with the bold assertions made
by Jenner and his friends forty years earlier, and show that
their anticipations had by no means been realised. The
credit of vaccination was however saved by the fact that
the then recent epidemics of small-pox had been mainly
among the poor, while the well-to-do classes had enjoyed
comparative freedom. The rational explanation of this

would have been, that the well-to-do enjoyed the advantages, which the poor at that time did not, of better sanitation, better nursing, and of better living.   Small-pox is known to be a dirt-disease, one that haunts ill-drained, ill-ventilated, and uncleansed tenements—"the beggar's disease" is, I believe, its popular name in Austria; and so it was not necessary to seek the explanation in what was also no doubt the fact, that in the first half of the century vaccination was very little practised among the poor in this country, who have indeed always shown themselves less ready to take up with the last medical fad than their more impressionable superiors.   But it was very easy and convenient to lay the blame for the recurrence of small-pox epidemics on the unvaccinated poor ; and there was the precedent of Germany for employing compulsion to secure the vaccination of the whole community.

There was also another reason why the medical profession should at that time regard compulsion with a favourable eye. In the early days of vaccination the operation had been performed by anyone and everyone, especially by clergymen and clergymen's wives.   As early as 1806 Dr Willan estimated the number of amateur practitioners at upwards of 10,000; but this was probably only one of the many exaggerations which characterised all references to vaccination in early times, and indeed in later times as well. Anyhow, the practice was not by any means confined to professional medical men, even as late as 1850 ; but a compulsory law would of necessity place it exclusively in their hands, and so would involve the State recognition of "duly qualified" men exclusively.   It would be the first step towards the establishment of a kind of State Medical Church, which has been, and is still, the dream of not a few professional men.

So a Bill, modestly entitled "Vaccination Extension,"

was introduced in the House of Lords, February 15, 1853, and was read a second time on April 4 ; and, after a short debate in Committee, in which Lords Lyttelton and Shaftesbury showed how well they had been coached by some medical enthusiast in the now well-known and illusory statistics, it was sent down to the Commons, where the second reading was carried *nem. con.*, and almost without debate, on July 19 ; the remaining stages being passed without any discussion at all. It may be doubted whether any measure of such grave consequence was ever hurried through the Legislature so lightly ; and the explanation doubtless lies in the fact that, when Parliament is guided by the opinions of professional experts, it loses sight of its own responsibilities ; and in this particular instance it certainly bowed to "doctor's orders" without a word ; and, except for a brief protest from Sir George Strickland, seemed to think nothing of this novel application of the "principle of compulsion." The assertion that the medical profession was unanimous in its belief in the protective power of vaccination rendered all other argument superfluous. The medical enthusiast who really passed this Act through both Houses was Dr Edward Seaton. Under the *alias* of "The Epidemiological Society," then founded and dominated by him, he furnished the statistics which were printed as a Parliamentary paper ; and certainly, if these statistics were a fair presentation of the case, there was nothing more to be said, assuming that blessings ought to compulsory. Sir Robert Peel indeed had urged, not many years before, that "to make vaccination compulsory, as in some despotic countries, would be so opposite to the mental habits of the British people, and the freedom of opinion in which they rightly glory, that I never could be a party to such compulsion." But Peel died in 1850 ; and, in 1853, there already existed strong and exaggerated notions as to the preventibility of disease, which

made short work of the old-fashioned doctrine as to the
"liberty of the subject"; and it was in that temper that the
Act of 1853 was passed.   It was not so much designed to
crush out opposition as to stimulate indifference.   That
there could possibly be wide-spread opposition, grounded
on disbelief in the efficacy of vaccination and on dread of
its risks, does not appear to have occurred to anyone; and
yet, if a fair and open enquiry had preceded this legislation,
it would have been impossible to ignore that prospect.
That there were plenty of materials for such an enquiry is
clear from the letter of John Gibbs, which Parliament had
the grace to print as an official paper in 1855; and that there
was at that date a more tolerant spirit abroad than prevails
now is equally clear from the fact that even the *Lancet* used
then to print admissions of the risks which vaccination
involved.   But, unfortunately, organised opposition came
too late.   The mischief was already done; and, Parliament
being now as impotent to undo its work as it is to do it,
repeal is only possible when an Act has either become
obsolete through neglect, or unworkable through persistent
and wide-spread opposition.

Into the history of subsequent legislation I do not propose to go; but two points deserve mentioning before I
proceed to another aspect of this many-sided question.

Repeated penalties in respect of the non-vaccination of
a child were first authorised by section 31 of the Vaccination
Act of 1867, which to all intents and purposes is the one
now in force.   A parent is liable under this section to be
proceeded against from time to time until the child is
fourteen years of age.   This was of course a departure from
the original idea of compulsion, which was mainly to
stimulate the indifferent.   The new procedure inflicted
punishment on the unbeliever; and a few moments' reflection will suffice to show that it is really for his heretical

c

belief and not merely for his inaction in not having his child vaccinated that he is repeatedly punished. For, if a parent, either from the experience he has had in his own family, or from what he has seen in the families of others, or from what he has read in the writings on vaccination of competent medical men, is convinced that the operation is not only useless but one that involves serious risk to his child's health and life, it would be in him an immoral act to present the child to be vaccinated; and to suppose that the law compels a man to act immorally is absurd. So it punishes him for holding an opinion which, in the judgment of the majority, is erroneous. It was prophesied, when this Bill was before Parliament, that this vexatious provision would provoke an agitation that would not cease until compulsion had been entirely repealed; and it had not been in force four years when a Select Committee (of which Sir Lyon, now Lord, Playfair was a member) unanimously recommended that repeated penalties in respect of the same child should be abolished. Yet the section is in force still to-day, and is likely to remain in force, until an enlightened and indignant people make short work of the whole foolish business. It is a striking instance of the impotence of the Legislature to correct its own mistakes.

The recommendation of the Select Committee, that repeated prosecutions should be abolished, was approved in the Commons by a majority of five to one (57 to 12) but was rejected in the Lords by a majority of one (7 to 8), after a brutal speech by the late Lord Redesdale, who entirely mistook the issue, and compared a parent, who for love of his child refuses to allow it to incur the risks of vaccination, to a man who repeatedly gets drunk. Grouse-shooting was already a week overdue when the Bill came back to the Commons (August 19th, 1871); and the Lords' amendment was accepted by the House on the recommendation of Mr Forster, who nevertheless could not avoid commenting on the absurdity of the unanimous recommendation of the Select Committee, arrived at after a patient enquiry, being thus rendered nugatory by the vote of a single uninformed peer. To that vote is due most of the bitterness and cruelty that have accompanied the administration of these Acts. While no single child, so far as I can ascertain, has ever been vaccinated in consequence of the infliction of repeated penalties, numbers of conscientious parents have submitted to imprisonment (in addition to the thousands who have been fined), because that seemed to them the more reasonable penalty to incur, rather than to be fined again and again for fourteen years on account of the same offence ; and also because the incurring of such a punishment as imprisonment for such a cause seemed more likely to bring about the ultimate repeal of the law. Yet, so deeply has the prejudice in favour of vaccination sunk into John Bull's mind, that, while at the present day the sins of the House of Lords are repeatedly collected and published to serve a political end, no one, so far as I know, has so much as mentioned this vote of August, 1871 ; though no other action of theirs has brought such bitterness and distress into hundreds of otherwise happy homes.

In 1880, a Liberal Government timidly attempted to repeal this odious provision ; but it retreated so soon as the medical corporations protested against such a sacrifice of their darling "principle of compulsion." And, as lately as 1893, we have had a fresh illustration of the way in which the bigotry of a handful of professional men can reduce the Legislature to impotence ; for, after the Royal Commission had sat for three years, and had heard evidence from both sides, although it contained a phalanx of devout believers in vaccination it went out of its way to report as a matter of urgency, for which it was not well to wait

until its final Report, that these repeated prosecutions
ought no longer to be possible.   That was the conclusion
at which they arrived "unanimously"; but the late Government declined to act on the Report, because, forsooth,
they had not yet read the evidence on which it was based ;
and you, Sir, when you introduced a Bill to give effect to
their recommendation, found that its progress was blocked,
week after week, until there was no time left to proceed
with it, by the action of a Scotch member, on behalf of
the British Medical Association.   Perhaps ultimately some
advantage will come from this exhibition of professional
bigotry and of Parliamentary impotence.   Repeated prosecutions are in some sense the logical outcome of compulsion ; for the policy of fining a disbeliever in vaccination each time he has a child born, and then leaving him
alone, is rather the policy of a Dogberry.   So that when
the public realises, as no doubt eventually it will, that no
body of men can enquire into this vaccination question
without coming to the conclusion that a thorough-going
policy of compulsion is impossible and defeats its own
ends, the public will perhaps see that, instead of mending
compulsion, it will be better to end it altogether.

In another way the amending Act of 1871 deprived us of
a safeguard of reasonable liberty which had before existed.
So far as I know, attention has never been adequately
called to the grave accentuation of the burden of compulsion which was the result of the repeal in its schedule
of section 27 of the Act of 1867.   Under that section
the Guardians had been directed that, after they had
received from the Registrar a list of the persons in default, they were "forthwith to make enquiry into the
circumstances of the cases" contained in the list, and to
prosecute if they found that the provisions of the Act had
been 'neglected.   This gave them the opportunity, after

the enquiry had been made, to select such cases for prosecution in which there did not appear to have been that "reasonable excuse" for not having the child vaccinated, which was also provided for in section 29 of the Act —a section which, by the way, remains unrepealed, though it is practically inoperative without the earlier one. As the procedure in vaccination cases is invariably summary, and the accused has no refuge in the common-sense of a jury, but is entirely at the mercy of the magistrate, who is naturally disposed to take what I may term a Churchman's view of the enormity of this heresy, there was a reasonableness in the cases being thus first sifted by a popular tribunal, the members of which might be expected to know something of the circumstances of the recusants, and so not to send up for certain conviction parents whom they knew to have grave cause for dreading the effect of vaccination. That is precisely how the law in some districts was at first carried out; and this reasonable administration prevented much hardship and discontent.

But this did not at all satisfy the medical officials of the Local Government Board, who, secure in their fortress at Whitehall, have acted, I fully believe, in the sacred name of Public Health, precisely, *mutatis mutandis*, in the same spirit as that in which mediæval ecclesiastics acted in the sacred name of Mother Church; and so the repeal of the section referred to was provided for in the schedule of the Bill; and the astonishing thing is that the whole measure passed through all its stages in the Commons without a single word of debate; such was the panic which possessed the House in consequence of the epidemic of small-pox then prevailing. Presumably this would not have been the case had the Bill been before the Commons in the shape in which it ultimately became law. Section 10 of the original Bill—the section struck out by the Lords, as noted above—provided for the cessation of repeated prosecutions; and this was a set-off against the aggravation of compulsion involved elsewhere in the measure. But, when the Bill had become an Act, no such mitigation was in it. Besides establishing throughout the country a new body of officers to prosecute defaulters, its chief effect was to deprive the Guardians of this reasonable liberty of enquiry, and to insist on their sending up to the magistrates everyone who was reported in default. For the last twenty-three years this has been the law; though its odious character has caused it to become inoperative in a large number of Unions; and from 1875 onwards the proportion of vaccinations to births has steadily decreased; latterly at an increasingly rapid rate.*

In practice compulsion has thus become a purely mechanical process. Both Guardians and magistrates protest that they have no option but to "carry out the law," which means, in the case of the former, no option but to prosecute, and in the case of the latter, no option but to convict and to inflict the full penalty. Of course there are exceptions; there are a few magistrates who admit a "reasonable excuse," such as the Act makes provision for; and there are others who are satisfied with merely nominal

* Even the stringency of the Act of 1871 did not satisfy the Local Government Board officials, who apparently desired to have quite a free hand in the administration of the law; and so, in 1874, another little Bill was introduced, "to explain the Act of 1871"; and this empowered the Local Government Board "to make rules, orders, and regulations with respect to the proceedings to be taken by the Guardians or their officers for the enforcement of the provisions of the Vaccination Acts of 1867 and 1871." This measure also passed through all its stages with barely any discussion. Its importance at the present time lies in this, that the powers thus entrusted to the President of the Local Government Board may very possibly allow of his putting an end to compulsion altogether by the issue of new rules. But such an administrative act would perhaps not be practicable, unless preceded by a resolution of the House of Commons hostile to the existing system.

fines ; * while over very large areas prosecutions have ceased altogether. So that the administration of the law, where not mechanical, is arbitrary, or has lapsed altogether; and it is this inequality which is one of the scandals of the situation. In one district refusal to have a child vaccinated is punished severely, as a gross act of insubordination, hard labour in some cases having been illegally added to imprisonment. In another, the law has been practically repealed for years. And further, there is no law in the statute book which is so obviously one that touches the lower classes exclusively. Why it is that the well-to-do have but seldom to complain of the injurious effects of vaccination is a point I will deal with later. My contention now is that, even if they decline to have their children vaccinated, they have rarely any occasion to complain about the compulsory law ; because in their case it is not enforced. The highest game at which a vaccination officer ever flies his kite is a Nonconformist minister ; the squire and the parson, and the dwellers in Belgravia or Mayfair, he regards as exempt from his jurisdiction. The officer can easily be " squared," if the parents are determined that there shall be no pretence even of the operation being performed ; but there is another loophole for escape, for the private medical practitioner is free to certify that he has " successfully vaccinated " the child, when he has done no more than produce a slight sore by touching the abraded skin with a drop of glycerine ; for there is no legal definition of what " vaccination " is. More will be said later on as to the variety of operations which the term covers.

On the whole, the administration of the law is such,

---

* Some few magistrates, who have come to realise the folly of enforcing such a law, adjourn the hearing *sine die ;* or else, after formal conviction, bind over the defendants to come up for judgment when called upon.

mechanical here and null there, strict here and lax there, that, if the Government should decide to retain compulsion in so far as it affects the careless and indifferent, but not to insist on it in the case of parents, who, so far from being indifferent, decidedly object to the operation being performed at all—and this really is the policy of those who advocate the cessation of second prosecutions on account of the same child—I would suggest, as a practical solution of the controversy, that, when the birth of a child is registered, the parent should be empowered to make a declaration that he objects to its being vaccinated, and should thereupon be free from further proceedings under the Vaccination Acts, he there and then paying a fine, assessed on the rateable value of his house, say at twopence in the pound, with a minimum of one shilling, and a maximum of twenty. Similar certificates of exemption ought to be obtainable at the same rate for other unvaccinated children under fourteen years of age; and in this way the majesty of the law would be vindicated, and a vast amount of irritation would be saved—guardians and magistrates sharing no less than parents in the general relief; and the funds thus obtained, which in some districts would be considerable, might be administered as compensation to those medical men who have suffered pecuniarily from the disuse of vaccination.

Vaccination not Scientific.

The primary scientific objection to vaccination, that it is a futile effort to guard against one disease by the implantation of another with which it has no pathological relation, has been brought into special prominence of recent years, because attention has been called to it by the important publications of Dr Creighton and Professor Crookshank; and it is by itself, when fairly considered, enough to discredit the whole business. But it by no means stands alone. The use of one disease as a prophylactic against another, even where there is a pathological relation, is a mode of treatment that is in many ways questionable, and the advocates of such treatment really trade mainly on the assumption that vaccination is a secure precedent for them. When that delusion has been dissipated, their theories will need reconsideration; and experiments performed in a new light may very likely yield other results. Not that there has been anything hitherto to lead one to suppose that vaccination (apart from its own alleged success) has opened a new era of preventive medicine.* It is a wide subject, and one on which I can only just touch in passing. But it is clear that the methods for treating phthisis and cholera, which at one time made the name of Koch famous, and were within a little of receiving premature official recognition, as vaccination did, have ended in a fiasco; though whether they would have so ended, had the State committed itself to the value of the operations, may be doubted. As things are, however, apart from certain so-called "chemical vaccinations," mainly the experiments of continental pathologists, which have attracted but little attention in this country, but are nevertheless of some interest, and are at any rate free from the risks which attend the inoculation of zoogenous poisons, there survives only Pasteur's treatment of hydrophobia, as offspring of the alleged success of vaccination; and whether that treatment is successful or not it is at the present time impossible to say. Of course there are the statistics issued by his friends

* In this connection it is worth pointing out that Auguste Comte found no place for Jenner in his Calendar, as he assuredly would have done had he believed in vaccination. Vaccination is either a mistake, or it is the most important and the most epoch-making discovery in the history of medicine. And Comte was familiar enough with medicine to have this alternative quite clearly before him.

and employees, which shew a marvellously low percentage
of deaths in the cases that have passed through his hands;
but there exist no statistics to place by their side, showing
what is the percentage of deaths in the cases of those who,
after being bitten by dogs presumably rabid, have enjoyed
no such treatment; while M. Pasteur's critics further call
attention to the fact that, whereas, in France, before 1883,
the deaths from hydrophobia averaged annually twenty-
three, that average has since that date (*i.e.*, since he com-
menced operations) increased to thirty-nine; while in
England they have decreased from an average of twenty-
six in the three years 1887-8-9 to an average of seven in
the three years 1890-1-2, in consequence, no doubt, of the
muzzling order, dated August 15, 1889, which effected a
form of isolation, and was, so far, a genuinely scientific
protection.

On the whole, the impression one carries away is that
(vaccination apart, for the sake argument) there is reason
to anticipate that a century hence all these schemes of
prophylaxy by the inoculation of disease will be regarded
as a bad dream in the history of medicine; and that the
future professors of that art will no more desire to call
attention to them than its present professors do to the
exploded methods of treatment by bleeding, blistering,
salivation, and so forth. Medical science should be free,
like all other branches of science, to revise its judgments;
and it is just the lack of freedom in respect to vaccination
which the compulsory law involves, that makes its place in
medicine unique and perhaps a little ridiculous.*

---

* Five and twenty years ago, *i.e.*, just before the great epidemic of
1871-2, there were enthusiastic medical scientists who dreamed that
preventive medicine had a splendid career before it, and that, after a
dozen or so specific " vaccinations," all of course to be made compulsory
in due time, none of us would die save of old age or accident. No one

That the enforcement of vaccination on every child or adult, irrespective of constitution or of other special conditions, is a thing apart from scientific medicine, needs only stating in order to gain acknowledgment. It is a commonplace in the art that treatment suitable for A is unsuitable for B ; and it must also be familiar to practitioners, who honestly note the immediate effects of vaccination, that, while in one case it has hardly any perceptible result, in another it produces severe constitutional disturbance.† This may in some cases be due to a difference in the virus used, as will be noted in a later paragraph ; but the fact that the children of one family will suffer severely, though vaccinated in different years and from different sources, while the children of another family, under similar conditions, will not suffer at all, indicates in the former case a constitutional susceptibility to the effects of cow-pox, which ought to be taken into account by the family doctor. But the law, as it stands, will not permit him to take it into account. He is permitted only to postpone the operation for two months, if the child is suffering from some specific disease ; he is not at liberty to certify, as he certainly should be, that in the case of such and such a child it is desirable to exempt it from vaccination altogether, on account of its constitutional liability to

has such dreams now. On the contrary, since cow-pox is at any rate a preventible disease, so far as human beings are concerned, it is more rational to hope that the "British Institute of Preventive Medicine" will justify its title and prove its scientific character by condemning vaccination as we now know it. In no other way is it likely to score any considerable or legitimate success.

† It is in fact the ordinary excuse that a doctor makes when it is complained that a certain vaccination has produced very severe results, possibly death, that other children were vaccinated about the same time with the same lymph, and that no harm came of it. Another familiar excuse is to assert, without a particle of evidence, that some " poisonous rag " must have been laid on the open wound.

suffer severely. The children of nervous and highly-strung
parents are undoubtedly liable to such risk ; and it is just
because doctors cannot legally in their case get free
of the operation altogether, that they are driven to such
shifts as have above been noted, which may mean the
certification as "successful vaccination" of an operation
which has been a mere formality.

Surely too it is rash and unscientific to inflict a disease,
even if it be a mild one, on infants of but a few weeks old,
whose life is in any case a precarious one. In this country
at the present time about fifteen per cent. of the children
born die within the first twelve months. I am not contending now that this high rate is partly due to vaccination,
for I propose to deal later with the risks of the operation,
as admitted even in the official statistics. But in relation
to medical science, which is supposed to have for its aim
the preservation of human life, is it reasonable to lay this
additional burden at an age when the risk from various
familiar causes is already so great, while the risk of small-
pox infection, a few exceptional cases apart, is practically
nil? It is of course useless to argue about the slightness
of this risk with people who are so ignorant as to suppose
that an unvaccinated child can start small-pox on its own
account. But it is worth while to remind those who know
that the infection must come from outside, how infinitesimal
is the chance of coming into contact with it, except of
course at the actual place or places where an epidemic at
the moment may prevail. Of catching measles, scarlet-
fever, or whooping-cough—diseases of which thousands of
children die every year—there is no doubt some risk. But
small-pox, in spite of all the fuss that the medical papers
make about it, is pretty nearly as extinct as the plague.
The average annual number of deaths from it in England
and Wales during the six years, 1887-92, the Sheffield

epidemic of 1887-8 being included, was only 318 ; and in
1890 the total number of deaths only amounted to 16 ; being
not one-third of the number of those that are admitted to
be annually caused by vaccination. Taking the number
of cases to be, as usual, about five times as many as the
deaths, and supposing each case to last a month, we find that,
at any given moment during the years 1887-92, there were
in England and Wales, that is out of a population of nearly
thirty millions, about 133 cases of this disease, or one case
among 220,000 people. Anyone able to appreciate the
force of these figures will see that infants, under ordinary
circumstances, really run as little risk of catching small-
pox as they do of being devoured by polar bears when
they take an airing in their perambulators.

Doctors disagree on this question of age, as indeed
they do on almost every point connected with the
subject. By their advice a law has been passed making
compulsory in England the vaccination of infants before
they are three months old ; and in workhouses the
medical officers often vaccinate infants within the first
week of birth. But in Germany the regulations, also the
work of medical men, strictly forbid the vaccination of
infants not yet three months old.* There is some lack
of scientific consistency in these contradictory directions.

In another way vaccination is, as practised, an unscientific operation, viz., in the uncertainty which shrouds
the nature and origin of the " lymph " or virus used.
This uncertainty has existed more or less from the beginning.
Jenner at one time advocated the exclusive use of matter
obtained from cow-pox that had originated in horse-grease ;
and, when cases of persons vaccinated with other cow-pox
were adduced, who subsequently were attacked by small-
pox, he explained that such was " spurious cow-pox,"

* Palmberg, *Public Health and its Appliances*, tr. Newsholme
(London, 1893), p. 366.

possessing no prophylactic power, and that the "true genuine life-giving fluid" must have its origin in horse-grease. This opinion he subsequently abandoned, when he found that it would be fatal to the general adoption of vaccination, if its origin in so offensive a disease were insisted on. Later operators obtained a new supply of lymph by passing small-pox virus through the cow; and other sources have been used in recent times. In fact, when Professor Crookshank instituted an enquiry into this all-important point, with a view to obtain a clear view of the pathology of vaccination as practised in England to-day, he found that the officials at Whitehall had no standard by which the lymph was judged. There was of course no doubt as to the immediate source of that obtained from the wretched calves exploited by the establishment in Lamb's Conduit Street; but of its ultimate origin, and of the origin of the "humanised lymph," sent to the office by practitioners in various parts of the country, there was no certainty at all. Some apparently could be traced back to genuine small-pox, though so weakened by transmission from child to child as to have lost the power of communicating that disease; while other lymph, with some amount of probability, could be traced to horse-pox (an undoubted variety of syphilis), other to sheep-small-pox, other to goat-pox, other to cattle-plague, and so on. Any kind of matter, in fact, that, inserted under the skin will raise a vesicle or a pustule, similar to that of the cow-pox, is good enough for what is called "vaccination"; and it is all equally protective. Indeed, a German doctor, Hufeland, has advocated the use of the drug popularly known as "tartar emetic," which produces a like effect, and is, he alleges, no less efficacious as a prophylactic. Its employment in lieu of any variety of animal lymph has this much to be said in its favour, that, being a mild, inorganic poison, its injurious effects are strictly limited; whereas any organic poison, such as the purest lymph actually is, may occasionally, by reproducing itself in the blood of the person inoculated, produce surprisingly severe results. No wonder that the offer of the Grocers' Company of a prize of £1000 to anyone who would discover a safe medium in which standard cow-pox lymph could be cultivated (so that in this way the danger of transmitting other diseases with the cow-pox might be avoided), has come to nothing, and that the prize has never been awarded. The law does not define what standard lymph is, nor can the officials who supply the lymph give inquirers any assistance. Surely there is some lack here of that precision which ought to be looked for in a scientific art.

There are other aspects in which vaccination, as practised, is not scientific. According to Jenner, a single operation in childhood secured life-long immunity from small-pox; and our vaccination laws have no other basis than the assumption that this is true. It would be ridiculous to insist on the vaccination of infants, who are mostly keepers at home, if, by the time they are old enough to attend school, and so mix with other children, with perhaps a remote chance of encountering small-pox infection, the "protection" afforded them by vaccination is worn out. Yet that the protection is thus very "fleeting" is what the majority of medical men now affirm; for indeed Jenner's proposition cannot be maintained in the face of notorious facts. Vaccination in infancy is an admirable protection, it appears, so long as there is no small-pox about for you to catch; but, as soon as an epidemic comes, you are no better off than the unvaccinated. This has been proved over and over again, both in England and on the Continent, by the fact that, during epidemics, the small-pox hospitals contain about the same proportion of vaccinated patients to unvaccinated as

is found in the country generally. So "re-vaccination" became the cry a few years ago; and the cry has quite lately
been extended to "frequent" or (what amounts to the same
thing) "recent vaccination," which we are now assured is
the only genuine and absolutely safe defence. Of course this
doctrine drives a coach-and-four through legislation which
insists only on vaccination in infancy; and it also renders
a little ridiculous the horror which many advocates have
professed to feel at the state of unvaccinated infants as
"centres of infection"; for it is a confession that the vast
majority of the population, including very likely the alarmists
themselves, are in the same parlous state.

Re-vaccination formed no part of Jenner's plan for the exter-
mination of small-pox. It was first practised in Würtemburg
about 1829, but it was not heard of in this country until 1844;
and, as recently as 1851, the National Vaccine Establishment
officially declared it unnecessary. Dr Seaton recommended
re-vaccination at puberty, but objected to a third repetition
of the operation. On the other hand, Dr Collingridge, the
active Medical Officer of Health for the Port of London,
advocates "thoroughly efficient *annual* re-vaccination"; and
Dr Bernard O'Connor supports the theory of Dr Warlomont,
of Brussels, who holds that vaccination is not efficient unless
it is "vaccinisation," that is, a repetition of the process every
four months, until the unhappy victim will not "take" any
longer.

It is a grotesque story; and it is wonderful that the
advocates of these repeated operations do not see that
their arguments destroy the basis of cow-pox prophylaxy
altogether. Dr Pearson, the contemporary of Jenner, and
the founder of the original "Institution for the Inoculation
of the Vaccine Pock," in 1799, saw this clearly enough, and
regarded re-vaccination not merely as unnecessary but as
impossible. He put the case bluntly and frankly :—"If a

child can be re-vaccinated, then it can take small-pox; *ergo*, vaccination is not an equivalent for small-pox; and where then is the good of it?" Perhaps he stated the case a little too tersely for it to be quite clear. If cow-pox cannot protect against cow-pox, or, in other words, if re-vaccination is possible, how can cow-pox protect against small-pox? In other words, vaccination is useless. The argument is perfectly sound, though it was urged in the belief that cow-pox was modified small-pox. If the modified form could not protect against the modified, how could it be expected to protect against the unmodified? If you cannot resist the attack of a cat, how can you resist the attack of a tiger?— to use the analogy between the two diseases which Jenner in his "Inquiry" employed. And the force of the argument is even greater—though, for that matter, it becomes superfluous —when, with modern knowledge, we have ceased to believe in there being any pathological relation between the two diseases. That re-vaccination, and, for that matter frequent vaccination, are quite possible, is now a matter of ordinary experience; and it has also been pointed out by Professor Crookshank that persons who have had small-pox are none the less susceptible of vaccination,—a further proof of the absence of any scientific relation between the two diseases.

Another instance of the unscientific confusion in which the whole of this vaccination business is wrapped is the disagreement among doctors as to the necessity of vaccinating in more places than one, and of producing what are called "good marks." Jenner was satisfied with a single puncture in the skin; and, according to his account, that secured life-long protection against small-pox. No one holds to that now. Four incisions are insisted upon by the Local Government Board; and I have heard a public vaccinator declare that he was not satisfied with less than seven; while a certain Dr Dixon, in his official report to the authorities at Bermondsey, asserted that, to make things really safe, there should be as many insertions of the lymph as there would be pustules on the body in a mild case of small-pox.* Nor must I omit to notice an entirely new doctrine as to the value of what are called "good marks," put forth as recently as last October by Dr Dalton, of the Metropolitan Asylums Board, and based by him on the observation of a thousand cases of small-pox. We used to be taught that, when vaccination "takes" severely, and the anxious mother is expected to rejoice on account of the saving gravity of the symptoms, the child, if it survived, would at any rate be absolutely secure against small-pox. We were expected to admire a process which brought so much foul matter out of the child; as if it would have been there even if the poison which produced it had never been inserted. But now, alas! according to Dr Dalton, all this is a mistake. The gravity of the effects of vaccination proves, he says, not that life-long immunity has been secured, but that the child is highly susceptible of small-pox, and, unless re-vaccinated, and that shortly, will almost certainly catch it and have a severe attack, should the infection chance to cross its path. Such is the criticism of an experienced small-pox hospital doctor on the theory which has been made so much of in recent years, and has been well supported by statistics, which showed that the vaccinated with "good marks" were, if under two years of age, absolutely immune from death from small-pox, and that at all ages only three per cent. of the cases of such persons proved fatal.†

* Why make this limitation of "mild"? Would it not be more reasonable to say "as many insertions of the lymph as the person in question would have pustules, if he caught small-pox"?

† It is a proof of the slowness with which criticisms on vaccination come to the knowledge of medical men that Dr Hugh Jones, in reading before the Royal Statistical Society, on December 19, 1893, an elabor-

At a meeting of the British Association some ten or twelve years ago, Dr W. Balthazar Foster (now better known as Sir Walter B. Foster, M.D.) is reported to have said that "it was incomprehensible how the virtue of vaccination could be regarded as an open question by any scientifically educated mind." In 1889, Professor Crookshank, a medical scientist of European reputation, concluded his study of the "History and Pathology of Vaccination" (Vol. I., p. 465) with the words, "Unfortunately a belief in the efficacy of vaccination has been so enforced in the education of the medical practitioner that it is hardly probable that the futility of the practice will be generally acknowledged in our generation, though nothing would more redound to the credit of the profession, and give evidence of the advance made in pathology and sanitary science." Clearly, in the case of vaccination, as elsewhere, science is by way of revising her judgments.

The Empirical Argument.

In the art of medicine empiricism has at times to do duty as science. Nor is it unreasonable that, when an explanation of phenomena is impossible, uniform experience of the regularity with which events succeed one another should give a quasi-scientific value to our conclusions as to their cause and effect. In other words, although no sound theory as to the relation be-

ate paper on "The Perils and Protection of Infant Life," thought it enough to say in passing, "It is unnecessary to discuss the prophylactic value of vaccination," and quoted the usual table showing the immense value of "good marks," apparently quite in ignorance of the facts that Dr Dalton's conclusions were inconsistent with that table, and that within the last seven years scientific and historical investigations, made by competent men, had indicated that vaccination has no specially prophylactic value at all, an inference which no one questions on scientific grounds.

tween cow-pox and small-pox warrants us in anticipating
that the former should prove a prophylactic against the
latter, if experience shows that, under varying circumstances,
cow-pox inoculation is invariably followed by immunity
from small-pox, the conclusion that vaccination has the
protective power that is claimed for it would be adequately,
albeit only empirically, established.

Very few persons have the opportunity of observing
at first hand whether these things are so ; and it is
unnecessary to point out that the conclusions that the mass
of people draw from experience which is necessarily on a
very limited scale, are largely coloured by the prepossession
with which they approach the subject.   Any scrap of
evidence that tells in favour of the opinion they hold is
treasured in the memory and stated for the benefit of others
from time to time ; any amount of evidence that tells the
other way is ignored, denied, forgotten, or explained so as
to make it consistent with the view that is so tenaciously
adhered to.   It is not dishonesty but unconscious bias.   I
know, for example, an eminent journalist, to whom the value
of vaccination has for years been as certain as the propositions of the multiplication table.   He was vaccinated and re-
vaccinated, and then had a severe attack of small-pox.   Did
it modify his opinion ?   Not a bit of it ; he is more devoted
to vaccination now than ever, for he is certain that, but for
vaccination, he would have died ; and it is useless to point
out to him that this assumption of his is quite groundless.
Of course, when the failure of vaccination thus affords
fresh reasons for believing in it, very slight evidence is
enough to render convincing its apparent success.   And
this is why it is so difficult at the present time to form a
fair estimate of the force of the empirical argument.
Immunity from small-pox subsequent to vaccination is
almost necessarily accepted as consequent on vaccination

by those who believe the official and professional doctrine ; though to those who take a wider view, and who have observed that no other infectious or epidemic disease is even supposed to have temporarily subsided or to have died out altogether in consequence of a prophylactic against it being adopted, there appears no necessity to accept vaccination as the cause.

The advocates of vaccination ought first to prove that nothing else could have brought about that diminution in the ordinary prevalence of small-pox in which we as well as they rejoice.   They ought to prove to us that, when in London, a hundred years ago, the soil was honeycombed with cesspools, and there was an annual death-rate of 70 or 80, as compared with 20 per thousand now, small-pox was only more prevalent because of the absence of vaccination. They ought to convince us first that neither sanitation, nor improvements in diet, nor the natural tendency of an exotic disease to wear itself out, can account for our comparative freedom from a disease, which is known to be specially deadly in the slums, among the ill-fed, and where it makes its appearance either for the first time or after a long period of immunity.   Until these things are done, the argument from statistics will only serve to convince those who were convinced already ; and it certainly will not make much impression on those who have taken the pains to examine the figures, and who see that the argument itself falls to pieces unless it is deftly handled.

It never was more deftly handled than by Sir Lyon (now Lord) Playfair in his speech in the House of Commons, on June 19th, 1883,* a speech which is said to have turned

* The occasion was a resolution proposed by the late Mr P. A. Taylor, to the effect that "it was inexpedient and unjust to enforce vaccination under penalties upon those who regard it as inadvisable and dangerous." The extraordinary rhetorical effect of Sir Lyon Playfair's speech may be gauged by the fact that, whereas, in 1871, a

more votes than any other ever delivered in Parliament, and which, in that case, brought about the continuance of the compulsory law for at least another decade. There is no reason to suppose that the speaker had any thought of using figures unfairly. The speech is that of a man genuinely anxious for the public welfare, and inspired by the belief, which fifty years of experience have done much to discredit, that legislation directed by modern science is able to "stamp out" infectious diseases.*   Thus, one sentence ran as follows :—"Parliament in 1853 passed an obligatory law, which remained without administrative means of enforcing it till 1871 ; but still, during this period of obligatory vaccination (1854-71) small-pox mortality fell (from 305 per million as it had stood in the preceding period of seven years) to 223 deaths per million. In that year (1871) a law was passed making it compulsory on Boards of Guardians

clause abolishing repeated penalties had been accepted by the House by a majority of 57 to 12, Mr Taylor's resolution was rejected by the enormous majority of 270 (286 to 16). The House had resumed a more rational temper by May 12th, 1893, when Mr Hopwood's resolution, "That the law compelling vaccination of infants and young persons is unjustifiable, and ought to be repealed," was rejected by a majority of less than two to one (136 to 70).

* The whole speech was given and was answered in detail by the late Mr William White, in a pamphlet entitled "Sir Lyon Playfair taken to pieces and disposed of." London, 1884. The title was gratuitously offensive, and probably hindered the criticism from being widely read ; which is the more to be regretted, since, as an answer, it was complete. Doubtless Lord Playfair had suffered from the disadvantage common to statesmen who have to speak in Parliament on a great variety of subjects which they have no leisure to study. A secretary is employed to get up the facts. He naturally takes it to be his business to collect and marshal only such facts as go to make a defence of the official position ; the result being that a specious case is made out, which falls to pieces when subjected to criticism. It will be the special advantage of the present Cabinet in dealing with this subject, that it contains in Lord Herschell an informant who has himself heard at least some of the evidence on the other side.

to appoint Vaccination Officers; and since that time the average small-pox mortality has been 156 per million."

Nothing could have been more gratifying to the members of the Legislature, who heard this speech, than thus to learn, on such excellent authority, how potent is the arm of the British House of Commons. For the speaker did not assert that these successive Acts of Parliament had resulted in an increase in the number of vaccinations, and that the decrease in the rate of small-pox mortality had in that way been secured. No doubt that was taken as implied; but it was not so stated, nor indeed would such a statement have been precisely true, so far as a comparison between the second and third of these periods is concerned. As a comparison between the first and second periods it would doubtless be true, but there are no statistics to produce. We have, however, the figures from 1852 onwards; and it is the fact that, from that date until 1876, the number of vaccinations did not quite keep pace with the increase of population; while, since 1876 up to the present day,—the period that has been freest from small-pox,—they have steadily decreased.* So that it is, apparently, the terror inspired by Acts of Parliament, and not vaccination itself, which causes small-pox to behave in this exemplary and docile way.

A further inspection of Sir Lyon Playfair's figures discloses the fallacy of the argument, which so profoundly impressed

* The year 1875 may be reckoned as the "high-water mark" of vaccination. The percentage of children who in that year escaped vaccination was only 3·8, and the number was under 5 per cent. until 1884. The steady increase of the number now escaping is best seen by the following table :—

1885	1886	1887	1888	1889	1890
5·8	6·4	7·1	8·5	9·9	11·3

and in later years, for which the returns are not yet to hand, the increase will probably be found to have been by "leaps and bounds." In London the percentage of children escaping vaccination has risen from 5·7 in 1881 to 13·9 in 1890.

the House of Commons. He was maintaining that increased stringency in compulsion resulted, time after time, in a substantial reduction in the death-rate from small-pox. But the Act of 1867, (which was the first to impose repeated penalties, and was thus the most severe of all the measures that have dealt with vaccination in this country—so severe and so odious in fact that it had not been in force four years when a Select Committee unanimously reported in favour of its repeal in that particular,) is not noticed at all; nor is the Act of 1874 noticed, which empowered the Local Government Board to keep a firm hand over the administration of the law. Surely these two brave blows in the cause of vaccination deserved honourable mention; and surely they inaugurated new periods in which the beneficial effects of the operation thus vigorously enforced would be displayed. Why are we not shewn that the decrease in the small-pox death-rate was continuous from 1853 to 1867, from 1867 to 1871, from 1871 to 1874, and from 1874 up to the date for which figures in 1883 were available? And why was 1847 selected as a date to start from, when there was no legislation at all in that year? These questions reveal the cleverness displayed in the selection of the periods; for the great epidemic of 1871-2 is in this way divided into two, the great number of deaths (over 23,000) in the year 1871 being thus diluted by being merged in the long preceding period of seventeen years, in which the mortality had been comparatively low, while a similar refuge is secured for the deaths (over 19,000) in 1872. Had the periods been really coincident with the dates of each increase in the stringency of compulsion (1853-67, 1868-71, 1872-74, 1875-80) the figures would have told a very different story.

As an illustration of the ease with which statistics can thus be played with, and made to prove anything you please, I commend to students of this controversy the following sentence, which is *not* from Sir Lyon Playfair's speech, but is nevertheless literally and strictly true :—" In the years 1861-2 the deaths from small-pox throughout England and Wales amounted to less than 3000. In 1867 an Act of Parliament was passed which made vaccination for the first time really compulsory, repeated penalties on account of default being now insisted on until the child should reach the age of fourteen years. *And what followed?* In the years 1871-2 the deaths from small-pox exceeded 43,000, being an increase of more than 1400 per cent. on the earlier period."

This epidemic of 1871-2 has always been the great crux of the advocates of vaccination, and Lord Playfair has not been alone in his efforts to slur over its disastrous testimony. The late Dr Guy, who read a paper on " Two Hundred and Fifty Years of Small-Pox in London," before the Statistical Society, on June 20th, 1882, proved to his own satisfaction, and doubtless to that of his hearers, that, thanks to vaccination, there had been no epidemic of small-pox at all in London during the nineteenth century; and this was done by assuming an epidemic to mean 10 per cent. of the deaths from all causes being due to the one particular disease in question, whereas in the year 1871 the ratio was only 9·837 per cent (Journal of the Statistical Society, Vol. XLV., p. 404). The paper is a very laborious one, and contains much valuable information; but when a writer plainly asserts (p. 414) that the question of the preventive power of vaccination is exclusively one of statistics, thus leaving out of account altogether, although himself a physician, the pathological side of the subject, which is more strictly allied to medical science, we have a right to expect that he shall not use the figures thus arbitrarily.*

* The kind of stuff that a learned man can acceptably lay before a learned society is illustrated by a phrase used by Dr Guy in this paper (p. 415)—" such fatal maladies as the ' Parish Infection.' " The

No one desires, and least of all have disbelievers in vaccination any desire to deny, that small-pox is now ordinarily
far less prevalent than it was a hundred years ago.   It is the
absence of any definite relation between the decline of small-
pox and the use of vaccination which we affirm ; and this
absence of any definite relation is illustrated as clearly as
anything can be by the reckless disregard for vaccination,
and even for Acts of Parliament, which epidemics are found
to manifest as they come and go, if only the figures are
allowed to tell their own tale.   That is the sole aim of our
criticism of the statistics put forth by advocates of vaccination,—to protest against their being so cooked and marshalled
as to indicate a relation where none really exists.   No
doubt some entirely trustworthy statistics can be quoted
to show that where vaccination is the rule small-pox is
rare ; but other statistics, no less trustworthy, can also be
quoted, and will be quoted shortly, which show just the
reverse.   The only safe conclusion in such a case is a
purely negative one, that the one set of figures does not
depend on the other.

Further Notes on the Argument from Statistics.

How comes it that the disparaging remark is so commonly
made about statistics, that they can prove anything?   It
is because they are, often enough, merely a mask behind
which a strong prepossession is striving mightily to establish
its case.   When confronted with statistical evidence that

name hardly sounds like that of a disease recognised as such in the
seventeenth and eighteenth centuries ; and it is in fact a mistake
(copied apparently from a statistical work of John Marshall), the
number of "parœch. infect.," or "parishes infected," being taken as
the number of deaths due to an otherwise unknown disease ; and, when
the weekly lists of these are added up for a whole year, a considerable
figure is the result.   See Creighton's "History of Epidemics in
Britain," Vol I. p. 396.

points to a conclusion unlikely for other reasons to be true, it is necessary to enquire from what sources these statistics have been drawn, whether there was any bias in those responsible for the original details, and whether there is any method of checking the returns. Especially is this the case when a double set of statistics comes from the same hand, and the bearing of the one series of figures on the other points towards some conclusion in which the person furnishing the statistics is known to be interested. Statistics of this kind are alive with prepossession; really trustworthy statistics should be innocent of all motive; they should state but the bare facts; they should be, so to speak, dead. The "live" statistics, on the other hand, must be treated as definitely controversial, and should only be accepted without hesitation when they perforce serve to tell against the known prepossessions of those who have prepared and issued them.

Thus the statistics issued by the Registrar General, showing the actual number of deaths from small-pox, are quite trustworthy, apart from occasional errors of diagnosis, which are probably too few to make much difference; and the same is true of the statistics of vaccination issued by the Local Government Board. Each department does its own work without reference to the other; and we may be tolerably sure that the records are strictly records of facts.

But it is impossible to have the same confidence in the statements as to vaccination which medical men are requested to append to certificates of death from small-pox. So great are their prepossessions in favour of the prophylactic value of vaccination, that it is perhaps hardly fair to expect them to certify that it has failed; and, in point of fact, in spite of the urgent and repeated requests of the Registrar General, they do usually omit any reference to vaccination. The following table illustrates this :—

Deaths from Small-pox in England and Wales.

	1887.	1888.	1889.	1890.	1891.	1892.
Vaccinated	42	91	4	4	3	55
Unvaccinated	111	269	2	0	17	106
No statement	353	666	17	12	29	270
Total	506	1026	23	16	49	431

With regard to this table, the cases about which no statement is made (about two-thirds of the whole number) may for the sake of argument be taken as vaccinated cases. This cannot, of course, be stated as a certainty; but it goes without saying that a medical man would readily certify an unvaccinated case as such, but would be unwilling to be equally frank in regard to a vaccinated one. Nor need the advocates of vaccination fear to grant this, as an hypothesis for the sake of argument; for even then, as the returns stand, the deaths of vaccinated patients would only be about three times as many as those of the unvaccinated; whereas the proportion of the one to the other in the population generally may be taken as eight or nine to one. Disbelievers in vaccination are not unwilling to admit that, in a population vaccinated to the extent of 90 per cent., the deaths of vaccinated persons from small-pox might be not more than 80 per cent. of the whole number; for the reason that the lack of vaccination is not the only condition that differentiates the unvaccinated from the rest of the population. Generally speaking the unvaccinated, if regarded as a class, would include very young children, who more readily succumb to infection, should they be brought into contact with it; but, what is more important, unvaccinated adults are mainly found among the waifs and strays of society, tramps, and the like, whom the compulsory law does not reach ; and such persons, from their habits of life, are far more liable than others to encounter small-pox infection, and, if they take it, to succumb to the disease.* So that a somewhat higher proportion of cases of small-pox, and of deaths from the disease, is to be looked for among the unvaccinated, without any need to regard their lack of vaccination as the factor in the situation.

Nevertheless, the disproportion, as shewn in the statistics of small-pox hospitals, or even in the Registrar General's returns interpreted as above, is too considerable to be accounted for satisfactorily in this way; and a further and fuller explanation, disastrous no doubt to the trustworthiness of the statistics in question, but proved to be correct in a sufficient number of instances, has been provided by the careful investigations of Dr Alfred Russel Wallace, F.R.S., Mr Wheeler, of Darlington, and Major-General Phelps, of Edgbaston.†

Briefly stated their criticisms amount to this :—

That there must be something wrong with the small-pox hospital statistics is clear from the extraordinary high ratio of deaths to cases which they indicate among the unvaccinated. The enthusiastic believer in vaccination finds no difficulty in believing that every unvaccinated person, brought into contact with small-pox infection, of necessity takes the disease and dies of it. Consequently, if the small-pox hospital returns show a ratio of 30, 40, 50, or even, of 60 per cent. of deaths to cases among the unvaccinated, he is surprised, if at all, at its moderation. But a person of wider information and of more sober judgment, knowing that in the eighteenth century, before vaccination was thought of, the proportion

* They are ordinarily also the vehicles by which the infection is carried from place to place. Legislation to check the spread of disease by tramps is urgently needed.

† For details see "Vaccination Proved Useless and Dangerous from Fifty-five Years of Registration Statistics," by Alfred Russel Wallace, LL.D., and edited with notes by Alexander Wheeler, 1889.

of deaths to cases was a little over 18 per cent., or less than one in five, sees at once that (unless we are to suppose that the doctors kill unvaccinated patients so as to maintain the glory of vaccination) there must be a mistake somewhere. The otherwise specially unfavourable conditions of the unvaccinated minority at the present day might explain a higher ratio (say up to 25 per cent.) of deaths to cases; but ratios of 68 or of 83 (such as were reported from two Rochdale Hospitals in 1881-2), are really incredible, when placed side by side with a ratio of 18 in the eighteenth century, also of course exclusively among the unvaccinated. On enquiry it appeared that all patients received at the hospitals used to be set down as unvaccinated, unless the marks were clearly visible. In cases of confluent small-pox (the more serious kind) the marks are temporarily obliterated by the disease, and only re-appear in case of recovery. Thus, vaccinated patients who recovered would be placed to the credit of vaccination; but, if they died, they would be registered as unvaccinated. In this way, while the general proportion of deaths to cases remained pretty much what it was before vaccination had been invented, hardly any deaths among the vaccinated were reported; but those who died were on that account reported as "unvaccinated," whose ratio thus became incredibly high.

It sounds almost like a joke, but there is no doubt about the facts; and, though attention was called as long ago as 1885, by Dr Alfred Russel Wallace, to the delusive nature of statistics thus falsified at their very source, the thing goes on merrily still; and in a recent small-pox hospital report, issued at Warrington, we even find it naïvely admitted that several patients who died were registered as "belonging to the unvaccinated class," because they were "vaccinated too late." If they had recovered, the recovery would have been credited to vaccination; so that this method of drawing up controversial statistics is distinctly a case of "heads I win, tails you lose." *

Occasionally, however, the small-pox hospital authorities do make admissions which shew pretty plainly the worthlessness of vaccination as a protection. Thus, in 1871, at the Highgate Hospital, 91 per cent. of the cases were reported as vaccinated, and, in 1881, 96 per cent.; and at Birmingham last autumn out of 117 cases 107 were vaccinated, 6 were unvaccinated, and 4 were doubtful. In all these instances the number of vaccinated patients suffering from small-pox would no doubt be greater in proportion to the unvaccinated patients than the proportion of vaccinated persons to the unvaccinated, taking the population as a whole; but this can only be accounted a mere accident. The excessive number of vaccinated patients is nevertheless a not infrequent phenomenon. Thus, to give further instances, there was an epidemic at Bromley in 1881, with 43 cases, all of them vaccinated. At Sunderland, in 1884, there were 100 cases, 96 of them vaccinated; and at Oldbury, in last year's epidemic, there were 123 cases of small-pox, of which all but 9 were vaccinated. Dr Gayton's evidence before the Royal Commission, that ordinarily the vaccinated patients are 80 per cent. of the whole number, corresponds accurately enough with what has been said above, that, while about 90 per cent. of the population may be

* See the letter of Mr Alfred Milnes in the "Times," September 9, 1892; Dr Birdwood's reply on the 13th, and Major-General Phelps' letter on the 19th. The death of a person from small-pox, who had been twice successfully re-vaccinated, was registered as if "no statement" about vaccination had accompanied the certificate; and other cases were set down as "unvaccinated," contrary to the fact. The Warrington report above referred to will be found in the "Vaccination Inquirer" for February 1894.

reckoned as vaccinated, the proportion of unvaccinated persons taking small-pox will probably be somewhat higher than their numerical proportion to the rest of the population, on account of other conditions, which render them more liable to the disease, and more likely to die if they have it.

The official returns in Italy of the epidemic of 1870 point to the same conclusion. Vaccination was then a common practice but was not compulsory, and it is hardly likely that more than 70 or 80 per cent. of the population were vaccinated. Yet, out of 55,897 cases of the disease, 76 per cent. were vaccinated.

That a small-pox epidemic does not pick out the unvaccinated persons, as believers in the operation would suppose, but takes people as they come, with a sublime disregard to their having been inoculated with the cow-pox or not, is further illustrated by sundry German statistics —and the German statistics may usually be relied upon as more straightforward than the English ones. Thus, at Bonn, in 1870, 41 vaccinated cases of small-pox were brought to the hospital before a single unvaccinated case was brought; at Cologne, at the same date, the number, under the same circumstances, was 173; and at Liegnitz, in 1871, it was 224; while at Neuss, out of a total number of 248 cases of small-pox between 1865 and 1873, not a single one was unvaccinated. *

These facts, and they are undisputed, certainly suggest the conclusion that, while vaccination gains a great reputation as a prophylactic from our ordinary freedom from the disease against which it is supposed to protect us, it is really quite useless when an epidemic makes its appear-

* *Encyclop. Britan.*, Vol. xxiv., p. 30. Further examples from Germany will be found in Dr Creighton's article, " Vaccination, a Scientific Enquiry," in the *Arena*—an American magazine—for September 1890.

ance. And that there is no relation between the use or disuse of vaccination and the presence or absence of small-pox, of such a character as to have any scientific value, is further shown by quite recent experience in our own country. There is, at any rate, this advantage to be gained from the comparative disuse of vaccination in sundry districts (in defiance of the law) that, whereas most of the statistics quoted above refer only to countries and periods where and when vaccination was uniform and universal, we can now see whether towns in which nearly all the children are unvaccinated do in fact suffer, as we had been led to anticipate, from their neglect of the great preservative; and we can compare them with other towns, similarly circumstanced in all respects save in regard to vaccination.

THE EVIDENCE OF SUNDRY TOWNS AND DISTRICTS IN ENGLAND.

I have recently taken the trouble to compare the tables issued by the Registrar General with those issued by the Local Government Board, independent, trustworthy, "dead" statistics, as I have above described them, taking for the vaccination statistics the period of six years, 1885-90—no detailed later ones have yet been issued—and, for the statistics of deaths from small-pox, the Registrar General's returns from 1887, which bring us, in the case of sundry large towns, up to the end of June this year; and they amply confirm what those who know that there is no patho-logical relation between small-pox and vaccination would have anticipated, viz: that neither is there any statistical relation. It is unimportant that the vaccination returns do not come down to date, because they vary far less markedly than epidemics do; and it may be taken as

E

certain that, where vaccination, as shown by the reports, was discredited and largely abandoned in 1890, there has been no subsequent return to the belief and practice, but rather a further departure from it.   On the whole, we are pointed to the conclusion that where there is least vaccination there also is least small-pox; but this again must be accounted a mere accident.*

Thus, to compare large areas first, the four best vaccinated counties in England are Westmoreland, Huntingdon, Somerset, and Worcester, containing a population of about 865,000.   The average vaccination default in these counties during the period named was very small, viz., 3˙9, and the deaths from small-pox during the six years 1887-92 amounted to 14.   The three least vaccinated counties are Leicester, Northants, and Bedford, with a population of about 1,050,000.   In these the average percentage of default was as high as 28˙3, and the deaths from small-pox, 12.   The numbers of course are too small in both cases for any sound conclusion to be based on them; but, at any rate, they do not indicate any serious consequences from the neglect of vaccination.

Turning next to sundry towns, and comparing the statistics of vaccination with the statistics of small-pox, we find it equally impossible to establish from the figures any positive relation between the two.   The tables which are here

* It should be pointed out that, while every effort has been made to render these figures, and those which are contained in the following tables, as accurate as possible, there may be in some cases a slight amendment required, as the Local Government Board and the Registrar General do not always follow the same boundaries : and in the Registrar General's preliminary reports deaths in small-pox hospitals are usually referred to the towns from which the cases came ; whereas in his Annual Report they are placed in the districts in which the hospitals are actually situated.   But the differences could hardly be of a kind to affect the general argument.

appended (pp. 68, 69) amply illustrate this. Table I. gives the twenty-two registration districts which have suffered most from small-pox during the seven-and-a-half years ending June 30th last. The table also shows to what extent vaccination had been neglected in these same districts during the six years ending December 31st, 1890. Later returns as to vaccination are not yet published; indeed those for 1890 have only just come to hand (on August 29th, 1894). Table II. shows the twenty-two poor-law unions (the boundaries of which correspond with sufficient accuracy with those of the registration districts) in which vaccination had been most neglected during the period above mentioned; and it shows also to what extent these districts have suffered from small-pox. *

Now, on the theory on which vaccination has been made compulsory—and it must be borne in mind that throughout I am criticising the reasonableness of a law which insists on the vacination of infants for the supposed benefit of the community—these two tables ought to be pretty nearly identical. Special prevalence of small-pox ought to be the result of neglect of vaccination, which is popularly supposed to act as a kind of bulwark, shutting the disease out; and specially-marked neglect of the great preservative ought to be followed by a smart epidemic. But what are the facts? what do the figures show?

* Sundry unions are included under the names of the towns to which they really belong. Thus Barton Regis is included under Bristol, Eccles-all-Bierlow under Sheffield, Aston Manor under Birmingham, &c. London is omitted from these statistical tables, partly because vaccina-tion varies so considerably over its huge and ill-defined area, that the figures would indicate nothing unless it were also pointed out in detail from what districts the cases come which are transferred to the hospitals of the Metropolitan Asylums Board at or near Dartford. But it may be noted, in passing, that the small-pox epidemic this summer in the neighbourhood of St John's Wood occurred in a district better vaccinated than London as a whole.

TABLE I.

Showing the 22 Towns or Districts (excluding London) which have suffered most from Small-Pox during the last 7½ years; and showing also how far they neglected Vaccination, 1885-90.

	DEATHS FROM SMALL-POX.									PERCENTAGE OF VACCINATION DEFAULT.						
	1887	1888	1889	1890	1891	1892	1893	1894*	TOTAL	1885	1886	1887	1888	1889	1890	AVERAGE‡
Sheffield . .	282	409	...	1	...	14	5	...	711	4·6	3·7	2·4	4··	4·5	5·4	4·1
Birmingham .	2	...	...	...	7	...	71	131	211	4·3	4·6	5·5	3·6	5·8	5·8	4·9
Bradford . .	...	3	1	...	...	4	115	26	149	7·1	8·0	10·5	7·3	20·6	24·3	12·9
Dewsbury . .	...	2	...	...	22	102	†	†	126	47·2	37·5	29·6	32·2	37·3	39·1	37·1
Bristol . . .	38	47	...	...	...	...	17	21	123	4·0	4·5	4·1	4·0	7·0	7·7	5·2
Oldham . .	...	13	...	...	...	15	65	21	114	18·4	27·6	44·1	60·9	71·0	74·4	49·4
Walsall . .	8	24	...	...	...	...	67	9	108	6·2	14·3	12·7	8·8	12·0	13·5	11·2
Halifax . .	...	1	...	...	...	52	35	2	90	9·8	13·0	28·2	44·8	60·0	69·6	37·5
Warrington .	...	2	...	...	...	56	17	...	75	4·3	3·6	4·1	4·6	6·0	5·1	4·6
Manchester .	...	1	1	...	...	...	48	17	67	3·5	4·1	3·5	3·7	4·4	4·9	4·0
Grimsby . .	13	48	...	...	...	...	1	...	62	6·4	7·2	4·3	5·6	5·3	6·8	6·9
Wakefield . .	...	20	...	...	1	11	25	†	57	3·7	3·9	3·0	3·4	5·1	4·6	3·9
Preston . .	1	52	...	...	...	...	...	1	54	7·9	6·4	8·2	7·1	10·9	8·5	8·1
Leeds . . .	1	18	1	...	1	8	20	2	51	1·8	2·1	4·2	2·2	5·7	5·1	3·5
Prestwich . .	6	39	...	...	...	4	†	†	49	7·4	7·1	8·2	7·1	10·7	8·6	8·2
Rotherham .	29	16	...	...	...	1	2	...	48	5·1	3·9	2·8	4·6	5·4	4·1	4·3
Chesterfield .	3	30	...	...	...	9	†	†	42	4·0	10··.	9·2	5·8	9·2	15·4	9·0
Wortley . .	17	17	...	...	...	5	†	†	39	3·8	3·6	2·4	3·9	5·5	7·0	4·5
Ashton-under-Lyne . .	...	34	1	...	...	...	...	...	35	7·4	7·3	8·1	5·9	11·6	12·9	8·8
Liverpool . .	2	2	2	...	2	15	9	2	34	4·7	4·8	5·7	4·7	4·3	4·4	4·8
Middlesborough .	18	5	...	...	...	2	7	2	34	3·0	2·1	2·6	2·8	3·9	4·1	3·1
Hull . . .	2	19	...	3	...	...	8	1	33	9·1	13·5	10·1	10·6	10·4	10·6	10·7

* To June 30th.   † Official details not yet to hand.
‡ These averages may be compared with the averages for the country as a whole, given on p. 55.

TABLE II.

Showing the 22 Towns or Districts (excluding London) in which Vaccination was most neglected, 1885-90; and showing also how far they have suffered from Small-Pox during the last 7½ years.

	PERCENTAGE OF VACCINATION DEFAULT.							DEATHS FROM SMALL-POX.								
	1885	1886	1887	1888	1889	1890	AVERAGE‡	1887	1888	1889	1890	1891	1892	1893	1894*	TOTAL.
Keighley . .	71'9	71'8	75'4	78'7	81'1	80'1	76'5	...	2	...	...	...	...	†	†	2
Leicester . .	52'1	69'1	72'2	77'0	79'8	78'7	74'8	...	...	...	...	...	6	15	...	21
Gloucester .	10'6	18'1	58'8	79'3	83'2	83'?	55'5	...	...	...	...	...	...	...	...	0
Oldham . .	18'4	27'6	4'1	60'9	71'0	74'4	49'4	...	13	...	...	...	15	65	21	114
Luton . . .	8'3	29'7	33'6	43'0	64'3	72'5	41'9	...	...	...	...	...	...	†	†	0
Eastbourne .	24'1	23'8	32'2	43'7	54'4	65'1	40'5	...	...	...	...	...	...	...	...	0
Halifax . .	9'8	13'0	28'2	44'8	60'0	69'6	37'5	...	1	...	...	...	52	35	2	90
Northampton	10'2	22'9	25'7	37'0	63'6	74'6	37'3	...	...	...	...	...	...	...	...	0
Dewsbury .	47'2	37'5	29'6	32'2	37'3	39'1	37'1	...	2	...	...	22	102	†	†	126
Barrow-on-Soar . . .	16'6	20'9	21'8	35'6	52'7	67'2	35'8	...	...	...	...	...	...	†	†	0
Kettering . .	10'4	22'2	27'1	36'8	46'3	53'3	32'7	1	...	...	...	...	...		†	1
Banbury . .	9'5	24'1	25'3	32'9	46'2	43'1	30'2	...	...	...	...	...	...	†	†	0
Billesdon . .	14'0	18'3	23'5	31'5	32'6	40'3	26'7	...	...	...	...	...	...	†	†	0
Wellingborough .	9'2	10'4	13'2	20'3	32'1	72'1	26'2	...	...	...	...	...	...	†	†	0
Falmouth . .	6'7	9'3	14'6	27'3	39'0	46'5	23.9	...	...	1	...	...	...	†	†	1
Thrapston .	4'9	7'5	9'5	26'1	36'6	51'1	22'6	...	...	...	...	...	...	†	†	0
Blaby . . .	10'4	13'2	13'3	19'7	24'3	47'7	21'4	...	...	...	...	...	...	†	†	0
Bath . . .	9'1	13'0	17'9	20'2	24'0	26'5	18'4	...	...	...	...	...	...	3	...	3
Cheltenham .	14'1	14'4	15'0	20'2	19'8	21'4	17'5	...	...	...	...	...	...	...	...	0
Dover . . .	12'2	17'4	18'2	21'6	12'8	16'8	16'5	...	5	...	...	...	3	...	...	8
Burnley . .	7'7	12'2	14'0	19'4	25'3	20'0	16'4	...	2	...	...	...	...	...	...	2
South Shields	11'9	13'1	13'9	23'1	18'8	16'0	16'1	...	1	...	...	...	1	...	...	2

* To June 30th. † Official details not yet to hand.

‡ These averages may be compared with the averages for the country as a whole, given on p. 55.

It appears, then, that in only three instances out of twenty-two do we find that the tables correspond; or, more correctly, only in three out of a total of forty-one places that come into the lists. Dewsbury, Oldham, and Halifax are these three; and I have had their names printed in italics for the sake of clearness. The advocate of vaccination is undoubtedly at liberty to point to these three, and to urge that their aggregate of 330 deaths from small-pox since 1887 is the penalty they have had to pay for their temerity in neglecting vaccination during six years, up to an average of 41'3 per cent on the number of children born. But what, then, are we to say of Sheffield, with its 711 deaths in spite of a very low average of vaccination default; and what of Birmingham, Bristol, Warrington, Manchester, and the other towns, which have also suffered considerably in spite of being vaccinated better than the country as a whole? Or again, turning to the other table, what are we to say of Keighley, Gloucester, Luton, Eastbourne, Northampton, and a dozen others, which small-pox has either not touched at all, or not appreciably, in spite of their great and growing neglect? But it is useless to pursue the subject. The figures, which, so far as I know, have never before been presented in a way which makes their significance unmistakable, tell their own tale; and only those who "will not be learned nor understand, but walk on still in darkness," can be blind to it.

If these statistics prove anything, they show that neglect of vaccination has involved no special disaster, and that insistence on it has provided no special security. On the whole the best vaccinated populations have suffered most.

Before this part of the subject is quitted, a word should be said as to Leicester, the town which has played the most important part in this vaccination controversy. For more than fifteen years Leicester has openly rebelled against the Vaccination Laws, and a very small percentage of the children born there are now vaccinated.* In 1871-2, when it was as well vaccinated as any other town in England, there were 358 deaths from small-pox; but from 1878 onwards there were not a dozen deaths from that cause, though the disease was imported on various occasions, until 1892; and when it then appeared that the prevalent epidemic had reached Leicester, the medical journals (which advocate vaccination with a peremptoriness and assurance such as no adverse experience has apparently any power to shake) displayed much excitement; and most of us felt some interest and curiosity, as we had been led to anticipate the most terrible epidemic of this or of any other century. But it did not "come off." Whether from carelessness about the isolation of patients, or from whatever cause, the disease lingered on for some months. Yet, during the whole period, in a town which numbers (including the suburbs) over 150,000 inhabitants, there were only 146 cases and 21 deaths; and the disease has since 1893 entirely disappeared. On the whole, perhaps it is to the advantage of the cause of those who desire the abolition of compulsory vaccination that there has been this very slight epidemic, if such it can be called, in Leicester; for it is an excellent instance to adduce of the now undeniable fact that, even at a time of small-pox epidemic, the disease does not of necessity spread amongst an unvaccinated population.†

By way of commentary on the statistics presented in this section—which are I believe substantially accurate, though I do not pledge myself to every figure—I cannot do better than quote from the "Report on Sanitary

* On April 3rd, 1890, the *Times* reported that out of 1200 births only 23 children were vaccinated.

† A full account of the epidemic, by Mr J. T. Biggs, was printed in the *Leicester Daily Post* in June, and reprinted in the *Vaccination Inquirer* in July this year.

Measures in India, 1879-80.* "'The vaccination returns
in India show that the number of vaccinations does not
bear a ratio to the small-pox deaths. Small-pox in India
is related to season, and also to epidemic prevalence. It
is not a disease, therefore, that can be controlled by vaccination, in the sense that vaccination is a specific against it.
As an endemic and epidemic disease it must be dealt with
by sanitary measures ; and, if these are neglected, small-pox
is certain to increase during epidemic times. Vaccination
has no power apparently over epidemic small-pox. It
would scarcely answer, in the face of these facts, to go on
vaccinating the people to protect them from small-pox,
while leaving them surrounded by such disease-causes as
the Reports would show to exist in all the villages affected."
Substitute in this memorable official confession, " England "
for " India," and you have the truth precisely stated. Its
application is indeed universal.

THE ALLEGED IMMUNITY OF RE-VACCINATED NURSES.

A favourite argument on behalf of vaccination is the
alleged immunity of small-pox hospital nurses who have
been re-vaccinated. Some years ago an official paper used
to be distributed at the public vaccination stations claiming
total immunity for such persons. The statement was
inaccurate, and it has now been formally withdrawn in
evidence before the Royal Commission, with the somewhat lame explanation that it was " a printer's error."
No doubt such nurses do usually keep free of the disease ;
but that their freedom is due to vaccination or re-vaccination is at least " not proven." Constitutional immunity
is a more reasonable hypothesis ; in some cases protection
is afforded by a previous attack ; and the process of

* Vol. XIII., 1881, p. 142.

"seasoning," not as yet satisfactorily explained,* may fairly be claimed as a cause of immunity from small-pox, no less than from other fevers, in the case of those who habitually attend the patients.† There are references to such immunity in the eighteenth century; while on the other hand we have recent testimony to there being no special security for re-vaccinated as compared with vaccinated nurses; and, though it is perhaps impossible at the present day, owing to the long-continued and almost universal prevalence of the practice of vaccination, to find unvaccinated nurses on whom experiments as to their immunity might be tried, I know of one unvaccinated doctor, who, so far, has not caught the disease while attending to his small-pox patients. On the whole, this argument from immunity, which, by the way is not so much used on behalf of vaccination as of re-vaccination, is not a very convincing one, when the facts are fairly and truly stated; but, as originally circulated by authority, it came no doubt with much rhetorical effect.‡

Unfortunately this is not the only misstatement that has persistently been circulated. Over and over again it has been publicly stated that, during the Franco-German war, the French, through having no compulsory vaccination law, lost 23,499 soldiers from small-pox; while the Germans, every man in their army being re-vaccinated, lost only

---

* An ingenious explanation, anticipating to some extent the conclusions of modern bacteriologists, occurred to the eminent discoverer Werner von Siemens in the course of a tour in the Caucasus in 1864. See "Personal Recollections" (1893), p. 297.

† Consumption also is now generally understood to be an infectious disease; but consumption hospital nurses enjoy absolute immunity from it.

‡ The Report of the Metropolitan Asylums Board for 1893, already referred to (p. 3), admits that several cases of small-pox occurred among the staff in that year.

3162.* It is highly probable that the defeated, depressed, and disorganised French did lose more by various diseases than the victorious and well-handled Germans; but that these particular figures must have been invented by some one (and invented for what end save for the glory of vaccination) is clear from the fact that it is admitted from headquarters on both sides that no records were kept during the war of the specific diseases from which soldiers died.

One other illustration may be given of the need that there is to use caution in accepting arguments based solely on statistics.

Mulhall states (" Dictionary of Statistics," p. 203) that in 1874 a law was passed in Germany making re-vaccination compulsory on all persons over twelve years of age. The wonderful effect of this law is illustrated by a table which shows that, whereas in the five years, 1871-4, the deaths in Germany from small-pox were 555 per 10,000 deaths from all causes, in the eight years, 1875-82, they were only 8. But the conclusion we are expected to draw from this is not warranted, for it is not the fact that re-vaccination was first made compulsory in Germany in 1874. The law then passed only consolidated and made uniform the vaccination laws already existing throughout the Empire. And, as early as 1835, re-vaccination of all children attending the public schools in Prussia had been made obligatory. Yet, in spite of the fact that re-vaccination had thus been the rule among the great majority of the population for thirty-five years, and that too among the poorer classes especially, for education was compulsory and so brought the children to the public schools, the deaths from small-pox in Prussia

---

* The number was given as 263 by Sir Lyon Playfair in the House of Commons, the figures apparently being quoted from Mulhall's "Dictionary of Statistics," in the new edition of which (1892) the statement still remains.

in the years 1871-2 amounted to the enormous number of 124,948.

Statistical evidence, if it is to be worth anything at all, must not consist of isolated facts, picked out here and there because they confirm a prepossession. True, in so vast a subject, involving a consideration of the effects of vaccination on hundreds of millions of persons, scattered throughout the civilised world, during a period which now extends over nearly a hundred years, it is impossible that all the facts should be got together and faced, even if we could rely (as we notoriously cannot) on the statistics not being falsified by those from whose pens they originally come. But there are in existence figures, not contested and doubtless substantially correct, which I submit prove adequately that there is no constant relation between small-pox and vaccination. Statistics on a large scale would by no means be necessary to prove the prophylactic power of vaccination, if only this constant relation could in a few well-ascertained instances be shown. "Show me" it has been publicly challenged in the newspapers, "twelve households into which, during an epidemic, small-pox gained entrance, but only in the case of the unvaccinated member or members of that household, and I will believe." Such evidence ought, ex *hypothesi*, to be easily producible, but such evidence has never been produced.

Conclusion on the Argument from Statistics.

A weakness discernible in the argument from statistics is the fact that the statistics of the day invariably support that particular form of the belief in vaccination which is at the time in vogue. In Jenner's day, when one insertion of the lymph through a single puncture in the skin was alleged to secure life-long protection, the statistics (at that date unofficial) amply proved the assertion. But, when the failure of this mild kind of vaccination could no longer be denied, the cry was raised that it was "not properly performed," and laborious statistics were issued showing the immunity of those who had "good marks," and especially of those who had a large number of marks. These statistics are still often quoted, but they are likely to go out of fashion, now that Dr Dalton has shown that "good marks" prove susceptibility rather than immunity. Statistics proving the value and indeed the necessity of re-vaccination are just now more in vogue; and, last of all, it is "recent vaccination," involving of course frequent re-vaccination, and so plenty of work for the doctors, which the medical journals are advocating as the only really safe thing. A little scepticism is perhaps pardonable under such circumstances as these.*

But it may be questioned further, whether the argument from statistics can legitimately be used at all, except by those who employ it as subsidiary to a scientific theory of vaccination. Mere empiricism is usually taken as synonymous with quackery; and certainly vaccination would never have obtained recognition as a legitimate operation, if it had not originally been based on a plausible theory, which pointed towards prophylaxy against small-pox as its probable effect. Statistics confirming such an anticipation have no doubt a legitimate place in the argument; but, so long as the Creighton-Crookshank doctrine of cow-pox remains unrefuted—and it has held the field now for some seven years, without even being called in question—the absence of any

---

* An interesting fact in relation to small-pox is that at the present time it is far more fatal to males than to females. Out of 2051 deaths from the disease in England and Wales in the six years 1887-92, 1231 were males and 820 females, the proportion being thus almost exactly 3 to 2. Yet re-vaccination is certainly more common among males than among females, being obligatory in the Army and Navy, and in some branches of the Civil Service.

scientific theory indicating a pathological relation between cow-pox and small-pox renders the appeal to statistics somewhat grotesque, and quite unworthy of the professors of a scientific art. The believers in the efficacy of any medical nostrum can produce testimonials (*i.e.*, statistics) to its value. Two men who believe that they have cured themselves of rheumatism by carrying a raw potato in the left-hand pocket of their trousers can issue statistics shewing that the remedy has, to their own knowledge, proved efficacious in 100 per cent. of the cases,—this use of magnificent percentages, when the actual numbers are very small, is a fallacious piece of rhetoric familiar to the students of this vaccination controversy—and it is obvious to add that, while testimonials to the curative power of this or that quack remedy are always to be had, even though there is some definite disease to be rid of first, testimonials to an alleged prophylactic power are far more readily obtainable, since nothing is necessary beyond keeping clear of the disease, which there may be no opportunity to catch ; and the evidence is proportionately worthless and misleading.

The medical journals, which, with pathetic persistency, publish small-pox hospital returns proving the value of vaccination, forget that, not only are statistics prepared by enthusiastic advocates, without any critical check, unsatisfactory evidence in any case to lay before those whom they wish to convert, but further, that such statistics can hardly be regarded as admissible evidence at all by those who realise that the scientific basis of vaccination has been overthrown. An illustration may make this clear. There is a good deal of evidence that electricity, in certain cases, has a curative power, though the subject is as yet an obscure one. When therefore we read cordial and sincere testimonies borne by persons of repute to the value of "electropathic belts," we are disposed to believe that such benefits might result from an electric current induced by the wearing of such a belt; and additional evidence serves to strengthen that conviction. But when it has been shown conclusively that the belts in question are not constructed so as to induce any electric current at all, the scientific basis (such as it was) of the alleged cures is destroyed; and no amount of evidence avails to restore our faith. Without imputing dishonesty to anyone who still testifies to cures effected, we are satisfied that such persons are mistaken. The cure, if not a delusion, was due perhaps to the warmth of the belt, or to some other cause wholly unconnected with it. Certainly it was not due to a non-existent electric current. Scepticism of this kind, which is wholly natural, is precisely parallel with the disbelief in the prophylactic power of vaccination, which grows steadily whenever the real state of the case becomes known; and no carefully prepared statistics, nor, for that matter, all the king's horses and all the king's men, can avail to restore the operation to that honourable place which it occupied when it was believed to possess a truly scientific basis.

Whenever an argument in favour of vaccination is produced, which is based solely on statistics and not on any scientific theory, the question should always be asked, " But is vaccination or re-vaccination, as the case may be, the only differentiating condition? " If it is not, the argument at once loses nearly all its weight. Thus, Dr M'Vail, of Glasgow, perhaps the ablest writer on the other side, in his " Vaccination Vindicated," produces some striking comparative statistics of small-pox mortality in the armies of the German and Austrian Empires respectively, and he ascribes the superior immunity of the Germans to their being invariably re-vaccinated, which the Austrians are not. But are all the other conditions the same? Is Vienna in all respects as healthy a town as Berlin? and are not Austrian soldiers often quartered amidst Oriental filth, such as would not be tolerated by Prussian officers in the neighbourhood of their barracks?

So, again, attention is sometimes called to the freedom from small-pox alleged to be enjoyed by the re-vaccinated soldiers of the British army. True, the mortality among them is, as one would expect among seasoned men, a little lower than the average throughout the country, so long as they remain in this country. But, when our re-vaccinated soldiers are sent to unhealthy quarters, as, for example, in India, the cases and deaths from small-pox, though they may not strike one as being very numerous, are yet such as, if stated as percentages to the total number of the British military force, would show a proportion that would mean a considerable epidemic if in London we had similar percentages of cases and deaths to the population.* Arguments based on figures alone are very misleading, unless care is taken to realise their true significance, and unless all the conditions on which they probably depend are given a fair consideration.

We, who disbelieve in vaccination, but hold that other causes beyond the natural dying out of an exotic disease have contributed to bring about our present comparative immunity from small-pox, are disposed to conclude that, if all the energy that has been spent in promoting vaccination had been devoted to really scientific prophylactic measures, sanitation, disinfection, isolation, and the like, the disease would probably have been banished from the country years ago; though, knowing the subtlety with which infectious diseases may gain an entry and re-establish themselves, we do not pretend that any such absolute immunity could be guaranteed. We admit that,

* This point is drawn out in detail in the *Vaccination Inquirer*, Vol. xvi. p. 71.

after all has been done, we may have to confess with the
Friar in " Romeo and Juliet " that

> " A greater Power than we can contradict
> Hath thwarted our intents."

But we do maintain, in any case, that a fair study of the
statistics, foreign as well as British, points to the conclusion
that, where all rational precautions have been taken, unless
the mysterious influence of an epidemic intervenes, there
is really no work for vaccination to do ; while, on the other
hand, if an epidemic does come, vaccination is seen to be
powerless, and it is on other measures that we have to
depend for protection.   So that, while vaccination in the
one case is superfluous, in the other it is ineffectual ;
and in either case its value as a method of hygiene
is *nil.**

THE ALLEGED RISKS OF VACCINATION.

But yet, in spite of disbelief in the protective power of
vaccination, the practice, as enforced by law, would never
have encountered the fierce resistance that has rendered
the Acts inoperative in many important districts, were it
not for the accompanying belief that it does harm instead
of good.   A mere innocuous " rite," bearing no religious
significance, could never have inspired such determined
opposition.

Many people are unwilling to admit that vaccination
ever does or ever can do any harm.   So great is their

---

* It is worth noting that, while Dr Creighton and Professor Crookshank, both coming to the study of vaccination with the usual professional prepossessions in its favour, lost their faith in it when they
examined its history and pathology, Dr Kolb and Dr Vogt, distinguished German and Swiss statisticians, also approaching the
subject with prepossessions in its favour, lost their faith from a
prolonged study of the statistics.

trust in a beneficent Legislature that they refuse to believe
in injurious results as a possible consequence of a legally
enforced operation. And there are medical men, who
ought to know better, but who nevertheless profess to
share this opinion. I have myself seen doctors smile
contemptuously when a death has been ascribed to
vaccination; and another I have known declare that in
the course of a long practice he had never observed a
single case of serious injury. Such a remark reminds
one of the saying of Rousseau, that "it requires much
philosophy to observe once what can be seen every day";
for others have a very different story to tell. An able
man, a believer in vaccination, for example, told me
that he thought it would be better for the practice to
be dropped, because his experience of its risks had
made him regard it as "paying too high a premium for
insurance"; and indeed the mass of medical evidence as
to the existence of serious risks is simply overwhelming.
Even the writer of the article in the *Edinburgh Review*
for October, 1806, though a strong advocate of the new
process, admitted that "violent cutaneous disorders" had
sometimes followed, and that he knew of "one or two
unfortunate cases in which the wound in the arm had
degenerated into a dangerous ulcer."

Jenner himself, liable as he was to be blinded by his
enthusiasm, admitted that he was alarmed at the severe
effects produced by cow-pox in sundry cases that he had
himself inoculated; indeed the whole history of vaccination, though much has been concealed, is strewn with
disaster and death. Nor is it easy to see how it could
have been otherwise, when one reflects on what vaccination really is. Why should cow-pox, alone among diseases,
never do any harm? Other diseases of animals, such as
glanders, or anthrax, or rabies, are known to be peculiarly

F

deadly when accidentally inoculated on to man. Cow-pox, no doubt, when affecting an animal otherwise healthy, is a comparatively mild ailment; and this, as has already been suggested, may be partly due to the fact that it is apparently a disease of human origin; but, whether we take Jenner's theory, that it is a form of small-pox, or Creighton and Crookshank's theory, that it is akin to syphilis, we still have to admit that it involves some risk. Dr Ballard, formerly Medical Officer to the Local Government Board, and a great believer in the value of vaccination, frankly admitted this :—

"Vaccination," he says, "is not a thing to be trifled with or to be made light of; it is not to be undertaken thoughtlessly, or without due consideration of the condition of the patient, his mode of life, and the circumstances of season and of place. Surgeon and patient should both carry in their minds the regulating thought that the one is engaged in communicating, the other in receiving into his system, a *real* disease—as truly a disease as small-pox or measles ; a disease, which, mild and gentle as its progress may usually be, yet nevertheless, now and then, like every other exanthematous malady, asserts its character by an unusual exhibition of virulence."

He is speaking of vaccination simply as the inoculation of cow-pox, and he has not in view in this passage dangers which many dread far more, viz. : the possible invaccination of other diseases at the same time.

This last is a point on which there is much difference of opinion, and I have no desire to press it unduly. Nevertheless, it is impossible to ignore the fact that there exists a vast mass of medical evidence (or of medical opinion, it may be better to term it, since rigid proof is seldom to be had), that such diseases as syphilis, erysipelas, eczema, and scrofula can be communicated or stirred up by vaccination; and the testimonies collected by Mr Tebb in various parts of the world amount to little short of a demonstration that the recrudescence of leprosy, which is causing so much alarm in tropical countries, is really due to this cause. *   It has been suggested by some one, evidently not very familiar with the subject, that, where a disaster results from vaccination, the doctor who performed the operation should be prosecuted.   But this would be altogether unfair; for it appears to depend rather on the child's constitution than on the quality of the lymph used, whether the operation "takes" severely, or, as is more common, results only in a slight fever, and a sore that does not last many days; while, as to the simultaneous communication of other diseases along with the cow-pox, it has been admitted by more than one expert witness before the Royal Commission that no microscopical examination of the lymph used can guarantee that it is the vehicle of cow-pox only.   There is, in fact, no bacterium specific to cow-pox lymph, though it is admitted to be an excellent medium for the cultivation of bacteria generally.   And, while so few inoculable diseases can be identified by any special bacillus, recognised as forming their *contagium*, it is clear that bacteriology can throw little light on the subject, apart from purely negative conclusions, such as the absence of any relation between cow-pox and small-pox.†   Of course,

* " The Recrudescence of Leprosy and its Causation," by William Tebb. London, 1893.

† While these sheets were passing through the press, there appeared (Aug. 29, 1894) in the Medical Officer's Supplement to the Twenty-Second Annual Report of the Local Government Board, a paper by Dr Klein, entitled, " On the Etiology of *Vaccinia* and *Variola*," in which he claims (p. 400 of the Supplement) to have discovered that "alike in variolous lymph and in vaccine lymph—and whether the latter be derived from the calf or from the human subject—one and the

even lymph that is by courtesy termed "pure" is full of microbes of one kind or another; but they are mostly quite harmless. The only really disquieting point in Professor Crookshank's evidence on the bacteriology of vaccine is that the lymph occasionally contains a bacterium characteristic of pus, thus indicating a risk of blood-poisoning.

It was the frequency with which syphilitic symptoms were alleged to follow vaccination that pointed Dr Creighton towards his conclusion as to the real character of cow-pox. For the medical details his book should be consulted ;* it is enough to say here that ulcers of a cancerous nature, slow to heal, and ultimately leaving the characteristic "good mark" behind, are the most familiar symptom ; while the persistency of the disease

same definite bacillus is demonstrable, a bacillus, namely, which contains bodies comparable with spores, but which cannot at present be cultivated in artificial nutritive media." Of course the paper is intended as a reply to Crookshank, though his name is not mentioned. If this alleged discovery can be maintained, it may give, no doubt, a prolongation of life to the vaccination doctrine, by providing for it a specious if an insufficiently established scientific basis. But, to be frank, the discovery will need independent confirmation, if it is to be accepted. Dr Klein's researches have before now had somewhat ambiguous results, notably in the case of the "Greenwich epidemic" last year. It is difficult to believe that at the eleventh hour an accommodating bacillus, dwelling, apparently as a "specific," in the lymph of two diseases known by other tests to be pathologically distinct, should reveal itself to an official observer, evidently to save the scientific credit of vaccination, though it was invisible under Professor Crookshank's microscope ; and, while Dr Klein's paper certainly deserves and will receive the careful study of competent men, at present the only conclusion one can draw from it is that the Medical Officers of the Local Government Board, meaning to fight for compulsory vaccination to the last, have realised that, unless they provide themselves with a scientific basis, they are bound to lose. See Postscript, p. 121.

* "The Natural History of Cow-pox and Vaccinal Syphilis," by Charles Creighton, M.D. London, 1887. The same theory is developed in his article "Vaccination" in the ninth edition of the *Encyclopædia Britannica* (1888).

in the system, long after the wounds have healed, a persistency which may manifest itself later in various disagreeable ways, is a further proof of its real character.

No doubt disasters consequent upon vaccination are but rarely observed, especially in the upper and middle classes. For one thing, observation depends on theory; and the old theory, which made cow-pox parallel with small-pox, naturally would not permit any such observations to be made after the period of a month or three weeks, had elapsed. For another thing, private vaccination is notoriously less severe—it is often enough not vaccination at all, in any real sense—than that performed at the public stations. It is mainly among those who have to go to these stations that disasters occur; and there are reasons for such a result apart from the vaccination itself. Poorly clad infants have to be taken to the place at the appointed time, whatever the season or weather may be; the mothers and their children, coming from a variety of unhealthy homes, have then to wait and associate; and this process has to be repeated eight days later, when the vaccinator has the right (penalty for refusing, twenty shillings) to open the vesicles so as to procure lymph for other cases; and in this second operation, followed by exposure to the cold, considerable risk must lie.

VACCINATION OCCASIONALLY A CAUSE OF DEATH.

Medical men, not public vaccinators, have frequently called attention to the hardships and dangers of this system; and the few cases of death registered as due to vaccination are probably all those of children operated on at the public stations, but subsequently attended by some other medical man; for at the eighth day the public vaccinator is not able to judge of the mischief that has been done; and he does not see the child again after that date. It is hardly likely that any medical man would certify as due to vaccination the death of a child whom he had vaccinated himself. Indeed, regard for the parents' feelings as well as for his own reputation would suggest that he should conceal the true cause; and the laxity of our method of registration makes such concealment very easy. I have never been on the look-out for injuries consequent on vaccination; but two cases of death from that cause (undoubted and ultimately admitted) which came under my notice perforce, were registered, the one as due to "convulsions" and the other as due to "syncope." Under these categories (as also under "debility"), which really involve no definite statement as to the cause of death, medical men, whether from incompetence, or indolence, or because for some reason they are unwilling to name the true cause, have long been accustomed to enter wholesale the deaths of infants under one year.*

Yet "convulsions" are a symptom rather than a disease; and they correspond in the infant to delirium in the adult, indicating that some disease or derangement (and there are several that cause convulsions) has reached an acute stage. Cow-pox is such a disease; and when a child is suffering severely from vaccination, but there is no indication of the presence of any other disease or of physical derangement, if the issue be convulsions and death, it is surely clear that "cow-pox" should be registered as the cause, and not the mere symptom "convulsions." Much the same may be

---

* Upwards of 36,000 in England and Wales are thus registered annually at the present time. Other "Anomalies of Death Certification" are dealt with under that title by Dr Allan, Medical Officer of Health for the Strand district, in the "Medical Times and Hospital Gazette" for May 5, 1894.

said of the deaths of infants ascribed under similar circumstances to "syncope" or "debility," when such deaths occur
during the crisis of the vaccination fever. Indeed, one
may go much further and maintain that in every case in
which an infant dies during the time of constitutional
disturbance following vaccination, or before the healing
of the vaccination wounds—a period often extending
over six weeks or more—"vaccination" should certainly
be entered on the certificate as a secondary or con-
tributory cause of death, even though the fatal issue may
have been mainly due to some other ailment; for the
reason that the death was probably due to the complication caused by the cow-pox fever. And, if death would
not have ensued but for that complication, vaccination
is in such cases the real and efficient cause, as being the
preventible one.

It is difficult, I know, to bring people to take this view
of the matter, though it is really the common-sense view,
and will be recognised as such as soon as the quasi-religious
belief in vaccination has waned. People feel that it is
monstrous—as indeed it is—to recognise in a State-enforced
operation a cause of disease and of death; and they are
ready to accept any evasion rather than admit it. They
are satisfied even with the stereotyped official denials made
in Parliament, though such denials would count for nothing
in the case of anything else. Occasionally a death alleged
to be due to vaccination receives the attention of the
authorities at the Local Government Board, and what is
called an "enquiry" is ordered. An inspector is sent
down, and, with a local medical man, he calls on the
wretched mother. Of course they mean to act fairly, but
they are convinced that vaccination could not possibly be the
cause; and it is not difficult for them, after a little cross-
examination, to make the mother bow to their authority,

though privately she may retain her own opinion. Parliament is then gravely assured that the death is not even supposed to have been due to vaccination ; and John Bull is confirmed in his belief in his own wisdom in making so harmless and so valuable an operation compulsory ; though, as I happen to know, a mouthpiece of the medical officials of the Local Government Board may ultimately feel ashamed of the lies which he has had to tell at their dictation.

Indeed, in spite of all the efforts that are made to conceal the truth, there exists now a considerable body even of official evidence to the risks of vaccination. The German regulations,* directing the vaccine lymph to be diluted before use with glycerine, and insisting on the most elaborate precautions, with the object of securing that only children in sound health shall be vaccinated, and that "humanised lymph" shall be taken only from the very healthiest cases, are a proof, not only of a paternal care for which everyone should feel grateful, but also of a recognition of the existence of serious dangers as possibly consequent on vaccination. These regulations, with various modifications, have been adopted by the Local Government Board ; and are supposed to be followed at the public vaccination stations ; but their great elaborateness makes them to a large extent impracticable, and it is certain that they are very imperfectly carried out.†

Then we have the Registrar General's returns, showing about fifty-two deaths annually due to "Cow-pox and other effects of vaccination," a number which Mr Alfred Milnes

* "Reichs-Impfgesetz," April 8, 1874. Among other precautions, vaccination during an epidemic of any infectious disease is forbidden. See Palmberg's "Public Health and its Appliances," translated by Newsholme. London, 1893. Pp. 365, 366.

† They are printed at length in the 17th Annual Report of the Local Government Board, and they came into force, March 17, 1887.

(who, as a Fellow of the Royal Statistical Society, may be trusted to be careful with his figures) estimates, after much enquiry, to represent about one in thirteen of the real number.* And, while the return moved for by Mr Hopwood in 1877 (Commons Paper, No 433) showed that the deaths of infants from certain specified causes had increased between 1847 and 1875—*i.e.*, coincidently with the enforcement of vaccination—at a rate considerably more rapid than the increase of the population would have warranted, in Leicester, on the other hand, the disuse of vaccination has been coincident with a reduction in the annual death-rate of young children from 107 per 1000 in 1868-72 to 63 per 1000 in 1888-9. I speak of coincidence and not of consequence, because the consequence is a mere inference, and the facts may be open to some other explanation. But the double coincidence is at any rate striking and worth recording.

On the whole it may be taken as adequately proved that vaccination, since its first introduction by Jenner, has brought about the deaths of some thousands of children; nor can we in regard to these have the consolation suggested by some who believe in vaccination but yet admit its risks,—that it is only the very weakest lives that have in this way been slightly abbreviated. Granting, for the sake of argument, that the State has the right to establish this form of infanticide, so as to rid itself of the burden of feeble and unpromising lives, the reply would be that it is not so much weakness, as constitutional susceptibility to

---

* Previously to 1881 it had only been officially admitted that "erysipelas following vaccination" might end fatally; and a coroner is reported to have refused to accept a verdict given in accordance with the medical evidence, on the ground that "vaccination is not a legal cause of death." This anomaly was remedied by Dr Ogle in the year above mentioned; and immediately the returns showed about double the number of deaths resulting from vaccination.

the fever of cow-pox, that makes the risk; and this susceptibility is certainly not peculiar to weakly children. Its
existence can only be ascertained by experiment; but
when the experiment has proved fatal in the case of one
child, it is natural to anticipate a similar susceptibility in
the case of other children of the same parents, who, as
having already paid tribute to the majesty of the law,
might fairly claim subsequent exemption from the compulsory Acts.

COMPULSION IN THE FACE OF ACKNOWLEDGED RISK.

It is impossible to leave out of account this aspect of
the vaccination question; for, although vaccination is
really discredited more by arguments which prove its uselessness than it would be (if its value were undoubted) by
proofs that it occasionally does harm, it is the dread of
vaccination, and not mere contempt for it, that makes
compulsion so odious and ultimately so unworkable. And
it is the existence of this dread which a statesman has
mainly to take into account. Medical men may be able
to prove to their own satisfaction in this or that particular
case that the ascription of death to vaccination was a mistake; but they cannot, on any theory of vaccination, prove
that it is always and of necessity harmless. That being so,
the dread in question remains a reasonable dread; and a
statesman, recognising its existence, need not trouble himself as to the exact measure of its reasonableness, when
he contemplates a repeal of the compulsory law. That a
number of persons are honestly persuaded of the seriousness
of the risk is sufficient reason for not putting pressure on
them. They may be mistaken; but that does not alter
the fact that their reasonable dread deserves consideration.
For myself, I dislike in such cases the use of the phrase
"conscientious objection" to vaccination. The word

"conscientious" has canting associations, and it is best not employed in this connection. It is rather a matter of common-sense than of conscience. A mother who loves her child will not allow it to pass the night in the open air without any covering, not because she has any "conscientious objection" to such a proceeding, but because she knows she would be a fool if she did. It is much the same with vaccination. To hold that it is useless and not free from risk may be an offence against medical orthodoxy, but you cannot prevent people from becoming persuaded that such is the case, unless you prohibit reading and thinking altogether. And, when parents are thus persuaded, it is merely in accordance with the dictates of common sense for them to refuse to have their children vaccinated. To discuss whether such persons should be prosecuted only once in the case of each child, or whether they should be prosecuted over and over again, until all their children are fourteen years of age, may be a useful way of employing the time of the House of Commons ; but, to anyone who takes a broad view of the situation, the idea of compulsion under such circumstances seems to be either immoral or grotesque.

OTHER OBJECTIONS TO COMPULSION.

Other points that a statesman has to take into account in regard to compulsory vaccination are, that it is at any rate unnecessary at the present time ; that experience has shown it to be impolitic ; and that the whole drift of public opinion all the world over is now steadily setting against it. A further point with which a Liberal statesman may be expected especially to concern himself is, that the compulsory law, while its existence is barely known to the well-to-do, presses with especial hardness on the poor. I will deal with this last point first, and very briefly, as I have already referred to it incidentally.

That the law, so lightly passed by the Legislature, was never intended to apply to persons whose station is above that of the lower middle class, is clear from the singular provision that the father of an unvaccinated child more than twelve months old is "summonsed" (if that is the word) to appear before the magistrate *bringing the child with him!* The father not unnaturally delegates this office to his wife; and, in a stuffy police-court, crowded with the riff-raff of the adjacent streets, I have seen half-a-dozen anxious mothers vainly attempting to keep their babies quiet while the criminal cases are first disposed of. If their efforts fail—as fail they must before two hours have elapsed—they have to wait outside in a draughty passage. What can be more ridiculous than such a provision, made too in the name of Public Health ! The law permits the parent prosecuting to be represented in court by another person; but this hardly enables a working man to send anyone but his wife in his stead; whereas a gentleman with a banking account can send a cheque to the Clerk of the Court, appointing him his representative, and begging him to fill in the amount of the fine. And to do this—*experto crede*—is more economical than to pay a doctor a fee every two months to sign a certificate for postponement. Guineas and half-guineas soon mount up; whereas the fine cannot exceed twenty shillings; and the Guardians, after a time, see the folly of prosecuting when the object aimed at is obviously unattainable.*

* It is only when people realise that vaccination is of no service either to the child or to the community, while it may involve serious risk to the former, that they are in a position to recognise how cruelly the compulsory law weighs on parents among the working classes, who can ill afford to pay a fine, and who doubt and dread the operation. They are quite as sensible as are their superiors of the ignominy of being bullied by vaccination officers, or of having "summonses" served on them by policemen; and it is worth remembering that the fine

This leads me to another point, the impolicy of prosecutions. This is especially true, and its truth all but a few vaccination fanatics allow, as regards repeated prosecutions. I admit that the dread of the first prosecution does induce some parents to have their children vaccinated ; and it is just that fact which gives some reasonableness to the otherwise Dogberry-like policy of prosecuting those who are likely to submit, while leaving the intractable alone ; for no such result follows when the law has once been defied. And it is in this way intelligible that sincere believers in vaccination should desire the continuance of the compulsory law, in so far as it secures the vaccination of a number of children whose parents have no particular view on the subject, but are likely to neglect the operation from sheer indolence unless some pressure is put on them. But it is difficult to find any motive for the insistence on repeated penalties, unless it be found in the natural tendency of all dogmatists to persecute. For it is the obvious result of such a policy to defeat its own ends. This was pointed out by Mr Forster, in the House of Commons, as long ago as 1877. He urged that those who had what he called "conscientious objections" to vaccination should be left alone, and that only those should be proceeded against who were in default from mere laziness. They are, he said, by far the greater number, and it was against them that the Acts were directed. Had his advice been followed, it is very likely

commonly inflicted on them is equivalent to a fine of about £200 taken out of a Cabinet Minister's official income. The late Mr Peter Taylor used, I believe, to quote as a specimen case of the administration of the law—though happily not a fair specimen—a working-man being given by the magistrate the alternative of "twenty shillings or seven days," after he had protested that he had "sworn before God over the dead body of his first child that he would never let it be done to another." Such legislation and such administration are surely calculated to bring the law into contempt, and to breed a generation of Anarchists.

that the whole question would have stood in a very different position to-day.

In Scotland, for example, where the law is administered in a far gentler spirit, and where the poor are more credulous and submissive than they are in England, pretty nearly every child is vaccinated, with hardly any occasion to use the terrors of the law. Thus, in 1891 (I quote from the Annual Report of the Board of Supervision), 14,127 persons were reported as being temporarily in default; but out of this large number only 45 were prosecuted, and, of these 45, only 25 had any penalty inflicted on them. Whether the Scottish authorities are canny enough to perceive that compulsion provokes enquiry, and that enquiry is fatal to faith, I do not know; but it is certain that their milder administration of the law has been more successful in securing the vaccination of nearly every child in the country—and voluntary re-vaccination at a later time is also the rule in Scotland—than the brutal methods which our guardians and magistrates have often employed. But this side of the question is barely worth discussing now; for it is certain that no amount of sweet reasonableness on the part of the authorities in England can at this date avail to rehabilitate a creed so unmistakably outworn.

A WAY OUT OF THE DIFFICULTY.

The non-necessity for vaccination at the present time will provide, some think, the way by which the medical profession, without any humiliating confession of having been in the wrong, may escape from its present untenable position. Vaccination may be said to have "done its work," now that the country is ordinarily free from small-pox; and the provisions of the Infectious Diseases Notification Act and of the Isolation Hospitals Act may

be claimed as affording another line of defence, likely
to prove sufficient under the altered circumstances. No
one will grudge them this refuge, if they avail themselves of it in time ; and, now that every Medical Officer
of Health throughout the country prefers isolation to
vaccination, or at any rate endeavours to supplement
the defects of the latter by the proved advantages of
the former, it is not easy to see on what ground (unless
it be affection for the "principle of compulsion") medical
men generally should be so unwilling to agree to a total
repeal of the existing law; especially since their present
uncompromising attitude (not indeed as individuals but
when acting as Colleges, Associations, and the like) is
doing so much to damage their reputation for scientific
insight and common sense.*

Sir Benjamin Ward Richardson, in reviewing Crookshank's work in the "Asclepiad," † showed that he personally realised the situation, though he was careful not
to commit himself on the main question. Speaking as a
medical man to his brethren, he said :—"If it be true that
we of physic have really, for well nigh a century past, been
worshipping an idol of the market-place or even of the
theatre, why, the sooner we cease our worship and take
down our idol, the better for us altogether. We have set
up the idol, and the world has lent itself to the idolatry,
because we, whom the world trusted, have set the example.
But the world now-a-days discovers idolatries on its own
account ; and, if we continue the idolatry, it will simply

---

* This new attitude of the Medical Officers of Health is the more
remarkable, because they are to a man, at any rate at the date of their
appointment, believers in vaccination. Only the orthodox on this
subject have any chance of obtaining an official post, for they only can
obtain the indispensable testimonials from the medical big-wigs.

† December, 1889.

take its own course, and, leaving us on our knees, will march on, whilst we petrify."

There can be no question as to the shrewdness of this forecast; the doubt is rather whether the medical profession have not already delayed too long to recognise the direction in which the tide is flowing. When, for example, we find the Council of the Royal College of Surgeons meeting the unanimous (interim) Report of the Royal Commission on Vaccination, which favoured an important relaxation in the compulsory law, by a resolution in which they declared that they "would regard as a national calamity *any* alteration in the law which now makes vaccination compulsory," and this, in spite of the fact that they were represented on the Commission directly by their own past President, Mr Savory, and other members of the College, we can hardly fail to realise the truth of the saying, that the two most odious elements in sacerdotalism, viz.: obscurantism and the spirit of domination, have in this nineteenth century passed over from the clerical to the medical profession. Men who could frame such a resolution certainly do not move with the times.

The Popular Protest against Vaccination.

A letter from Dr Yarrow to the *Lancet* (May 19, 1894) admitted that vaccination was becoming more unpopular. "Discredited" would perhaps be a more accurate expression than "unpopular"; but, however the fact may be stated, the witness of the vaccination returns quoted above (p. 55) is unmistakable. Nor do they stand alone; for the returns of prosecutions and convictions under the Vaccination Acts show that the persons imprisoned or fined are double as many during the later decade as they were during the previous one. The total number

of persons proceeded against under the Vaccination Acts
in the years 1873-89 was 34,286. Of these 136 were
committed to prison, 19,482 were fined, 14 were
" bound over," and 7354 had " other punishments."
The number proceeded against rose from 972 in 1873
to 2881 in 1888, when a decline began to set it, not
because more children were vaccinated, but because more
Boards of Guardians had become sick of the game.

Another important record, throwing light on the real
state of public opinion, will be found in the details of
the house-to-house census, taken in about a hundred
towns and districts under the auspices of the London
Society for the Abolition of Compulsory Vaccination.
These records of opinion have been ignored by the
press, and by the well-to-do public generally, because
they have been collected by the despised and detested
"anti-vaccinators." But there is no reason for supposing that they are in any sense unfair; and they show
that, in a great variety of districts throughout England,
as many as 87 per cent. of the people—mostly working
men, no doubt—are opposed to vaccination being compulsory, while about 68 per cent. do not believe in it
at all. It seems pretty certain that, if our Vaccination
Laws were submitted to a popular vote, on the plan of
the Swiss *referendum*, they would at once be swept away.*

Another testimony to the drift of public opinion on this
subject is to be found in the British colonies. In some of
these, viz : in Canada, Queensland, and New South Wales,
there has never been any compulsory law ; in New Zealand
there is such a law, but it is not enforced; and in Tasmania

* The fact that very few petitions to Parliament against the compulsory law are presented is no criterion of popular feeling. Petitions
are the luxury of well-organised movements that have plenty of money
behind them ; and of new movements especially ; for a little experience
proves their utter futility.

the law has been repealed.* Similar progress can be reported from some parts of the Continent, at any rate from
countries in which liberty is still of some account.   In
Switzerland not only was the Federal Law of Vaccination
rejected in 1882, at the *referendum*, by the largest majority
that had been known, but the Cantonal laws are also, I
am told, not enforced, and re-vaccination on admission
to the army has been dropped, as it has been also in
Holland.   Even in State - ridden Germany, where it is
little short of blasphemy to suggest that any legislation
is wrong and should be repealed, there is a growing movement in favour of liberty ; and it is a significant fact that
the Emperor does not permit his own children to be vaccinated.†   France indeed, where there had been no compulsory law at all at the time when the famous statue of
Jenner was erected at Boulogne, and where there is still
no law enforcing the vaccination of infants, is somewhat
retrogressive on this question, new regulations coming
into force from time to time, which make vaccination a
necessary preliminary to admission to the public schools
or the public service ; and in Italy a most stringent law,
enforcing vaccination in infancy, and re-vaccination between
the ages of eight and eleven, came into force as recently as
January 1, 1892 ; the authorities having decided to attribute
to the non-universality of vaccination a persistency of small-

---

* In the United States of America the vaccination of infants has
never been compulsory ; and a decision of the Supreme Court of the
State of New York, in June, 1894, practically deprived the Health
Commissioners of the powers which they had previously claimed to
enforce the vaccination or re-vaccination of adults.

† See *Vaccination Inquirer*, Vol. xiv., p. 71.   (July, 1892).   A
similar inconsistency, interesting as showing how little real belief in
the official doctrine prevails even in official circles, is to be found in
the fact that Professor Crookshank, whose work on vaccination is
practically an incitement to a breach of the law, has quite recently
been made a J.P. for the county of Kent.

pox in certain localities, which would more obviously be explained as due to the notoriously insanitary conditions under which the poorer Italians live. France and Italy are thus disappointing from the point of view from which I approach this subject; but in both countries there are medical men of repute who disbelieve in vaccination altogether; and, as science becomes more and more international, the civilised world must ultimately come to the same conclusion on all questions such as this.

THE ATTITUDE OF THE PRESS.

One difficulty that still to a great extent stands in the way of those who desire a repeal of the compulsory Vaccination Law has been and is the persistent hostility of the Press. There is no evidence to show that this hostility is based on any special knowledge of the subject possessed by journalists and editors; on the contrary, ignorance, arrogance, and flippancy chiefly characterise the paragraphs that from time to time treat of the follies and iniquities of "anti-vaccinators" in the columns of newspapers otherwise so highly respectable as the *City Press* or the *St James's Gazette*. A writer who can describe a disbeliever in vaccination as " an advocate of free-trade in small-pox" has yet to learn the very elements of this controversy; and another paragraph writer, who speaks of the delight it would give him if he could inflict physical torture on parents who prefer to go to prison rather than subject their infant children to the admitted risks of the operation, has evidently been born some centuries too late. But it is as much by persistent silence as by silly misrepresentation or envenomed criticism that the Press has retarded the due recognition of the essential justice and the scientific soundness of this cause. The *Daily News*, for example, that has been in other respects for the last quarter of a century the most ably conducted organ of Liberalism in the world, has uniformly excluded, at any rate until quite recently, all letters or communications that contained statements to the discredit of vaccination. Doubtless this has been done with the best intentions, so as not to encourage what from the official point of view is a dangerous heresy; but such a policy of suppression looks a little foolish when, after years of waiting, the heresy in question is on the point of being acknowledged as the true account of the matter. The *Times* has similarly used its tremendous influence, though perhaps less persistently. Letters from representative men on the anti-vaccinist side it has occasionally admitted during the holiday season; but the grossest unfairness was exhibited in its extended notice of the (so called) Fourth Report of the Royal Commission, containing the evidence given between July 1890 and July 1891, and at last published in February this year. The article was evidently the work of a medical member of the Commission, for it was printed a fortnight before the Report was issued to the public; and it consisted exclusively of professional criticisms on the non-professional evidence of opponents of vaccination in Leicester,—an easy task, and one satisfactory probably to the writer, but unsatisfactory to readers who recognise that knowledge may be accurate, though not expressed in technical language, and that working men and their wives, who live habitually with their children, may be better able to appreciate what has caused a death in the family than a medical man who looks in when all is over, and is prohibited by professional prepossession from admitting that the cause was vaccination. Leaving that on one side, however, the worst feature of the article in question was its passing over in absolute silence, as if unworthy of even being mentioned, the elaborate and

important evidence of Professor Crookshank, which occupied the Commission for nine days (July 9, 16, 23, 30,
August 6, November 12, 19, 26, and December 3, 1890),
and extends over some 110 pages, closely printed in double
columns. This evidence is probably the fullest indictment
of vaccination on scientific grounds that has ever been
made; and, taken in conjunction with the same writer's
two volumes already referred to, and Dr Creighton's evidence before the Royal Commission (December 4 and 11,
1889, and January 22 and 29, 1890), and his four publications on the same subject, it constitutes that case which
elicits no reply from the other side, beyond an appeal to
statistics which I am surely justified in describing as
questionable.   The motive for this silence is obvious.
The average well-to-do Englishman reads his *Times*, either
at home, or in his office, or at his club.   It is his ordinary
source of knowledge, so far as current events are concerned.
What the *Times* does not notice, he does not notice.   For
a thousand men (including legislators and justices of the
peace, who are under a kind of obligation to inform themselves on this vaccination question) taking this newspaper
article as giving them all that is worth knowing about the
Fourth Report of the Vaccination Commission, there will
be barely one who will turn to the actual Blue Book, and
will see for himself what it really does contain, and will
endeavour to form a fair judgment on it.   The obscurantism
of the Press is thus effectual, at any rate temporarily; but,
though ignored in this country, as far as is possible, Professor Crookshank's evidence and Dr Creighton's evidence
will be attentively studied by medical scientists on the
Continent, and it will not ultimately be without effect.
For the time, however, as indeed for a long time past, the
hostile attitude of the Press (in which I include the un-
willingness of magazine editors to admit an article that

might offend medical orthodoxy in regard to this vexed question) must be accounted one of the chief difficulties in the way of those who have lost faith in vaccination and desire that it should no longer be enforced by law. *

Anti-Vaccination Literature.

The works of the two writers just named have finally removed the reproach that used to be levelled against anti-vaccination literature as being intrinsically poor stuff. But it is by no means clear that those who used to affect such contempt had really read what they thus condemned off-hand. A cause which is a popular one, in the sense that the majority of those keenly interested in it, for reasons mentioned above, will be found among the poorer classes, is sure to be supported to some extent by literature of a popular kind and of inferior value. † We do not look for carefully balanced arguments or for literary style in

* At a meeting of the British Economic Association on June 27, 1894, Mr Balfour, as reported in the daily papers, referred to the vaccination question as one in which he took "a remote interest," it being "a quarrel between the doctors on the one hand, who think they have settled the matter in a scientific spirit, and a section of the people on the other hand, who have not studied it in a scientific spirit at all, but are determined that their feelings shall override science." This deplorable misunderstanding of the present position of the controversy is presumably a result of that conspiracy of silence on the part of the Press above referred to.

† The number of writers and of publications against vaccination is at any rate evidence of a wide-spread feeling, even though they may not always display scientific or literary power. "A Catalogue of Anti-Vaccination Literature," printed in 1882, showed :—

	Writers.	Publications.
British . . .	100	205
American . . .	17	36
German . . .	39	104
French and Belgian .	8	29
Dutch . . .	2	4
Swedish . . .	3	7

hand-bills and posters hastily drawn up and circulated wholesale when parents are being sent to prison, or are having their furniture sold under distraint, for the sole crime of loving their children and of believing that they know best how to take care of them. Publications of this kind apart, there existed already, before Dr Creighton first appeared on the field in 1887, certain books and pamphlets that deserved far more attention than they obtained. Omitting all publications dated 1882 or earlier, there was Dr W. J. Collins' pamphlet, entitled "Sir Lyon Playfair's Logic" (1883), which is a most temperate and judicial criticism of the speech referred to above (p. 53); and there were the two works of the late Mr William White, unfortunately entitled, I admit, but forming in all respects (apart from the identification of cow-pox with syphilis, the key-stone of the arch, necessary for the confirmation and explanation of those observations which indicated the uselessness of vaccination and of those which indicated its dangers, which it was left to Dr Creighton and Professor Crookshank to supply in 1887 and 1889), a careful and complete answer to the arguments used by the advocates of vaccination. * Other publications, well deserving notice, might be mentioned; but I must content myself with naming an able and convincing criticism of the statistical arguments, written by the eminent naturalist, Dr Alfred Russel Wallace,† and a monthly periodical, (indispensable to those who want to know the progress of the anti-vaccination movement, but read, I am disposed to

* "Sir Lyon Playfair taken to Pieces and Disposed of; likewise Sir Charles Dilke." Presented to the Third International Anti-Vaccination Congress, held at Berne, September 27th to 30th, 1883. "The Story of a Great Delusion." 1884.

† "Vaccination proved Useless and Dangerous from Twenty-Five Years of Registration Statistics." 2nd Ed., 1889.

fear, exclusively by those who are already supporters of that movement), ably edited by Mr Alfred Milnes, F.S.S.*

It is not in fact any lack of earnest and well-informed writers, but of unprejudiced readers, that hampers this movement. So much contumely has been poured on anti-vaccinists as "faddists," "fanatics," and what not, that very many people would be ashamed to be seen reading a publication put forth by an adherent of that cause. Things are not indeed so bad with us as they were some years ago in Germany, when the writings against vaccination of the late Dr Nittinger, of Stuttgart, were treated as seditious, and were confiscated by the police; but much of the old bitterness, as between ortho-doxy and heresy, still remains; and men will not sit down to read works which advocate a cause they have long been accustomed to despise. And, if this is true of laymen, it must be truer still of professional men, whose orthodoxy is so chaste that they will not, for example, even allow a homœopathic periodical to lie on the table in their public library. It is really only the prejudice and timidity of readers that anti-vaccination literature has to fear.

THE ROYAL COMMISSION.

Many people anticipate that this vexed question will be settled by the final Report of the Royal Commission, which is expected to be published this year. That the Report will contribute towards a settlement is certain; but it is hardly possible that it can do more. If so comparatively small a detail as the repeated prosecution of defaulters could not be settled by the unanimous decision of a Select Committee in 1871, followed up by the

* "The Vaccination Inquirer and Health Review." London, E. W. Allen. The sixteenth annual volume is now in progress.

unanimous decision of a Royal Commission in 1892, it
is not to be expected that the larger question will be
settled by a Report which is certain not to be unanimous.
Other circumstances, connected with the appointment and
the procedure of the Commission, suggest that, although its
work in collecting evidence is of permanent value, and its
preliminary so-called Reports, containing this evidence,
will be a quarry for anti-vaccinists so long as the controversy
continues, the actual conclusions and recommendations of the
majority of its members are not likely to be in accordance with
what I claim to call the progressive view of the subject.
In the first place, there was no thought, when the Commission was appointed, that it might possibly result in an
exposure of the futility of vaccination.   It was appointed
in order to shelve a troublesome subject, and to provide a
loop-hole for escape from the interminable series of questions
asked in Parliament as to the administration of the Vaccination Laws.   Its appointment was wholly in the hands of
believers in vaccination ; its enquiry, it was thought, would
be brief, and would quickly result in the "pricking of a
bubble," *i.e.*, in the discomfiture of the anti-vaccinists ;
and there was barely any pretence of treating the question
as one in which either side had a right to equal represen-
tation.   The proportion seems to have been suggested
rather by the number of medical men understood to be on
either side in the country at large.   A similar rule was
observed in the appointment of the German Commission
in 1874.   It consisted of eighteen members, of whom three
were opposed to vaccination.   But such a rule had not been
adhered to in other enquiries.   When the Gold and Silver
Commission was appointed, the advocates of bi-metallism
in this country were fewer than they are now, and were
probably numerically not one tenth of their opponents.
Yet an equal number (four on each side) represented the

contending parties on the Commission; and, as had been
anticipated, the parties were still equally represented
when the Commission issued its final Report.   On the
Vaccination Commission it is true that a certain number
of laymen (eight) were placed, who might be expected
to form their opinion solely on the evidence brought
before them. None of them, I believe, had already expressed any definite opinion on the subject, but some of
them had confessed to doubts, and they were therefore
likely to prove impartial judges.   But the medical profession was represented on the Commission by six to one
in favour of vaccination.   Of the ability and high character
of each of the six there could be no reason to doubt; but
how could it be expected of professional men, men moreover past the age when the judgments and opinions of
earlier years can readily be reconsidered and revised, that
they would find themselves free to take a wholly unprejudiced view of a question on which their definite opinions
had long been before the public in print?   A study of the
evidence already published discloses the fact that they
habitually treated witnesses opposed to vaccination as
hostile witnesses; and their policy, as advocates of the
practice which they had been commissioned to weigh in
the balance, is in other respects unmistakable.   If ever
there was an enquiry which it was desirable for the public
to follow day by day, it was surely this one.   Yet the
majority decided that it should be conducted with closed
doors; with the result that when, at long intervals, hundreds
of columns of closely printed evidence were published as
Parliamentary Blue Books, the vast mass of material was
at once buried under its own weight, and the enquiry was
thus rendered to a large extent nugatory.*

* Only once during the enquiry was there any publication of evidence
while it was thus still in the confidential stage ; and that was in May

Further, the strength of the existing case against vaccination depends, first on the pathological argument,
which proves the absence of relation between cow-
pox and small-pox, and then, as a subsidiary argument,
on criticisms of the current statistics, which, collected
under the influence of an erroneous theory, are used to
prove that vaccination, whatever it may be, is at any
rate efficacious. The incidental risks of vaccination—*i.e.*,
risks which may exist apart from the essential nature
of the disease inoculated—and the anomalies of the compulsory law, are not the arguments which constitute the
strength of our case, though in themselves they have
considerable importance. Yet, incredible as it may seem,
it was only these minor points that the majority of the
Commissioners were at first willing to take into consideration at all. To them apparently the vaccination question
was merely a question of policy. That there existed a
clearly defined scientific case against vaccination itself seems
only to have dawned on them after the enquiry had already
lasted some time. Certainly, before Dr Creighton had
given his evidence they regarded such an idea—I judge

1890, when a paragraph went round the papers to the effect that the
evidence of Surgeon Parke, who accompanied Stanley across Africa,
had profoundly impressed the Commission with the value of vaccination.
Some time afterwards (Christmas, 1890) when the second Report was
published, it proved to be merely hearsay evidence (for he had been
500 miles away from the place where the events occurred), and therefore
such as would have been ruled inadmissible had it been on the other
side ; and in substance all it amounted to was that the vaccinated companions of the travellers, *i.e.*, men seasoned by climate and a variety of
other circumstances, were mostly found to be insusceptible to an epidemic of small-pox which carried off a number of natives to whom the
disease had before been a stranger. There is no necessity to refer to the
condition of being vaccinated or not, susceptibility or insusceptibility
under such different circumstances. The evidence is criticised at length
in the "Vaccination Inquirer" for January 1891.

from the proceedings contained in the First Report—as too extravagant to deserve consideration; and we know that it was only after a sharp struggle that Professor Crookshank was permitted to give evidence at all. Indeed, every effort is still made to ignore his evidence; while by a majority the Commissioners have recently decided not to hear Major-General Phelps as a witness, though his testimony would have been of the utmost importance, as showing how statistics, which make the unvaccinated almost invariably die, and the vaccinated almost invariably recover, are utterly untrustworthy, being falsified at their very source. The Commissioners excused themselves from hearing him, on the ground that they had not proposed to themselves to base any conclusions on those particular statistics which he had examined with such damaging effect. But this was hardly a sufficient reason for excluding his evidence. No one suggested that the Birmingham and King's Norton Small-pox Hospital returns were less trustworthy then those prepared elsewhere; the point was that General Phelps, as a Guardian in the locality, had enjoyed facilities for investigation which are unfortunately very rare; and his evidence, if received, would not only have shown that in such and such particular cases an incorrect and misleading entry had been made, but would also have indicated a line of enquiry worth following out at much greater length, if the conclusions of the Commissioners were ultimately to rest on a sure basis.

One other instance of unfair dealing must not pass unmentioned. The evidence of witnesses opposed to vaccination had throughout the enquiry been submitted, while still in the proof or confidential stage, to witnesses—chiefly to one witness—taking the other side, with a view to its being criticised and rebutted. There would have been no objection to this, were the same favour shown to either side impartially. But the evidence given in favour of vaccination between July 1890 and the autumn of 1893, was all withheld from the opposite side until November 1893, when an enormous amount of printed matter was submitted, all at one time, and at a date when the hearing of witnesses was understood to be nearly over ; while the evidence thus tardily divulged needed weeks for careful examination and for the preparation of counter-evidence, where necessary, that should disclose its weak points.

There are thus, it would appear, serious grounds for maintaining that a permanent solution of this vexed vaccination controversy cannot be looked for from a Commission constituted such as this was, especially when sundry features in its procedure are taken into consideration. It is no settlement of the real question at issue, if, after hearing the evidence of a number of poor and respectable parents, who have been shamefully treated under the provisions of the compulsory Acts, the Commissioners, in a fit of condescending generosity, unanimously report that such persons ought not to be punished more than once. That is a very small matter in comparison with the question whether a scientifically discredited operation, dangerous as well as useless, should be in any degree enforced by law, or even be encouraged by an elaborate system of State endowment. Another enquiry, with fair play for both sides, will be needed before that question will be satisfactorily answered.*

* In a letter to " Vanity Fair," dated November 5th, 1892, Mr Tebb called attention to one very remarkable testimony to the changed position of the vaccination question which the Royal Commission had incidentally brought to light, viz. : the retreat of former advocates, Lord Playfair, Mr Ernest Hart, and Sir George Buchanan, who have all declined to face the risk of cross-examination.

The Prepossessions of Medical Men.

A consideration of the action on the Royal Commission of the strong majority of medical men introduces the question sometimes raised as to whether medical men are really prejudiced in approaching this subject; and, if so, on what grounds. There are vaccination enthusiasts who maintain that it is in the most heroic spirit of self-sacrifice that the profession encourages vaccination; for without it the disease which they thus so easily repress would bring much grist to their mill. This, however, is a begging of the whole question. From my point of view the doctors have had, since vaccination was invented, every shilling's worth of small-pox that they would have had without it; and they have had in addition an easy and not unpleasant operation to perform, which, it is the simple truth to say, has brought in hundreds and thousands of pounds to the medical exchequer. I do not impute a directly sordid motive as at the bottom of the professional interest in vaccination. I have known and know a number of medical men, and I am sure there is not one among them who would advocate vaccination, not believing in it himself, merely because he thereby increased his income. But doctors, perhaps more than any other professional men, act as a corporation and not as individuals; and it would be affectation to assert that they, as a body, have no pecuniary interest in the matter at all. Here is a popular belief, which has to the profession a capital value that may be estimated at some millions sterling; * and what corporation would be so unselfish as to discredit such a belief, until the time came when it could be maintained

* This capital value will, of course, be more than doubled if a belief in the universal necessity of " recent vaccination " can be established in the public mind.

no longer ? *   And so much evidence in favour of vaccination is forthcoming, and will be forthcoming so long as the
belief in it remains, that a medical man, even if he privately
entertain some doubt, is almost justified in silencing such
a doubt ; or at least he is not bound to disclose his doubt
by refusing to perform the operation.   It is the laity and
not the medical profession that will first abandon vaccination.   For the profession has an interest in the matter
more deserving of respect than a merely pecuniary one.
So committed has it been for nearly a century past to
the value of this operation, that its prestige must suffer
severely when the confession of a mistake has to be made ;
and that confession will be postponed as long as possible.
Vaccination is indeed a *damnosa hæreditas* from credulous
and unscientific predecessors ; but, so long as the medical
profession, as a whole, is satisfied that its interests are best
served by maintaining the value of the operation, we cannot
look to that quarter for aid in the work of emancipation.
As Burns puts it :—

> "When self the wavering balance shakes,
>   It's rarely richt adjusted."

Only individuals here and there, men to whom medicine
is really a science, and who do not dread, or perhaps
can afford to despise, the evils threatened by the trade-

---

* The annual payments out of public funds on account of
vaccination amount to more than £110,000 ; but the aggregate
receipts of private practitioners must be largely in excess of this,
though it is impossible to form even a rough estimate ; and the amount,
especially on account of re-vaccination, varies largely from year to
year.   When there is, as there has been recently, a slight epidemic
of small-pox in the country, and the *Lancet* calls our attention to it,
assuring us meanwhile that it is "a disease which no one need have
unless he pleases," the harvest reaped in Harley Street and thereabouts
is, I have been assured, something prodigious.

unionism which has enmeshed their profession,—only these few can be looked to for a plain and straightforward account of this strange delusion. For the great majority, the fact that a practice is in possession is sufficient justification for maintaining it.

I should be sorry if these remarks were interpreted as a generally hostile criticism on medical men and their profession. The medico-politician I do indeed distrust, as a serious foe to liberty; for members of Parliament are so much in the habit of bowing to "doctor's orders" when he recommends them a month at Monte Carlo in the season, or, should that be beyond their means, an extra glass of whisky in the evening, that they are predisposed similarly to give their vote for coercive measures, asserted to be necessary in the sacred cause of Public Health, on the word of a medical man, who may be taking only a very narrow view of the subject, and may indeed be incapable of a statesmanlike consideration of what the proposals involve. And, what is true of the medico-politician as an individual, is truer still of the action of the Medical Associations, Colleges, and the like. Corporate action deadens the sense of personal responsibility; and it is certain that, in this vaccination business especially, much that is simply tyrannical has been done at the dictation of these bodies, or by direction of medical men holding official positions—that is to say, by professional men who cannot be called to account by those over whom they rule.

But there is another side to all this. The "beloved physician" belongs to no one place or time. The skilful, experienced, sympathetic, and judicious medical man must always be a welcome visitor where accident or disease has brought anxiety and alarm; and the triumphs of modern surgery, no less than the heroism necessary and forthcoming when a dangerous epidemic is abroad, must ever command sincere admiration. Much self-denial goes to the making of a good doctor ; and it would be ungenerous not to recognise frankly and fully the services that are daily rendered by men of education and refinement, of whom the most hard-worked are often the least fairly paid.

THE DIFFICULTY OF AROUSING INTEREST IN THE SUBJECT.

One difficulty in the way of securing a revision of judgment on this vaccination question is the unwilling-ness of people to think about it at all. The question is said to be settled ; the matter is declared to be of no importance ; the subject is voted a bore. Others will even go further, and recoil from an enquiry, as if it were almost profane. In truth, the little girl who replied to her Sunday-School teacher that "circumcision under the Law of Moses was a type of vaccination under the Gospel" really showed a true appreciation of the quasi-religious position which vaccination holds in the public mind. The belief has at any rate this in common with a theological belief, that, to those who hold it, it is more certain than the premises on which it is grounded ; and it is difficult to shake a prepossession, however unreason-able, that occupies a position such as this.

A first step towards a due understanding of the subject is made when people come to realise that, though medicine is or ought to be a scientific art, it is really full of uncer-tainties throughout. " Dr Chassaigne " has recently been insisting on its limitations ; * and, if what he says is true—

* "Vous demandez des certitudes, ce n'est sûrement pas la médecine qui vous les donnera. . . . Certes, il est des maladies que l'on connaît admirablement, jusque dans les plus petites phases de leur évolution ; il est des remèdes dont on a étudié les effets avec le soin le plus

H

as it undoubtedly is—of curative medicine, of "treatment" generally, which has the whole past experience of the human race to inform and guide it, how far more true must it be of preventive medicine, which is but a thing of yesterday, and, having little or nothing else to boast of, is obliged to stake its reputation on the alleged success of vaccination.

Possibly fiction, which M. Renan told us was to be in the future the means of conveying all knowledge, might penetrate the hedge of prejudice and secure a hearing that would result in a revision of judgment. There would be no lack of realistic material ; for Mr Tebb, who years ago was active in the cause of the slaves in North America, declared before the Royal Commission that their sufferings were in his judgment less than those of poor parents in England struggling against the tyranny of the vaccination law.

The object that might be attained by such a treatment of the subject would be the awakening of sympathy for those mothers, and especially for those among the poor, who, reluctantly submitting to this cruel and useless law, are condemned, if not to witness a loved child's legally-inflicted death—and it must be remembered that even the official returns admit that since 1881 one death per week on the average has been due to this cause—at any rate to days and nights of anxious watching, if the course that the disease takes is severe. Such sympathy would not be of

scrupuleux ; mais ce qu'on ne sait pas, ce qu'on ne peut savoir, c'est la relation du remède au malade, car autant de malades, autant de cas, et chaque fois l'expérience recommence. Voilà pourquoi la médecine reste un art, parcequ'elle ne saurait avoir une rigeur expérimentale : toujours la guérison dépend d'une circonstance heureuse, de la trou- vaille de génie du médecin. Et, alors, comprenez donc que les gens qui viennent discuter ici me font rire, quand ils parlent au nom des lois absolues de la science. Où sont-elles ces lois, en médecine? Qu'on me les montre !" *Lourdes*, p. 198.

the conventional, counterfeit, loquacious kind, with which we are but too familiar, but such that stimulates and enables the sympathiser to understand—*durch Mitleid wissend*— what causes have led to the trouble, and to work quietly but determinedly for their removal.

Or, if literature should fail, painting might succeed, and a realistic presentation at the Royal Academy of one of the wretched calves at the Vaccine Institute, with its stomach shaved clean of hair and punctured in some sixty places for the production of cow-pox lymph, might shock the British public into a sense of the disgusting folly of the situation. Or, better still, an imaginative artist, following out the idea of Van Eyck's "Adoration of the Lamb," might produce a most telling picture of our nineteenth century calf-worship. Angels should be represented as catching in goblets the "life-giving fluid" as it issues from the poor beast's festering sores, and groups of Medical Men (the Council of the Royal College of Surgeons having a prominent place in the foreground) of Poor Law Guardians, of Justices of the Peace, of Vaccination Officers, of Jailors and Policemen, all duly supported by Members of both Houses of Parliament, should be picturesquely grouped around, singing the praises of the Great Preservative. There has, in truth, been no such calf-worship since the days when the children of Israel encamped beneath Mount Sinai; though on that occasion, if the records are to be trusted, the representative of the Law was not on the side of the superstition.

CONCLUSION.

It has been my aim in writing this letter, while pointing to larger works in which the history and pathology of

vaccination have been adequately handled by specially
qualified men, to show, not only that vaccination is and
from the first has been a mistake, but how it was possible, and
even natural under the circumstances, that such a mistake
should have been made.   That the history of vaccination
might form an additional chapter in Sir Thomas Browne's
Pseudodoxia Epidemica, or an extended section in Mr
Caxton's " History of Human Error " is to many persons
an altogether incredible idea.   They forget how much
that is false, and for how long a time, mankind has in
all ages believed.*   They do not test Jenner's advocacy
of vaccination by the application of Aristotle's doctrine
as to the sources of persuasion, which shows, correctly
enough, that it is not the cogency of the arguments used,
but the acceptableness of the man, and the acceptableness
of his message, that really command assent.   They forget
how Fashion, Authority, and Interest are more potent guides
of conduct than science or common sense.   They leave out
of account the influence of Enthusiasm and of Custom,
and they ignore the passion for coercing all to march in
line, which so often possesses those who have their fingers
on the springs of legislation.

I do not anticipate that my arguments will suffice to
change the opinion on this subject of men who have long
been accustomed to regard the belief in vaccination as
worthy of all acceptation ; but I do think the considera-
tions I have urged should suffice to show that disbelief
in vaccination cannot fairly be described in a disparaging

---

* An interesting illustration of the persistency of an error, which has
a pseudo-scientific basis, is to be found in the popular belief in the
influence over the weather possessed by the "changes " of the moon.
It is easy to demonstrate the scientific baselessness of the belief, and
three or four times a month it can be tested and shown to be a mistake.
But the belief prevails and will prevail.   Fortunately it is harmless
and not compulsory.

sense as "a fad," and to prove further that the doubts
concerning it are so reasonable and well-grounded that
it is not a fit subject for compulsory legislation. The
term "faddist" is indeed a relative one, and the faddists
of one generation may prove in the next to have been
pioneers. The Lollards, for example, were the faddists of
the fifteenth century, but they were the heralds of the
Reformation. And so, when anti-vaccinists are contemptuously classed by their opponents with anti-vivisec-
tionists, anti-opiumists, vegetarians, teetotallers, spiritists,
phonetic spellers, Anglo-Israelites, and what not, it is
well to insist on a distinction, and to claim. that only
such opinions as are ill-supported by argument, and are
obviously of a fantastic and trivial kind, shall be stigmatised
as "fads."

How weak is the faith in vaccination, even of those who
profess such belief in it that they insist on enforcing the
practice by law, is evidenced by the very fact that they do
thus insist on the vaccination of others. If the protection
is absolute, why worry about other people? if it is not
absolute, whence comes your right to enforce it? Faith
indeed has grown cold among medical men as well as
among the laity. Could any doctor now be found, who, in
spite of his brave confession of belief, would be willing to
imitate Jenner's foolhardy experiment in permitting his own
vaccinated child to sleep in the same bed with a small-pox
patient? We are now within a very short time of the
centenary of Jenner's great "discovery." How will it be
celebrated? Will his statue in Kensington Gardens be
decorated, after the manner of "Primrose Day," with
wreaths and flowers? or is it not more likely that, if vaccination is still compulsory at that date, an indignant Hyde
Park "demonstration" will chuck it into the Round Pond?
Such a demonstration—apart from any lawless incident—

might very well be arranged for now, and is perhaps the only thing calculated to persuade our easy-going legislators that the question is an important one, and that many people are in earnest about it. But funds and organisation are needed to carry out such a scheme; while anti-vaccinists are for the most part poor and isolated. Speakers could easily be found, for all the Labour members of the House of Commons (and many others) are opposed to compulsory vaccination; the difficulty would be to get the bunting, the breaks, and the brass-bands; for these things cost money. It was done, however, at Leicester in 1885, when the Mayor, amidst the wildest enthusiasm, burnt the Vaccination Acts in the market-place; and a similar demonstration in London in 1895 might set the whole country free.

But to conclude, Sir, my letter, which has run to much greater length than I had thought of when I began, may I make one or two suggestions as to the way in which the Legislature might deal with the Vaccination question without delay. If the case against vaccination is accepted as adequately proved, many will urge that an immediate repeal of the compulsory law is hardly enough. The whole of the State establishment of vaccination should at the same time be abolished, so that no further official sanction or encouragement to the practice should be given. Some would even go further, and demand that an operation condemned as futile and perhaps dangerous should be made illegal, as the old system of inoculation was made in 1840. I would not ask for so much; rather I would urge that the prohibition of inoculation should be withdrawn, save in so far that persons inoculated should be prevented from involving other persons in the risk of infection. For freedom is surely the best atmosphere for the progress of science, medical or otherwise; and, though it might be right to prohibit the vaccination of children, or of young persons unable to give a rational consent to its being done, it would be absurd to prevent intelligent people from using an alleged prophylactic which has been so long and so firmly believed in.   Freedom for both sides is really all that need be asked for.   If, after compulsion has been withdrawn, the practice slowly dies out, it will be time enough then to put an end to the National Vaccine Institute.

Meanwhile, it is much to be hoped that there may be nothing like a serious epidemic of small-pox during the time that the question of compulsory vaccination is being considered by Parliament : for experience has shown that, oddly enough, it is not the apparent success of vaccination but its obvious failure in the face of epidemics that stirs up the official world to make the burden of compulsion heavier.   The dates of the various Vaccination Acts are sufficient illustration of this.*

What I hope is this, that the Government, in view, not only of the final Report of the Royal Commission, but also of the facts I have noted above as to its constitution and procedure, will feel satisfied that compulsion ought forthwith to cease, and will resolve to carry this through. I do not wish to suggest ignoble motives for undertaking what ought to be done on account of its own inherent justice; but it is more than probable that some hundreds

---

* Activity in the administration of the law is stimulated by the same cause.   A somewhat grotesque instance may be quoted.   At Ashford, in Kent, in the autumn of 1891, there was a slight epidemic of small-pox, traced to the importation of foreign rags.   As there had been considerable resistance to the compulsory law in the district, the authorities at once began proceedings against the detested "anti-vaccinators."   But on enquiry it was ascertained that the disease had only attacked vaccinated persons.   An attempt was made to obtain publicity for these facts ; but it was of no use.   See the "Vaccination Inquirer," Vol. XIII., pp. 109 and 122.

or thousands of votes at the next General Election will be determined by the attitude taken by the Government on this question; for it is widely felt that this is a matter which has been neglected too long. Not much time need be spent upon it, if the Government would first proceed by resolution in the House of Commons, and would then introduce a measure of repeal in the House of Lords. A bare resolution passed in the Lower House would suffice to render the Acts inoperative throughout the country, as they are already in very considerable districts ; for indeed the authorities, by their own confession, are becoming sick and ashamed of administering a law for which they are careful to disclaim responsibility. A resolution, " That in the opinion of this House the time has arrived when the practice of vaccination should cease to be enforced under penalties," would. if proposed by the Government, easily command a majority ; for many sincere believers in vaccination hold that it has now " done its work," and that it is better to rely on sanitary measures, or the compulsory notification of infectious diseases, and on the isolation, so far as practicable, of cases. No doubt the motion would be opposed ; but it could not fail to pass, if the case were clearly and firmly stated. That then being carried, the Lord Chancellor could introduce in the Upper House, a measure embodying the resolution ; and, as having been for three years the presiding Chairman of the Royal Commission, he would be listened to and would command assent as an expert on the subject; and it is quite possible that the Bill might get through. Further action would then in one sense be unnecessary, as the law would be practically repealed ; and in another sense it would be imperative, so as to secure the executive from the ignominious position of being unable to carry

out a law which still remained on the Statute Book.
Under such circumstances even the most resolute ob-
structives in the House of Commons might relent, and
allow the repealing Bill to pass as an uncontentious
measure. A widespread feeling of relief would accompany
the final stages of the Bill; for compulsory vaccination
has been for years a vexed Parliamentary question; while
the bitterness it has stirred up throughout the country
at large need not be further referred to. That you, Sir,
may put your hand to this work of justice, and may
secure the emancipation of your countrymen from a law
so foolish and odious that it can hardly fail to be regarded
a century hence with a mixture of amusement and amaze-
ment, is the sincere wish of,—Yours, &c.,

ARTHUR W. HUTTON.

September 16, 1894.

POSTSCRIPT.

Dr Klein's Alleged Discovery.

I HAVE made above (p. 83) a note on Dr Klein's paper
On the Etiology of Vaccinia and Variola, which was issued
with the Local Government Board's Medical Officer's
Supplementary Report just as these pages were passing
through the press (August 29). I anticipated that the advocates of vaccination would hail its appearance with
delight, as rescuing them officially from the ignominious
position of having no scientific theory of vaccination to
adduce; and so it has proved. In a leading article on
September 7th, the *Times* called attention to this "highly
important paper," and asserted that "the experiments of Dr
Klein . . . appear to place the identity of the two forms

of disease [cow-pox and small-pox] beyond a doubt."
The article in question was probably the work of a
medical member of the Royal Commission; for it referred
to evidence as yet unpublished.

As I have made a special point of the dissimilarity
between cox-pox and small-pox, there is some likelihood
that inattentive readers will conclude that Dr Klein's
paper has knocked the bottom out of my argument. I
therefore append some criticisms on its conclusiveness :—

1. It is a small matter, but one worth noting, that
Dr Klein, as an apt disciple of Jenner, assumes in the
title of his paper the conclusion which he has to prove.
Such at least is the inference one would draw from the
single use of "etiology" with the two diseases. They
have one and the same cause—viz., the bacillus that I
have discovered.

2. Another small matter, but one deserving attention,
is the silence, both of Dr Klein and of the writer in
the *Times*, concerning Professor Crookshank's elaborate
and prolonged researches in the same field. He must,
if possible, be forgotten.

3. Independent observation by other skilled and unbiassed bacteriologists is necessary to confirm the existence of this new bacillus alleged to be common and
specific to the two diseases. It must be remembered
that scores of microscopes, on the Continent and in
America no less than at home, have been for years
searching for this much-desired microbe, but (Dr Klein
apart) in vain.

4. Assuming, however, that the discovery is a genuine
one, to what does it amount? Does it mean that vaccination, discovered by Jesty in 1774, or, if you so
prefer it, by Jenner in 1796, approved by the profession
since 1800, and enforced in England since 1853, has

had all this time only an empirical basis, but is now at last, in 1894, proved to be a genuinely scientific operation? They who eagerly welcome Dr Klein's paper should not forget what a confession it involves.

5. But the discovery (granted, for the sake of argument) is quite inadequate by itself to transform vaccination into a scientific operation. Bacteriology is still in its infancy, and it has doubtless something to unlearn as well as much to learn. Every Medical Congress introduces to us with much enthusiasm a new bacillus, specific to this or that disease; and wondrous results are promised, or are even alleged as already realised. But how very, very little does it all come to after a few months or years! Even those bacteria which have been longest and most closely studied are of dubious service in diagnosis, as they who watched Dr Klein's reports on the cholera last year must have noticed. The distinction between *cholera nostras* and the Asiatic variety is better drawn by the old-fashioned method of clinical observation than by bacteriology.

6. And, while bacteriology is thus, so far as I can judge, of second or even of third-rate importance in the diagnosis of disease, the distinction between cow-pox and small-pox has been firmly established on pathological grounds which cannot easily be gainsaid. No mere bacillus will avail to set aside the observations of Auzias - Turenne, Boens-Boissau, Creighton, and Crookshank; and, while it is best for a layman to leave to professional men the technical details which indicate the difference between the two diseases, it may be pointed out that the vaccine vesicle, though it has, no doubt, some superficial resemblance to the variolous pock, is really unlike it, in being of an ulcerous rather than of the true exanthematous character; while the " marks " that the two diseases

leave behind—the foveated scar of the one and the indentated "pit" of the other—can readily be distinguished even by a non-professional eye; though the fact that "marks" are commonly left in both cases is enough to satisfy those who wish to believe in the identity of the two diseases. And, finally, the non-infectiousness—in the ordinary sense—of cow-pox is a very notable distinction. The mildest case of small-pox may, by aerial infection, convey the disease to others, even in its severest form; while the most severe case of cow-pox can only be transmitted to another when the lymph actually touches the person where the skin has been abraded. This is really a decisive differentiating test.

On the whole, I am disposed to conclude that Dr Klein's paper, so far from rehabilitating vaccination, will rather tend to discredit bacteriology as a method of diagnosis.

A. W. H.

PROFESSOR CROOKSHANK ON DR KLEIN'S PAPER.

AN earlier portion of Dr Klein's paper (pp. 391-5) gives details of experiments made by him, and by Dr Simpson, of Calcutta, chiefly with the view of raising a fresh stock of vaccine lymph from genuine small-pox virus. On June 23rd, 1892, Dr Klein inoculated a calf at the Brown Institution with "lymph of variolous pedigree," making "forty-seven cutaneous insertions in the usual manner." On June 28th, this animal "had splendid vesicles typical of *vaccinia*." Other experiments were less "successful"; but "scrapings" from the calf aforesaid were used by Dr Cory to vaccinate three children, with "characteristic *vaccinia*" as the result. An effort to test the effect of the vaccination by subjecting the children to re-vaccination at a little later date was thwarted by "our failure to induce the mothers in question to bring back their children, after the first vaccination had to their satisfaction been happily got over." This is intelligible.

It is mainly with reference to this portion of Dr Klein's paper that Professor Crookshank writes as follows :—

" In answer to your letter, I must state most emphatically, that we do not know the nature of the *contagium* of cow-pox, or of human small-pox, or of any of the diseases from which so-called "vaccine lymph" has been cultivated for the purpose of obtaining protection from small-pox.

" With regard to Dr Klein's experiments on behalf of the Local Government Board, which have been recently noticed in the *Times*, I am bound to say that they have not added in the least to the information we previously possessed.   Lymph for vaccination has been over and over again obtained by inoculating calves with human small-pox; but this does not prove the identity of two such totally different diseases as natural cow-pox and human small-pox.   If Dr Klein, or anyone else, had ever succeeded in converting cow-pox into human small-pox, that would be evidence of a different kind; but it never has been done.   On the other hand, lymph producing the familiar appearances of vaccination has been obtained by attenuation of small-pox, without resorting to the calf as a medium of cultivation; and similarly, lymph for the purposes of vaccination has been raised from horse-pox, sheep-pox, and cattle-plague.   To argue on this ground that all these diseases are identical is therefore absurd."

" Edgar M. Crookshank,
"Author of 'The History and Pathology of Vaccination'
(2 vols., 1889), and Director of the Bacteriological Labora-
tory, King's College, London."

" Saint Hill, near East Grinstead, Sussex,
" *Sept.* 20, 1894."

Attention may also be called to a letter in the *British Medical Journal*, September 15, 1894, in which Professor Crookshank defines and defends his position. The letter was written on August 1; but was kept back by the editor for six weeks, apparently with the aim of printing simultaneously some kind of rejoinder (*q.v.*).

I subjoin the professional records of the three medical men on whose criticisms of the current belief in vaccination my own disbelief is mainly based (see above, p. 4). They are taken from the "Medical Directory" for 1894:—

COLLINS, WM. JOB, 1 Albert Ter., Regent's Park, N.W.— M.S. Lond. 1885, B.S. (Honours) 1881, Certif. Pub. Health (Gold Medallist) 1887, B.Sc. (2nd in Honours in Physiol.) 1880, M.D. 1883, M.B. (Univ. Schol. and Gold Medallist in Obst. Med., 1st Class Honours in For. Med.) 1881; F.R.C.S. Eng. (exam.) 1884, M. 1880; (*St Bart.*); Senator of Lond. Univ.; Mem. Lond. Co. Council; Jeaffreson Exhib. St Bart. Hosp. 1876; Fell. Sanit. Inst.; Mem. Ophth., Anat. and Path. Socs.; Mem. Middle Temple Inn; Vis. Surg. Lond. Temp. Hosp.; Roy. Commissioner on Vacc.; late Asst. Demonst. of Anat. St Bart. Hosp. Med. Sch., Ophth. House Surg. and Res. Midw. Asst. St Bart. Hosp., and Surg. Western Ophth. Hosp. Author of "Specificity and Evolution in Disease," 1884 and 1890; "Spinoza," 1889; "Rationalism in Medicine," 1890. Contrib. "Cases of Ocular Motor-Paralysis," *St Bart. Hosp. Reps.*, 1883; "The Capsulo-pupillary Membrane, with some Varieties of its Persistence," *Ophth. Hosp. Reps.*, 1888; "Action of Various Aromatic Compounds upon Bile-Secretion," *Rep. Brit. Assoc.*, 1888; "Associated and Related Ocular and Dental Diseases," *Trans. Odont. Soc.*, 1891; "Surgical Treatment of Empyema," *Lancet*, 1889; "Traumatic Hydronephrosis," *Brit. Med. Journ.*, 1892; Evidence before University for London Commissioners, *Blue Books*, 1887 and 1893.

[Dr Collins' tract, "Sir Lyon Playfair's Logic," 1883, referred to above (p. 103), is not included in this list, being

now out of print.   Dr Collins' father, who bore the same
name, was induced, by his experience as a public vaccinator,
to abandon his belief in vaccination.   He refused to have
his own children vaccinated, and he published two tracts
(*Twenty Years' Experience as a Public Vaccinator*, 1866,
and *Have you been Vaccinated?* 1867), showing how he
had come to recognise the futility and the risks of the
operation.]

CREIGHTON, CHARLES, 32 Gt. Ormond St., W.C.—M.A.
Aberd. 1867, M.B. and C.M. 1871, M.D. 1878 ; M.A. Camb.
(*propter merita*) ; (*Aberd., Edin., Vienna, and Berlin*) ; formerly
Demonst. of Anat. Univ. Camb.   Author of "Contributions to
the Physiology and Pathology of the Breast and its Lymphatic
Glands," 1878 ; "Bovine Tuberculosis in Man," 1881 ; "On the
Autonomous Life of the Specific Infections" (address in Path.
Brit. Med. Assoc., 1883) ; Art. "Pathology," *Encyc. Britan.*,
1884 ; and other works.   Contrib. "On Infection of Connective
Tissue in Scirrhus Cancers of Breast," *Journ. Anat. and Physiol.;*
"Physiol. Type of Giant Cells of Tubercle, &c.," *ibid.;* "Illustrations of the Pathology of Sarcoma," *ibid.* ; "A Pathol. Func-
tion of the Periosteum," *ibid.;* "Homology of the Suprarenals,"
ibid.; "Formation of Placenta in Guinea Pig," *ibid.;* &c.

[The above list of Dr Creighton's publications is very in-
complete, all his writings on vaccination, for example, being
omitted.   The following additions may be made :—" Hand-
book of Geographical and Historical Pathology" (translated
from the German of A. Hirsch), 3 vols. 1883-6 ; "Illustrations of Unconscious Memory in Disease, including a
Theory of Alteratives," 1886 ; "The Natural History oi
Cow-pox and Vaccinal Syphilis," 1887 ; Article on "Vaccination" in the *Encyclop. Britan.*, 1888 ; "Jenner and
Vaccination," 1889 ; "Vaccination: a Scientific Enquiry,"
Arena, Sept. 1890 ; also sundry articles in the earlier
volumes of the "Dictionary of National Biography," ed.
Leslie Stephen ; the sections on "Public Health," in the

work entitled "Social England," now in course of publication; and "The History of Epidemics in Britain" (Cambridge University Press), the second and concluding volume of which is expected to be published this autumn.]

CROOKSHANK, EDGAR MARCH, Saint Hill, East Grinstead, Sussex—M.B. Lond. (Honours in Obst.) 1884, M.R.C.S. Eng. 1881 (*King's Coll.*); Exhib. and Gold Medallist in Anat. 1st M.B. Lond. 1879; Fell. King's Coll.; Mem. Roy. Micros. Soc. and Path. Soc.; Prof. of Comp. Path. and Bacteriol. King's Coll.; late House Surg. King's Coll. Hosp., and Civil Surg. Med. Staff Egyptian Campaign (Medal and Clasp, Tel-el-Kebir, and Khedive's Star).   Author of "Manual of Bacteriology," 3rd edit. (transl. into French); "Photography of Bacteria"; "History and Pathology of Vaccination."   Contrib. "Evidence on Medical Service in Egypt," *Blue Book*, 1883; "Report on the Antiseptic Methods Employed at the Field and Base Hospitals of the Egyptian Expedition," *Lancet*, 1883; "Remarks on the Cholera Bacillus of Koch," *ibid.*, 1885; "Report on the Typhoid Fever Epidemic at Worthing," *ibid.*, 1893; "On Flagellated Protozoa in the Blood of Diseased and Apparently Healthy Animals," *Journ. Roy. Micros. Soc.*, 1887; "On the So-called Hendon Cow Disease in its relation to Scarlet Fever," *Path. Trans.* and *Rep. Agric. Departm. Privy Counc.*, 1887; "Anthrax in Swine," "Tubercular Mammitis," "History and Pathology of Actinomycosis," *Rep. Agric. Departm. Privy Counc.*, 1888; "Evidence before Royal Vaccination Commissioners, 1891"; several Papers in *Trans. Internat. Med. Cong.*, 1892, &c.

FURTHER NOTES

ON THE

VACCINATION QUESTION

A LETTER ADDRESSED BY PERMISSION TO THE

RIGHT HON. ARTHUR JAMES BALFOUR, M.P.

First Lord of the Treasury

BY

ARTHUR WOLLASTON HUTTON, M.A.

Formerly Scholar of Exeter College, Oxford
Librarian of the National Liberal Club

FURTHER NOTES ON
THE VACCINATION QUESTION.

DEAR SIR,—In the autumn of last year (1894) I addressed
to Mr Asquith, at that time Home Secretary, a public letter
on the Vaccination Question. Since that date further evidence on the question has come to light, especially with
reference to the results of the repeal of compulsion in
certain parts of Switzerland; and I am indebted to you for
your permission to address to you a supplementary letter
on the subject, the contents of which I trust you will consider in connection with the long-delayed final Report of
the Royal Commission, whenever that makes its appearance.
Whether that Report is unanimous in recommending the
repeal of our compulsory law—and this is not unlikely,
since already in its interim Report the Commission has
unanimously recommended that the law should not be
further enforced in the case of parents who are willing to
pay what amounts to an exemption-fee of not more than
twenty shillings in the case of each child—or whether, as
is perhaps more probable, there will be two Reports, one in
favour of and the other adverse to a continuance of compulsion, it is certain that the Government will have to take
some action in the matter. Over a very large extent of the
country the law is practically repealed already; and, if a
majority of the Commissioners report in favour of compulsion being continued, the difficult question will have to be
faced as to how it is to be restored; for this will only be

possible, if possible at all, by means of fresh legislation.
Advocating, as I do, a total repeal of our compulsory law,
together with complete disestablishment and disendowment
of the State apparatus by which this useless and mischievous
animal poison is (doubtless with the best intentions) transmitted throughout the country and injected into the bodies
of healthy infants, I am not sure whether I ought not also
to advocate, as a means to that end, the passing of a new
and stringent Vaccination Law.   If I may be excused a
paradox, it is the weakness of our present law which constitutes its strength.   Its existence is only tolerated because
all that it does is, in a flabby, casual way, to punish a small
percentage of those who disobey it, its victims being almost
invariably selected from the defenceless poor.   But let a
new and stringent law be passed and be enforced everywhere without respect of persons, subjecting every child to
the rigid preliminary examination and the four punctures
officially insisted upon by the Local Government Board
as necessary for " efficient vaccination," and the measure
would within twelve months be swept from the Statute-book
by an aroused and indignant nation.

CONSERVATIVES AND COMPULSION.

But I do not anticipate that, whatever the Commission
may report, the present Government will attempt to pass
any measure of this kind.   The medico-politicians, of whom
Mr Ernest Hart may be taken as a type, men who believe
less in progressive medical science than in " State Medicine " and " the principle of compulsion," have, if I mistake
not, a disappointment in store for them.   The change of
Government is not likely to prove so advantageous to their
plans as they had supposed.   It is true that a considerable
number of those who in 1893 supported Mr Hopwood's

resolution against compulsory vaccination are from various causes, unconnected with the present subject, no longer to be found in the House of Commons. But their places have been supplied by others equally opposed to our present system ; and it is satisfactory to learn that an enquiry recently made discloses the fact that, of some sixty members who have publicly pledged themselves to vote against compulsion, about one-half are Unionists. The question, indeed, is one that has nothing whatever to do with party politics ; and although it is true that the anti-vaccinist cause has mostly been championed in the House of Commons by Liberals of the old school, it is also true that the tendency to *doctrinaire* legislation, of which the Vaccination Law is an indubitable specimen, has of late years been rather a characteristic of the new Liberalism ; while Conservatives have recently been reminding one another that it is their traditional policy to avoid unnecessary interference with personal liberty, and to refrain from (an expression which includes, I should hope, to repeal) harassing legislation. It is, moreover, reassuring to remember that it was in his Radical days that Mr Chamberlain spoke of "that blessed word *compulsion.*" Indeed I have reason to believe, that he is, on this question, distinctly sympathetic with the views which I express. Probably he has noted that in the recent small-pox epidemic, 1892-4, Birmingham, despite its scrupulous care about vaccination, showed ten times as many deaths as Leicester, which has wholly neglected it for many years past.*

Fads and Faddists.

The word *doctrinaire*, which I have used above, reminds me with how little propriety the advocates of vaccination

* For the same reason, doubtless, the Guardians have now ceased to enforce the law in Birmingham.

speak contemptuously of their opponents as "faddists." A moment's reflection makes it clear that the boot is on the other leg; unless, indeed, it be the case that when the State endows and enforces a fad it is a fad no longer. Vaccination originally possessed every attribute that constitutes a fad; and it is not easy to say when those attributes were lost. Time and use have given it a certain respectability; but its prophylactic value is to this day a matter of dispute; it is destitute of a scientific pathological basis; and its history is a history of apologies for its failures. I cannot see how the members of the original "Committee on Vaccine Inoculation" were not in the strict sense faddists, when, setting aside unfavourable evidence, they recommended Jenner for a grant of public money, a grant which in 1803 committed the whole official world to a belief in the merits of vaccination, and was thus the original ground for its legal enforcement some fifty years later. Again, I cannot see why Dr Seaton and his Epidemiological Society were not faddists when they gained the ear of Parliament for their plea for compulsion in 1853; nor, finally, can I see why Dr Farquharson was not a faddist when, in 1893, he repeatedly and successfully used the obstructive forms of the House of Commons to prevent the Vaccination Law from being relaxed in accordance with the unanimous recommendation of the Royal Commission. It depends on your point of view. The editors of the *Sun* and of the *St James's Gazette* will have it that *we* are the faddists who are working for the repeal of a law which is an unique example of the legislative enforcement of belief in a doubtful medical dogma. When that repeal has been accomplished, and the practice has fallen, as Professor Crookshank is confident it will, into desuetude, time will show whether vaccination was ever anything more than a fad temporarily glorified by Act of Parliament.

THE ROYAL COMMISSION.

Meanwhile let me recall certain facts in regard to the Royal Commission now sitting. Appointed in 1889, if it should not have issued its final report (as now seems likely) before May 1896, it will have been in session for as long as seven years. For an inquiry of this nature such a prolonged period is probably unprecedented ; and the fact alone suffices to show that they who in 1889 spoke with such confidence of the speedy endorsement of the value of vaccination which the enquiry was sure to effect, were somewhat premature in their boasting.   I for one make no complaint as to the slowness with which the enquiry has been conducted. I wish, certainly, that it had not been conducted with closed doors ; for the publication after each session of a summary of the evidence taken would have beyond all things been serviceable in educating the general public as to the real state of the case.   And, though the Commission may report and Parliament may legislate, it is really with an educated general public that the decision must ultimately lie. That the evidence obtained at so much cost and labour should thus remain sealed, except to the eyes of the very few who have the opportunity, the industry, and the intelligence to study profitably some thousands of pages of Blue-books, closely printed in double columns, is surely to be regretted by everyone who does not love darkness rather than light ; but the protracted nature of the enquiry, followed by two years of hesitation as to the conclusion to which the enquiry points—for the taking of evidence ceased in 1893—must impress every one who thinks at all with the conviction that a conclusion, whatever it may be, reached through so much doubt and difficulty cannot possibly afford a sound basis for penal legislation, and indeed that there never ought to have been any penal legislation in connection with such a subject at all. In my first Letter I criticised freely—perhaps too freely—the composition and sundry points in the procedure of the Royal Commission (pp. 104-9), and I still hold that it was little short of absurd to give to elderly medical men the duty of "enquiring" into a matter, which, in their judgment, had been settled long ago. The convictions, even though they be the illusions, of a life-time, are not lightly laid aside, so as to admit of the reception of new light. Men with scientifically trained minds, but not professional men, and lawyers accustomed to weigh evidence, would have been the proper judges; while the medical men would have been in their right place as witnesses. But I quite admit that, having stated these objections, the appointment of the Commission, and its final as well as its interim Report, cannot fail to be of service towards the settlement of this vexed question. If the general impression conveyed is no more than this, that the subject is one full of doubts and difficulties, that is really enough for those who demand that the compulsory law should be repealed. We do not want or expect either the medical men on the Commission or medical men in general to do penance in a white sheet, and to confess that they have been altogether in the wrong. That would be too much for human nature. But we do expect them to admit, at any rate tacitly, that it is a controversy in which we of the opposition can make out a fair case; for, having admitted as much as that, they will see, what the clear-sighted among them have seen long ago, that it is contrary to the best interests of their own profession for a practice thus open to criticism, and certainly not indispensable, to be enforced by law.

The Moral Objections to Compulsion.

As I understand the matter, the cause which I advocate can be argued most conveniently under three heads.

First, the orthodox doctrine as to the nature and effects of vaccination may be impugned on scientific grounds pathological and statistical. Secondly, the objection to vaccination being enforced by law is arguable on moral grounds; and finally, it must be urged on the legislature that the repeal of compulsion is eminently expedient, and that experience has shown that such a policy need cause no alarm. And in the course of the argument it should be indicated how, although the popular belief in vaccination is unsound, there are intelligible reasons why such a belief should have grown up and should apparently have been confirmed by experience. It will be my aim in what follows to deal briefly with each of these points; and, as the moral argument is the least interesting, and perhaps also the least likely to carry weight with members of Parliament, I will dispose of that first. There is the less reason for my dwelling on it at any length, as I have recently stated it elsewhere as fully as the space then granted to me would admit. * But there are sundry points in this moral argument which deserve serious consideration.

Our law does not empower any official to vaccinate any child without the parent's consent. So far so good. But it punishes parents who act as if they did not believe in vaccination, and it is thus the penal enforcement of a creed. For a parent to submit his child with a good conscience to vaccination he must believe these three things:—1. That vaccination protects against small-pox; 2. That the child will stand in need of such protection; and 3. That the operation is free from risk. Now a parent may quite reasonably deny every one of these propositions, and can support his denial, if he likes, by abundant evidence. And if, while disbelieving the creed thus forced on him by the law,

* " The Moral argument against Compulsory Vaccination " in *The Humanitarian* for September 1895. Vol. vii., p. 177.

he submits his child to vaccination, having a bad conscience all the time about it, there can be no doubt that he acts immorally. Our vaccination law is thus to be condemned for the same reason that we condemn Test Acts and all legislation which insists on an action being performed that can only be performed rightly when prompted by a sincere belief. *

Again, our compulsory law violates the principle of progressiveness in medical science, and interferes with the just liberty of medical men. It is a common-place of applied science that it lacks finality, that it should ever be free to revise its judgments ; for it is of its essence to be always learning something new. And this is especially true of medicine, which is rather an art, or at best a scientific art, than a science ; so uncertain and so variable are its methods, and that necessarily, on account of the varying character of the subject-matter with which it has to deal. And medical men who do not blindly follow routine must see that the law interferes with their legitimate liberty of advice. To many such a one, believing, if you will, in

* In a period of temporary theological reaction, when we are called upon to believe in creeds, not because of evidence that proves them true, but because the notion that they are true is so agreeable, Paley's remarks on creeds may seem too old-fashioned to deserve notice. But they are at least equally forcible when applied *mutatis mutandis* to medical creeds :—" Though some purposes of order and tranquillity may be answered by the establishment of creeds and confessions, yet they are at all times attended with serious inconveniences. They check inquiry ; they violate liberty ; they ensnare the consciences of the clergy by holding out temptations to prevarication ; however they may express the persuasion, or be accommodated to the controversies, or to the fears, of the age in which they are composed, in process of time, and by reason of the changes which are wont to take place in the judgment of mankind upon religious subjects, they come at length to contradict the actual opinions of the church, whose doctrines they profess to contain."—*Moral and Political Philosophy*, Book VI., Chap. x.

vaccination, but not so far gone in the superstition as to hold that an unvaccinated child can actually start small-pox on its own account, it must have occurred as the right advice to give to parents, especially if resident in the country :—" The risk of small-pox infection is practically *nil ;* you had better defer vaccination until some such risk appears ; and meanwhile your child, with its health un-impaired by the effects of vaccination, will pass more easily through the inevitable troubles of infancy." But this sensible advice the law forbids him to give. All he can do is to sign a certificate of postponement for two months, and that only if the child is suffering for some definite disorder, which he has to name. Yet the doctors as a rule prefer this tangle of red tape in which their own freedom is involved, rather than let parents be free from a law which incidentally establishes the supremacy of medical men.

Further, if " the rights of man " be not a mere phrase, is not the implantation of disease, when the best instincts of our nature bid us strive to maintain our bodies in good health, a violation of one of those rights, none the less objectionable because the implantation is according to law ? Of course the operation is performed with the best inten-tions ; but no one can say for certain either that it is necessary, or that it will be effectual, or that it will anyhow do no harm. And this law, for the repeal of which I am pleading, makes this attack solely on the bodies of infants, who are of course helpless in the matter, although the doctors mostly agree that adults, even if already once vaccinated in childhood, need the operation none the less ; while, as administered, it is grossly partial and comes down with severity only on poor parents here and there. I could enlarge on these and on similar points indefinitely, but this is enough to indicate how our system of compulsory vaccination is open to criticism on moral grounds.

The Scientific Criticism on Vaccination.

The fact must not be overlooked that it was on the assumption that vaccination is a *specific* defence against small-pox that compulsion was and could alone be justified. The recognition of a casual antagonism between cow-pox and small-pox—a matter on which I will say more later—would not have sufficed. And this specific character of the protection can hardly be maintained apart from Jenner's doctrine of the substantial identity of the two diseases. That is why so much importance was attached by orthodox believers in vaccination to Dr Klein's alleged discovery of a bacterium common to the two. The *Times* (see above, p. 121) recorded the discovery with a sigh of relief; for, if it can be maintained, the scientific explanation may be given that the vaccinated person is exempt from a subsequent attack of small-pox, *because he has had it already.* That is in fact the *raison d'être* of the specific protection.*

Now I am not going again over the same ground in regard to the recent criticism of the Jenner doctrine by Dr Creighton and Professor Crookshank, and their maintenance of the theory that cow-pox is pathologically a totally distinct disease from small-pox.† That theory commended itself to me so soon as I read their account of it; and, in

---

* I pass over, as commonly accepted, the implied assertion that one attack of small-pox is a specific protection against a second.   But it is certain that there have been cases of a second attack ; and it has been ingeniously suggested that the number of such cases bear the same proportion to the number of persons who have had small-pox once as these latter do to the whole population.   If this could be established it would of course upset the whole theory of vaccinal protection, even after admitting that vaccination is a modified attack of small-pox. But there are no statistics in existence by which the theory can be either established or refuted ; and certainly the popular impression is that one attack does preclude another with almost absolute certainty.

† See above, pp. 19-23.

spite of Dr Klein, I believe that it continually finds more acceptance. How indeed could it be otherwise when that theory alone explains all the facts? The Creighton-Crookshank theory, while it excludes the notion that cow-pox is a specific defence against small-pox, does not exclude the notion that in a casual, uncertain, fleeting manner the former may be antagonistic to the latter, and so, now and again, be actually a defence against it. As much as this was admitted by Professor Crookshank before the Royal Commission; and, though the admission is inconsistent with the tenets of strict anti-vaccinists, I am not myself unwilling to make it, because it brings vaccination into line with other facts observed by medical men, and also because it helps us to get at a rational understanding as to how the older and bolder theory of vaccination, false though it be, has succeeded in obtaining widespread and prolonged cre-dence. Given then this admission as not inconsistent with the Creighton-Crookshank theory, and all the facts can be ex-plained, as they can not be explained by the Jenner theory. Vaccination frequently produces ulcers of a syphilitic char-acter, even when the greatest pains have been taken to secure " pure lymph." Certainly, because that is the nature of the disease implanted. When there is an epidemic of small-pox about, vaccinated people seem to take the disease pretty nearly as freely as the unvaccinated. Certainly, be-cause in cow-pox there is no specific defence against small-pox. And yet, on the other hand, there is a good deal of evidence to show that the recently vaccinated are, on the whole, less liable to attack, and that, if they do take the disease, they get over it more quickly. Very likely; some such antagonism has been observed in the case of other diseases which are not pathologically related to each other; but it is a subject on which as yet little is definitely known. Speaking before the British Medical Association on July 31st,

1895, Sir William Broadbent said incidentally, "Apparently one virus may be antagonistic to another, and an attack of small-pox has often seemed to cure phthisis." Read this, "an attack of cow-pox has often seemed to prevent small-pox"—and this let us grant is the case—and you have perhaps a key to the whole of this vaccination controversy, for you have here an explanation as to how the belief arose and has been maintained, while you have no extravagant pretensions as to the universality or certainty of the defence. Let us grant that in some sense vaccination is a prophylactic against small-pox, but only in an uncertain, casual way. It may prevent small-pox just as small-pox itself may cure phthisis; but, accepted thus, it will no longer hold an unique position in medicine. It must come down from that high pedestal on which blind enthusiasm placed it long ago, a pedestal which State patronage, endowment, and enforcement have made so strong. It must take its place alongside of other medical prescriptions, as tentative, perhaps promising, but by no means as infallible ; and it must be regarded henceforth as a matter between physician and patient, whether the one will recommend it in this or that case, or regard it as unnecessary under the circumstances, and whether the other will choose to submit to the operation, or will prefer to face what in any case can only be regarded as a slightly increased risk. Obviously, if recent scientific criticism of vaccination really does in this way dethrone it, and leave it indistinguishable from other forms of medical treatment, plausible, perhaps valuable, but far from being infallible, compulsion is henceforth out of the question. An equally good case could be made out for Sir William Broadbent's alleged remedy for phthisis being made compulsory ; yet neither he nor anyone else would dream of such enforcement. Nevertheless, the case for compelling consumptive patients to submit to small-pox inoculation might be very plausibly stated. The mortality from phthisis is immense and increasing; the disease is now generally recognised as infectious; there is no known cure for it, unless it be that "small-pox often seems to cure it." Surely, then, such a remedy should be insisted on under penalties for the welfare of the community. Eighteenth century statistics can be quoted to show that the mortality from inoculated small-pox is *une quantité négligeable;* so that there is medical authority to persuade parents and patients that, while there may be much to gain, there can be nothing to lose. I am not advocating, of course, any such compulsory law; I am only using the illustration to show how easily enthusiasts can make out a plausible case for legislative enforcement, where a sober-minded statesman, or an average well-informed man of the world, will see at once that the idea of coercion is absurd.

The Repeal of Compulsion in Switzerland.

The main obstacle in the way of repeal is the fear that possesses men's minds that, when compulsory vaccination is gone, small-pox will again over-run the country like a plague. When this belief is held sincerely, as undoubtedly it often s, it deserves honour or at least respect; but at the same time it should be clearly pointed out that such a belief could not possibly be held as certain by intelligent men, were it not for the obscurantist attitude of the editors of our newspapers and magazines, who, influenced themselves by the same dread, lest they should help forward the movement that makes for repeal, obstinately refuse to make public well-ascertained facts which prove as clearly as the case admits of proof, that these fears are without foundation. I am not troubling now about the distinction that may be made between the repeal of the law and the actual disuse of vaccination, in so far as they affect the prevalence of small-pox. Where there has been no agitation against the law, it might very likely be quietly repealed without making for some time any serious difference in the number of vaccinations performed ; but where it is repealed in consequence of local agitation, the effect is at once considerable. And the table given above (p. 69) showed clearly that widespread disuse, consequent upon local repeal, in such towns as Keighley, Leicester, Gloucester, Luton, Eastbourne, Northampton, and elsewhere, has led to no evil results. Further reports published since that table was prepared only confirm the evidence which it affords ; and a fresh and most important confirmation of it has within the last few months come to hand in the shape of a letter entitled "The Results of the Repeal of Compulsory Vaccination in Switzerland,' addressed last June to the Minister of the Interior in Wurtemburg by Dr Adolf Vogt, physician and statistician, of Berne.* His testimony cannot be set aside as that of a mere theorist or layman, and no sensible man would disregard the facts which he chronicles, merely because they tell against the necessity for compulsory vaccination. From 1850 to 1856 he was a public vaccinator in the Canton of Berne, where the practice was compulsory from 1849 until the present year. After 1856 he was in active service as physician during several small-pox epidemics at home and abroad. In 1871 he was director of the sanitary inspectors who had charge of the French soldiers interned in the Canton. For many years he was Professor of Hygiene and Instructor in Health Statistics in the local High School ;

---

* *Die Folgen der Aufhebung des Impfzwangs in der Schweiz ; Brief an Seine Excellenz den Herrn Staats Minister des Innern von Pischek in Stuttgart.* Pp. 16. Stuttgart, 1895. With this should be read an earlier publication of Dr Vogt's—*Die Pockenseuche und Impfverhältnisse in der Schweiz.* Pp. 78. Bern, 1882.

and since 1877 he has written several works on small-pox
and vaccination, mainly with reference to the special circumstances of Switzerland. The whole of his recently published
letter deserves careful study ; but I must confine myself now
to a summary of its chief contents.

Detailed death-statistics for all the twenty-five Cantons of
Switzerland begin with the year 1876. At various dates,
but in all cases some time before 1876, vaccination had been
made compulsory in twenty-two of the Cantons ; and in three
of these, Zug, Fribourg and the Grisons, re-vaccination was
(and is) also obligatory. The three Cantons which have
never had any compulsory law are Geneva, Uri, and Aargau.
In the latter, however, there is the singular provision that,
while vaccinated cases of small-pox are isolated at the public
expense, unvaccinated patients have to pay the cost of their
isolation. It would be interesting to know how this arrangement has worked, but Dr Vogt gives no particulars. In
1876, 89 per cent. of the population of Switzerland were
under a compulsory law. Since 1876 twelve Cantons have
abolished compulsion, so that in 1895, 68 per cent. are free.
The dates are as follows ; but it should be noted that in two
or three instances the date is that when the law ceased to be
enforced, the formal repeal following a few years later :—
Glarus, May 1876; Basle (town), November 1878; Basle
(country) and Obwald, July 1882 ; Zurich, May 1883 ;
Lucerne, June 1883; Schaffhausen, July 1883; Outer-
Appenzell, April 1884 ; St Gall, November 1884 ; Thurgau,
January, 1885 ; Schwytz, November 1894 ; and Berne,
February 1895.

In 1881-2, the pro-vaccination party made a determined
effort to check the tide of opposition to compulsion, and
they succeeded in passing a Federal Law on Epidemics
which would have made vaccination compulsory throughout
Switzerland, irrespective of Cantons. But the *referendum*

K

was at once demanded, and on July 30, 1882, the law was rejected by 79 per cent. of the voters, a larger number coming to the poll than on any previous occasion. Only in one Canton (Neuchâtel) was there a majority in its favour. In the same year, 1882, the Federal Council, recognising the trend of popular feeling in this matter, abolished the obligatory re-vaccination of recruits.

The process of repeal, which went on steadily until January 1885, was in that year checked by a small-pox epidemic, more serious than any that had occurred since 1871. This was not unnaturally attributed by many to the growing disuse of vaccination ; but confidence was restored when the year following the epidemic died out in the natural order of things, and without any recourse to fresh measures of compulsion, since which date Switzerland has been freer from small-pox than it ever was before ; and, now that the important Canton of Berne, the seat of the Federal Government, has, in February this year, repealed its compulsory law, it is thought that the ten Cantons which still retain their local law will shortly follow suit.

How a Belief in the Beneficial Effects of Compulsion is Fostered.

Leaving Dr Vogt and his Swiss statistics for a moment, I may point out how this incident of the Swiss epidemic of 1885, and similar experiences elsewhere, tend to confirm, though quite unjustifiably, a belief in the necessity of compulsory vaccination. Small-pox, throughout all its recorded history, has been and is a disease that ebbs and flows. The annual statistics show this with sufficient clearness; but statistics at shorter intervals, monthly or weekly, are better, as they indicate the precise date of the culmination of an epidemic, whether great or small. It is in vain—and I

challenge the believers in vaccination to prove me wrong in
this matter—that a constant relation, or anything like a constant relation, between this ebb and flow of the disease and
the presence or absence of vaccination is attempted to be
established.   Yet occasionally, I admit, some such relation
can be indicated ; but it is perfectly intelligible without
recourse to the hypothesis that the one phenomenon is
dependent on the other.   The epidemic of 1885 was very
plausibly attributed by many in Switzerland to the growing
disuse of vaccination ; but they who were familiar with the
natural history of small-pox knew that, although it is an
expiring disease, it still recurs in slight and local epidemics,
and that some such return of it was to be expected, whether
there were compulsory vaccination to meet it or no ; and so
they kept their heads cool, and soon found the justification
of their confidence, when the epidemic in due course declined.   Similar experiences are likely to lead to similar
doubts elsewhere.   If men were logical they would abandon
the practice of vaccination at the time when a violent epidemic has proved its futility.   The practice was far more
universal in England in the years 1853-70 than it has been
in the last ten or fifteen years.   Yet it did not prevent the
great epidemic of 1871-2 ; and, if in the height of that epidemic men had recognised its uselessness and had repealed
the law, the subsequent decline of the epidemic, which
would certainly have been experienced none the less, would
have justified their action.   As it was, however, a fresh Act
was passed in 1871, thus giving to Lord Playfair the opportunity to assert that the inevitable decline was really due to
the appointment of vaccination officers under that Act—a
truly whimsical notion to anyone who takes a broad view of
the whole subject.   But, human nature being what it is, a
repeal of compulsion, whether local or national, is only
possible when small-pox is at its lowest ebb ; and then the

subsequent recrudescence of the disease, almost as inevitable as the return of the tide, is triumphantly claimed as a consequence.

A similar fallacy is noticeable elsewhere. Small-pox appears in some town or district; an alarm is raised; the ocal authorities take action; special facilities for vaccination and re-vaccination are afforded; recourse to it is urged even by a house to house visitation; and some thousands submit to it. (This, by the way, is an incidental proof of the non-necessity of compulsion; for these vaccinations are, almost without exception, extra-legal, and could not be enforced on unwilling subjects.) In due course the epidemic subsides, and the usual paragraph appears in the papers that it has been "stamped out" by vaccination. But where is the proof? Did not and do not epidemics subside at times or in places, when or where there was or is no vaccination? I am willing to admit (for the sake of argument, and because my aim is not to prevent people from voluntarily submitting to vaccination, but merely to get rid of compulsion) that in some casual, uncertain way the vaccination may have helped to check the epidemic; but certainly there neither is nor can be any cogent proof that the local epidemic in question would not have subsided at the same date and in the same measure if there had been no attempt made to affect it by vaccination. That the local authorities do admirable service in checking epidemics by such rational methods as isolation, etc., I of course fully admit; but that is not the present question.

FURTHER NOTES ON DR VOGT'S SWISS STATISTICS.

That Switzerland as a whole has not suffered from the partial repeal of compulsion is clear from the following table, which shows the actual number of deaths from small-pox during a period of eighteen years :—

1876,	8	1882,	22	1888,	17
1877,	105	1883,	24	1889,	3
1878,	48	1884,	64	1890,	32
1879,	135	1885,	426	1891,	26
1880,	173	1886,	182	1892,	35
1881,	168	1887,	14	1893,	15

Total, 1497 ; Annual average, 83.

Anyone who is determined to regard the epidemic of 1885 as a consequence of the *referendum* vote of 1882 can divide the above period of 18 years into two periods of 9 years each, and can so prove that the repeal of compulsion has resulted in a small increase in the number of deaths from small-pox (750 in the later period as compared with 747 in the earlier); but a fairer judgment is obtained if the 18 years are taken as three periods of 6 years each ; in which case the annual average shows a rise from 106 to 122 in the first and second, and a fall to 21 in the third. The third period thus shows just one-fifth of the mortality of the first, the repeal of compulsion over so large a portion of the country notwithstanding.

Dr Vogt very pertinently calls attention to the striking contrast between the Canton of Uri and that of Zug. In some respects the two are much alike, neither Canton containing any large urban community, while the mean population during the period, 1876-93, was in round numbers 21,000 in the one case, and 23,000 in the other. But in regard to vaccination the difference is about as great as possible. In Uri it has never been compulsory, whereas in Zug both vaccination and re-vaccination have been compulsory since 1865. Has anything been gained by this strenuous enforcement of the practice? During the

18 years small-pox has visited Uri only twice (in 1880 and 1885), with a total of 6 deaths, thus giving a mean annual small-pox death-rate of 2·4 per 100,000 living; while during the same period small-pox has visited Zug 6 times (in 1877, 1879, 1880, 1883, 1885, and 1886), with a total of 39 deaths, thus giving a corresponding death-rate of 10·4, or more than four times as great. Dr Vogt gives similar statistics for other Cantons, which seem almost to point to the conclusion that compulsory vaccination, so far from excluding small-pox, really seems to attract it; but he honestly points out a contrary experience in the Canton of Zurich, which repealed its compulsory law in 1883, and had 20 deaths from small-pox in the 8 years immediately preceding repeal, and 136 deaths in the 8 years succeeding. That this, however, was a mere coincidence and not a consequence of the repeal is clear from the experience of other Cantons, as, for instance, Lucerne, which also abolished compulsion in 1883, and had 76 deaths from small-pox in the 8 years immediately preceding, as compared with only 3 in the 8 years following; the Canton thus escaping the epidemic of 1885 altogether.

One important point Dr Vogt establishes incidentally, and that is that small-pox is a disease which favours urban as compared with rural districts, and that it is the question of density of population, rather than the presence or absence of compulsory vaccination, which really determines whether an epidemic shall be serious or slight. The figures are very convincing on this point. Taking Switzerland as a whole, it appears that during the period under review there has been in the urban districts a mean annual small-pox death-rate of 7·45 per 100,000 living; while in the rural districts the corresponding death-rate has been only 2·32. In relation to compulsory vaccination the same distinction holds, while the advantage—a small one—is on the side of those Cantons in which compulsion has been abolished, probably because they have substituted other and more rational precautions. Where compulsion has been repealed the rural death-rate is 1·71, and the urban death-rate 7·42 per 100,000 living. Where compulsion remains in force the figures are 2·80 and 7·54 respectively. So far as I can judge, Dr Vogt clearly proves his case that Switzerland has positively gained in regard to small-pox mortality since the repeal of compulsory vaccination. His pamphlet should be read by those who dread that a similar measure of repeal in our own country would be followed by a grave disaster. There is really no evidence that such a dread has any rational foundation.

Practical Difficulties in the Way of Repeal.

The case for repeal, when considered as a whole, is so undeniably strong, that it is difficult to realise what is also undeniably true, that repeal will be impossible, unless the Government, or some member of it, is so convinced of its expediency, if not its necessity, that a firm attitude in regard to it is assumed. Let me briefly recapitulate the case. You have the fact that the medical profession is itself divided on the value of vaccination. On the one side stand the great majority, accepting, without enquiry, the orthodox doctrine that vaccination is a specific defence against small-pox, as being in fact the infliction of the same disease in a mild form. On the other side stand men with minds cast in a more critical mould, who, after patient and independent enquiry, decide that it is nothing of the kind. And to this opinion, they who fairly face the facts are slowly coming round. Then you have the fact that the students of the history of epidemic diseases say there is nothing in the decline in the ordinary prevalence of small-pox since about 1780 that is inexplicable, without taking vaccination to have brought it about. On the contrary, small-pox has declined everywhere, irrespective of vaccination; it shows no notable tendency to recrudescence where vaccination has been abandoned; and when it does re-assert itself in a severe epidemic, as in 1871-2, it does so with a sublime indifference to the efforts of the vaccination law-makers. Presumably, but for the insanitary conditions brought about by the Franco-German War, there would have been no severe epidemic in 1871-2; and no severe epidemic is now to be looked for, apart from similar conditions, with which, of course, vaccination has nothing to do, unless it be by way of hindering recourse to rational scientific precautions.

Then, further, the law is not one that can be let alone as a matter of indifference, doing no harm, even if it does no good. That it does a certain amount of harm is officially admitted. A thousand deaths recorded by medical men as due to vaccination are now on the registers at Somerset House; and, though I am myself satisfied that this number is not one tithe of those that are really due to this cause, it is enough to call peremptorily for a repeal of the law.

The registers, of course, are silent as to the pain and misery caused to hundreds of thousands of infants and their mothers, where death did not result; and all this suffering has been absolutely profitless, if the orthodox doctrine about vaccination be not true. This side of the subject brings us back to the moral argument against the practice being enforced under penalties, to which I do not wish again to refer, though, in my judgment, it is by itself strong enough to condemn our existing system altogether.

But, however strong the case may be, it is the fact that it is next to impossible to get it fairly considered by the public generally that is likely to prove the greatest obstacle in the way of repeal. It is a subject which the editors of our newspapers and magazines detest, and they will allow no reference to it, unless it be an occasional sneer at the ignorance and fanaticism of the anti-vaccinists. I will give my own experience. The editors of the principal magazines that lie on the table in clubs or in public libraries decline at the present time even to consider an article that protests against vaccination being compulsory. It is not with them a question whether the article is well written or not, or whether its statements are correct. The subject alone rules it out. So again with the newspapers. At this season of the year they are very liberal in admitting correspondence on all sorts of subjects, most of them of little or no public interest. On September 17, it was noted that the *Times* had as many as fifty-two letters on thirty-five different subjects. Yet a day or two previously the editor had thrown into the waste-paper basket a letter from me, in which I had given very briefly, and with barely any comment of my own, the facts detailed by Professor Vogt as to the results of repealing compulsory vaccination in Switzerland; facts which, in view of the pressing question as to the continuance of compulsion in England, are of the utmost public importance. No doubt these men are guided by what seems to them a lofty motive. They have themselves the fullest faith in vaccination, having presumably never looked into the subject; and they dread the responsibility of shaking the faith of others. They act in regard to medical orthodoxy precisely as a Spanish Inquisitor acted in regard to theological orthodoxy. They are determined that, so far as in them lies, evidence unfavourable to orthodoxy shall remain hidden from the public; and, when this line is taken, as I believe it is, by the editors of all the London daily papers with one or two exceptions, a very serious obstacle is thrown in the way of securing a well-informed public to support a measure of repeal. This editorial obscurantism, coupled with the closed sittings

of the Royal Commission, must necessarily result in a decision to abolish compulsion (should that be the Government's policy) coming upon very many people as a surprise.

And another serious obstacle there is that may hinder the
Government from making repeal their policy, even though
the Report of the Royal Commission should clearly suggest
it. It is an obstacle that on more than one occasion has
proved fatal to the restoration of public liberty in regard to
vaccination. After discussion and enquiry have indicated
the rightfulness of the policy of repeal, up comes Mr Ernest
Abraham Hart with his deputation, " earnestly deprecat-
ing " any concession ; and the distracted statesman finds
a refuge in doing nothing. Deputations have their importance, certainly ; but their significance is apt to be over-
rated. An eager, energetic man has no difficulty in getting up
several such shows, which imposingly come as representing
learned or professional corporations ; but, in point of fact,
they need only represent that one man and his marionettes.
And it is not clear that the opinion of Mr Hart on vaccination deserves more weight than that of the Royal Commissioners. What he really knows on the subject must
remain uncertain, for, having shrunk from giving evidence
before the Commission, his knowledge has not been tested
by cross-examination. But he appears to make no account
of the history and pathology of vaccination, or of the
history of epidemic diseases generally, as bearing on this
question, but to be satisfied with the bare evidence of
small-pox hospital doctors. Not that this satisfies him
altogether ; for in a letter to the *Times* (which accords to
him large type, and as much space as he may require) in September last year, he found it necessary to misquote his own
authorities in order to make them quite satisfactory.*   And

* When these misstatements had been corrected by Mr Alfred Milnes,
the *Times* repudiated Mr Hart :—" Although we have given insertion

yet—such is the inscrutability of human affairs—Mr Ernest
Hart " looks largely " in the medical world. He is the
editor of one of the leading medical journals, and he is
Chairman of the Parliamentary Bills Committee of the
British Medical Association ; while, in regard to this particular question of compulsory vaccination, he is really the one
man on whom the maintenance of the law has depended.
I was wrong in supposing (p. 53) that the wonderful
statistics quoted with such effect by Sir Lyon Playfair in
the House of Commons in 1883 were the result of his own
independent investigation ; they were taken bodily from an
article of Mr Ernest Hart's in the " British Medical Journal "
in 1881 ; and in his latest publication on the subject,†
Mr Hart boasts of having " ignominiously defeated " the
bills to mitigate the severity of our existing law, which a
Liberal Government introduced and withdrew in 1881, and
again in 1892.   And he evidently anticipates that he will
similarly triumph over similar measures in the future ; for,
posing as "your Committee," he recommends, among other
grotesquely tyrannical things, that re-vaccination should be
made compulsory, and that opponents of compulsory vaccination, like myself, should be " dealt with as guilty of a
criminal offence."   But Mr Hart should be on his guard.
His dream is all of " State Medicine."   He sneers at private

to Mr Ernest Hart's letters, we are in no way concerned to adopt or
defend all his statements, and Mr Hart himself, we presume, would not
claim to be an original investigator, or to have any information on the
subject which is not at the disposal of the public generally " (Sept. 7,
1894).   To which may be added the caustic criticism of the editor of the
"Medical Times and Hospital Gazette" (Oct. 6) :— " Mr Hart has put
himself into a very awkward position, and he will have some difficulty in explaining how he could make such an assertion "—that vaccinated children never die of small-pox.   Of course he was too shrewd
to attempt any explanation.
    † " Essays on State Medicine."   No I., Compulsory Vaccination.
1894.

practitioners ("sixpenny doctors," he calls them), who give
certificates of insusceptibility to vaccination, and points
triumphantly to the official vaccinators, who take care that
there is nothing of the kind.   But he may rest assured that
his State Medical Church (which exists in some measure
already) will be quickly disestablished and disendowed, if
he should succeed in carrying his absurd proposals.   I
seldom attend a public meeting, but in the autumn of 1894
I was present at an anti-vaccination demonstration at Mile
End Old Town, where nothing struck me so much as the
angry cheer with which the two thousand persons present
greeted the phrase, "We will have no domineering medical
priesthood."   And so say all of us.   Medical dogmas are
at least as variable as theological dogmas ; and Englishmen
of all political parties may be trusted to resist determinedly
any attempt to treat as "a criminal offence" active disbelief in one of those dogmas, even though it may for some
years have enjoyed the support of the State.

Conclusion.

But in spite of the attitude on this question assumed by
sundry newspaper editors and by an official clique in the
medical profession, I am satisfied that there is in the country
generally, apart from the class who depend exclusively on
the *Times* for information, a growing preparedness for the
repeal of compulsion.   My letter to Mr Asquith brought me
into communication with a considerable number of medical
men, and, though they mostly maintained their belief in the
efficacy of vaccination, there was hardly one who did not
admit that it would be better for the practice to be no
longer enforced by law.   And there are indications that
even the official clique will surrender compulsory vaccination
if only they are given the right to enforce something else

under penalties. The compulsory removal of small-pox patients to an isolation hospital will perhaps be accepted as the price. Now we are all agreed that the isolation of persons suffering from an infectious disease is the precaution best calculated to prevent the progress of an epidemic. The question, therefore, is whether compulsion is an indispensable element in the exercise of that precaution. We have no such compulsion now; and has there been any experience since and where adequate isolation hospitals have been provided, showing that patients cannot be brought into such hospitals without compulsion? Surely not. Everywhere, with exceptions that only suffice to prove the rule, patients and their friends have been only too glad to avail themselves of the accommodation provided. And I maintain that, as a matter of principle, in so delicate a matter as the removal of the sick from their homes, the force that should be employed is not compulsion but attraction. Given isolation hospitals—and we do perhaps need fresh legislation making it obligatory on the local authorities to provide them—as admirably equipped and managed as many rate-supported hospitals are now, and there will be no need for compulsory removal. The arguments in favour of it may be very plausibly stated, but when you come to practice, there is necessarily friction. We are beginning to learn in England, what they have already learned in the United States, that the wholesale appointment of inspectors and other petty officials to carry out the provisions of some coercive measure does not really tend to social welfare. These men, who are all subservience to their official superiors, are often most offensive and domineering as well as incredibly stupid in carrying out their instructions. There are always exceptional cases to which a general law is not applicable, and these officials are just the men to be incapable of recognising such exceptions.

Hence arises friction, bitterness, and opposition, which tend to bring locally into discredit the whole system of the public care of the sick. The moral authority of a competent medical man, backed up by the reputation of a well-managed hospital, will be found to suffice without any need for compulsion, while the absence of compulsion is itself a guarantee of the work being done in a kindly, as well as in an efficient manner.

A compulsory law that intrudes itself into matters of domestic concern is, in fact, only to be tolerated when it can be shown that such a law is absolutely indispensable for the public welfare. And can any man, in view of the evidence as a whole, honestly say that our vaccination law is thus indispensable? Of course the editor of a medical paper, anxious to keep up his reputation for consistency, may say so in one of his leading articles. He may say so again when he introduces a deputation to a Cabinet minister. And an official report, drawn up in Whitehall, may take the same line, though with reservations. But take the men who write and say these things away from the conditions of professional and official life, invite them to dinner, and then, when their feet are on your fender, and your cigars and port are at their side, ask them what they believe to be *la verité vraie* about vaccination, and under such conditions, which will lead the most orthodox clergyman to confess that he doesn't for a moment believe that Moses wrote the Pentateuch, your medical Torquemadas, on whose assurances at other times the whole fabric of compulsion has been built, will make—or rather, but for my warning would have made — admissions fatal to the *raison d'être* of a penal law.

And if it be allowed that compulsory vaccination is not an indispensable condition of public health, the expediency of repealing it, in view of the intensity of the feeling which it has aroused, and of the thousands of otherwise blameless citizens who have suffered under its provisions, becomes obvious. To leave the law in the Statute-book, but not enforced, as the provision for repeated prosecutions has been left since 1892, would satisfy nobody. And with the compulsory clauses would go the vaccination officers, and the duty of Boards of Guardians in regard to prosecutions, a duty which all that perform it at all perform unwillingly. But the National Vaccine Institute, the public vaccination stations, and the officials connected therewith, would remain, anyhow for a time. Not however, it may be presumed, for any long time; since the evidence that the anti-vaccinists have accumulated* most distinctly goes to show, not merely that compulsory vaccination can be dispensed with, but that vaccination itself is probably useless, and is certainly not infrequently harmful. State patronage is in that case hardly more defensible than State enforcement. But I would go even a step further than this. To repeal the law is little else than to confess that the law ought never to have been passed. It is an admission that persons punished under the law have suffered unjustly. The question then arises whether they have not a legitimate claim to compensation. I do not, of course, mean that they would claim compensation for the loss of a child from the effects of vaccination. That is not for a moment to be thought of. But to reimbursement of the actual sums taken from the pockets of persons convicted under the Acts, whether by way of fines or of costs, such persons have undoubtedly a moral right; and a clause in the Act by which compulsion is repealed, setting aside a sum of

* "The anti-vaccinists are those who have found some motive for scrutinizing the evidence, generally the very human motive of vaccinal injuries or fatalities in their own families or in those of their neighbours. Whatever their motive, they have scrutinized the evidence to some purpose; they have mastered nearly the whole case; they have knocked the bottom out of a grotesque superstition."—*Jenner and Vaccination*, by C. Creighton, M.D., p. 352.

money—it would not be a large one—to make good such claims for reimbursement, claims that could easily be verified by the court records, would, I am sure, be widely recognised, anyhow among the working classes, as a great act of justice.

That you, Sir, will go as far as I do in this matter is hardly to be expected, though I nevertheless hope it may be so. I speak as one who in his own family has had experience of the possibly fatal risk that vaccination involves, and since I had that experience, now some ten years ago, I have seen evidence accumulate that convinces me that the law against which I protest is as foolish as it is odious. I am also satisfied that, although no one of those in high places likes to be the first publicly to condemn that law, such is the tyranny that the established order of things has over men's minds, making them, as Lowell says,

> " Slaves, who fear to be
> In the right with two or three,"

nevertheless public opinion is already well-prepared for the repeal of compulsion; and I believe also that if one strong man would put his foot down, and would resolve that, what is really a scandal in regard to the respect due to the law, as also in regard to the home-rights of parents and the freedom of medical science, shall, without further delay, come to an end, his action would be hailed with almost universal approval; while time would soon show the baselessness of those fears that have kept the law unrepealed so long. With the hope that you, Sir, may prove to be the strong man that I have in view,

I have the honour to remain,

Your obedient Servant,

ARTHUR W. HUTTON.

October 21, 1895.

CORRECTIONS AND NOTES

LETTER TO MR ASQUITH.

L

CORRECTIONS AND NOTES

TO THE

LETTER TO MR ASQUITH.

P. 3. *The Frequency of Errors in Diagnosis.*

The Metropolitan Asylums Board Report for 1894 shows that, in that year, out of 1263 cases notified as small-pox, as many as 155, or 12½ per cent., were found, on arrival at the hospital, not to have contracted that disease. If medical men are thus frequently mistaken in their diagnosis, when they know that their judgment will be revised by the small-pox hospital doctor, and that, if he reverses their decision, they may possibly be liable for damages, how frequently may they not be mistaken when there are no such checks on their judgments ! This consideration points towards a great uncertainty in all registration statistics, and shows how misleading arguments may be which are based on such statistics, especially when percentages are drawn from small numbers. There is an important paper on erroneous diagnosis of small-pox in the *Lancet* for July 20, 1895.

P. 6. *Post hoc, ergo propter hoc.*

The popular but unverifiable belief that our present ordinary freedom from small-pox is a consequence of, and not merely a coincidence with, the use of vaccination has a kind of parallel in the popular belief that the Great Fire of London stamped out the Plague. The sequence of events

was certainly close enough to make such an idea plausible,
and doubtless the Fire made London a less congenial
habitat for filth diseases of all kinds than it had been
before. But that the Plague really died out from what in
default of better knowledge we must call "natural causes"
is shown by the fact that it had practically come to an end
before the Fire broke out, and that it declined simultaneously in the country and on the Continent.

P. 11.   *The Fewness of Pock-marked Faces at the
Present Day.*

One hears occasionally of people who say they are satisfied that vaccination has been an inestimable blessing
because they see now-a-days so much fewer pock-marked
faces than they or their elders used to see in years gone by.
It is therefore worth while to consider what force there is in
this argument.   Granted the facts (vague as they are, both
as to date and to numbers, and incapable of being stated
with accuracy), what do they prove?   Simply that there is
less small-pox now-a-days than there was in years gone by.
Who denies it or doubts it?   We all alike rejoice in it; but
the connection between vaccination and this decline in the
ordinary prevalence of small-pox remains to be proved.   It
is at least conceivable that small-pox is dying out for other
reasons; and where then would be the evidence in favour
of vaccination?   Or again, if it be said that after the great
epidemic of 1871-2, when the disease was as fatal and as
prevalent as it had been in the eighteenth century, there
were still very few pock-marked faces to be seen, and that
vaccination must therefore have mitigated the disease, does
the argument hold good?   Surely not.   The fact, if such it
were, need only prove that, whereas in the previous century
unvaccinated persons often recovered, even after a severe

attack, which left them disfigured for life, in the later
epidemic, whether vaccinated or not, they mostly succumbed
when the attack was severe, and so their faces were no more
seen.   Or better nursing might have avoided the "pitting"
—which I believe depends more on skin-texture than on
the severity of the disease—or better living during the last
three-quarters of a century might have resulted in a better
physique generally, so that the disease was more easily
thrown off.   In short, the fact, so far as it is a fact, is perfectly explicable without any reference to vaccination ; and
as an argument it only avails to confirm the faith of those
who believe in vaccination already.   It causes no perplexity
to those who do not believe.

P. 17.   *Jenner and the Cuckoo.*

I have no wish to attach undue importance to this incident, and I think that Jenner's latest biographer, Dr Norman Moore, perhaps unintentionally, states the case against
him too strongly.*   But I cannot agree with a critic who
complains that the matter is altogether "irrelevant."   That
is not so ; it throws light on Jenner's character.   The incident shows that we cannot regard him as a careful and
conscientious observer of natural phenomena ; and it furnishes us with an earlier indication of that shallow facility
with which he found a pseudo-scientific explanation of a
very simple matter which needed no such explanation, thus
preparing us for his pseudo-scientific account of the relation
between cow-pox and small-pox, the speciousness of which
led to the belief in vaccination.

* My own explanation of what Jenner says he observed will be found,
if anyone cares to see it, in *Nature Notes* (Elliot Stock), Vol. VI. p.
15 ; and with this may be compared a further communication to *Nature
Notes*, Vol. VI. p. 76, and a letter in the *Lancet*, July 2, 1892.

P. 18. *Jenner inoculates with " Swine-pox."*

A correction is needed here.   I have confused " swine-
pox " with " swine-fever," and so have made Jenner inoculate
experimentally with an animal disease (the date should be
1789) when he was really, like other small-pox inoculators
at the time, only trying to find some milder human disease
that would serve for inoculation, and with this object employed matter taken from a case of what we should now call
" chicken-pox."   The mistake does not affect my general
argument ; but I was wrong, of course, in inferring that
Jenner dropped " swine-pox " because of its " disgusting
associations."

P. 40.   *A mitigated form of Compulsion suggested.*

A critic having concluded from what I say here that I am
not in favour of the total repeal of compulsion, I am in the
humiliating position of having to confess that these suggestions were meant to be taken humorously, as the last sentence
should show.   Such a solution of the controversy could only
be a temporary one, and it would only gratify those who
delight in red tape for its own sake.   If I do not insist that
the whole of the State establishment of vaccination should
be abolished at the same time as compulsion, so that no
further official sanction or encouragement to the practice
should be given, it is merely because, as a matter of policy,
I doubt the wisdom of attacking more than one thing at a
time.   The vested interests in connection with the National
Vaccine Institute are numerous and strong, and to touch
them might delay for some years the remedying of what is
really the one crying evil—viz., the hard enforcement of the
law against poor and defenceless parents here and there.

P. 41.   *Vaccination and the Anti-toxin Treatment of Diphtheria.*

Many people have a vague impression that the principle of vaccination has found a further development in the method of treating diphtheria, introduced since my letter to Mr Asquith was written ; and they further think that we are on the eve of fresh discoveries in scientific preventive medicine, that will reflect honour on Jenner's use of cow-pox, as having furnished the *idée mère* of these discoveries. Thus vaguely stated it is difficult to reply to the argument, though it may be pointed out that the *idée mère* may just as well have come from the caldron of Macbeth's witches. There are, however, two entirely distinct principles in the modern medical use of animal substances as either prophylactic or curative ; and a brief consideration of this fact will show that vaccination is no precedent for the anti-toxin treatment, the merits of which are still under discussion ; nor will that treatment, should its merits be established, do anything to rehabilitate vaccination. The principle of vaccination is to take diseased animal matter, and by its inoculation into a healthy person to give that person henceforth immunity from a certain disease, because the diseased animal matter will have given him the disease in a modified form already. Vaccination indeed, as we now understand the matter, is a blundering application of its own principle ; for cow-pox is not a modified form of small-pox ; but that is not the present point. On the other hand, the principle of the anti-toxin treatment is to enable a person already diseased to throw off that disease by introducing into his system a fortifying element taken from an animal observed to be insusceptible of that disease.

Now, as the cow is insusceptible of small-pox, just as the horse is insusceptible of diphtheria, a true " vaccination," corresponding with what we may term the new " equination "

in the treatment of diphtheria, would be to inject into the
blood of a small-pox patient the serum obtained from the
blood of a healthy cow. And there is, of course all the
difference in the world between such an operation as this
and vaccination as commonly understood. Jenner then is
in no serious sense the precursor of Roux, nor is Roux a
re-incarnation of Jenner.

P. 48. *Dr Collingridge and " Annual" Vaccination.*

Quoting from Mr Milnes' "Vision of Vaccine," I ascribed
to Dr Collingridge the advocacy of "thoroughly efficient
annual re-vaccination." On his warmly denying that he had
ever stated or held such an opinion, I took some pains to
refer to the original authority, and in the *Times* for July 14,
1881, I found that, in a special report to the London City
Corporation, Dr Collingridge had expressed the opinion
that "until the Vaccination Act was carried out in its
entirety, and until re-vaccination became general, with
thoroughly efficient annual vaccination, there seemed but
little chance of avoiding serious outbreaks." On my
referring Dr Collingridge to this, he informed me, as he
ought to have informed me when he first wrote to complain,
that the word "annual" was a misprint for "animal."

There would have been nothing very wonderful if Dr
Collingridge had really insisted on the necessity of "annual
re-vaccination." He would only have shown himself a
definite and uncompromising advocate of what others term
"recent vaccination," and equally insist on its necessity.
But his testimony to the absolute necessity of "animal vaccination" is far more interesting and important. Believer in
compulsion as he is, Dr Collingridge holds that our existing
compulsory law is of little or no use ; for it makes provision
neither for re-vaccination nor for calf-lymph ; and poor
parents demanding calf-lymph at public vaccination-stations,

believing rather in its greater safety than in its greater efficacy, have before now been roughly handled by the authorities of the Local Government Board, which also refuses to pay his otherwise duly-earned bonus to a public vaccinator who acts on Dr Collingridge's advice.

P. 61.   "*Forty-five years of Registration Statistics.*"

The above is the correct title of Dr Alfred Russel Wallace's tract, and not " Fifty-five," as it stands on p. 61, or "Twenty-five," as it stands on p. 103. I do not understand how the double press error escaped my notice, for with the work itself I was familiar.

Pp. 68, 69.   *The Statistical Tables.*

Further Reports of the Registrar-General and of the Local Government Board, which have come to hand since the above were compiled, make little or no practical difference in their significance. To the statistics of deaths from small-pox the following particulars may, however, be added for 1893 :—

Prestwich	...	53	Banbury	...	—
Chesterfield	...	47	Barrow-on-Soar		—
Keighley	...	12	Billesdon	...	—
Dewsbury	...	8	Falmouth	...	—
Blaby	...	4	Kettering	...	—
Luton	...	1	Thrapston	...	—
Wortley	...	1	Wellingborough		—

The deaths here entered under Prestwich appear mostly to belong to the Urban Sanitary District of Manchester, and were already entered under that heading. It will be observed that, except at Oldham, Halifax, Leicester, Keighley, and Dewsbury, there was, even in the epidemic year 1893, practically no small-pox in the 22 districts entered in the second table as foremost in abandoning vaccination.

In the year 1894, for which the statistics are not yet complete, there were 185 deaths at Birmingham (with Aston), 27 at Bradford, 23 at Manchester, 23 at Oldham, 22 at Bristol, 20 at Liverpool, and 10 at Walsall, but no serious prevalence of small-pox elsewhere ; and in the latter part of the year the epidemic, which had begun in 1892, almost entirely died out.

In the first six months of 1895, apart from 18 deaths in Birmingham and the neighbourhood,—now free from the disease,—13 at Liverpool, 8 at Derby, 3 at Oldham, and 2 at St Albans, there have been barely any to record throughout the country.

Meanwhile the percentage of vaccination default has increased rapidly. In the year 1891 it was 13·4 for the country generally (see the earlier annual percentages on p. 55) ; and if this rate is maintained until the year 1896, that is to say, until the earliest date when proposals for legislation on the subject can be entertained, Parliament will have to face the fact that, in spite of the law, one out of every four or five infants born will be growing up unvaccinated. In London the practice is being abandoned very largely; and in the country the following Unions may be added to those given on p. 69, as showing, in 1891, a default of over 25%:—

Ashby-de-la-Zouch.	Derby.	St. Alban's.
Ashton-under-Lyne.	Hinckley.	Scarborough.
Axbridge.	Ipswich.	Skipton.
Basingstoke.	King's Lynn.	Tetbury.
Bedminster.	Lewes.	Tewkesbury.
Brackley.	Loughborough.	Tonbridge.
Bradford.	Melton-Mowbray.	Uckfield.
Bury (Lancs.).	Norwich.	Westbury-on-Severn.
Coventry.	Nuneaton.	Weymouth.
Darlington.	Saddleworth.	Wheatenhurst.

This is a goodly number of recruits for one year; and when those for the years 1892, 1893, 1894, and 1895 are added, it may well be doubted whether, whatever the Royal Commission may report, the Government will care to incur the odium involved in authorising so many thousands of prosecutions as a restoration of compulsion would mean. Delay, in short, will have won the day.

P. 71. *The Number of Cases of Small-pox at Leicester in 1892-93.*

The figure here given (136) is incorrect. According to the Local Government Board's Reports it should be 320, with 21 deaths. Where I got the figure 136 from I cannot remember, but I passed it as correct in reading the proofs, because it gave a percentage of deaths to cases of between 15 and 16, corresponding fairly enough with what the percentage used to be. But the actual percentage at Leicester was, if the returns are correct, under 7, while throughout the country in this particular epidemic it was 9. Either, then, the medical men at Leicester made many mistakes in their diagnosis, and notified erroneously other diseases as small-pox—and this is not impossible, since they had barely so much as seen a case of small-pox for many years—or else, in a large manufacturing town, in which the vast majority of the young children are unvaccinated, small-pox during an epidemic year took an exceptionally light form. See the *Times*, Oct. 11, 1894, p. 8.

P. 72. *The Immunity of Re-vaccinated Nurses.*

Those who feel the force of this argument—and they are not a few—should read " The Legend of the Small-pox Hospital Nurses saved from Small-pox by Re-vaccination "

(5th edition, 1895. London: E. W. Allen. Price 2d.). It is not argumentative, but, by giving, with the necessary references, cases in which re-vaccination failed, and other cases in which there was immunity without vaccination or re-vaccination, it is convincing.

P. 74. *A further Note on the Argument from Statistics.*

The great difficulty, which really amounts to impossibility, of using in argument accurate small-pox death-statistics for this country may be illustrated by the following Table, which shows, side by side, in a sufficient number of cases, the Returns of the Registrar-General and of the Local Government Board :—

Deaths from Small-pox in 1893.

	R.G.	L.G.B.		R.G.	L.G.B.
Bristol ...	6	19	Halifax ...	49	33
St George ...	—	5	Keighley ...	12	8
Barton Regis	21	—	Manchester	2	49
Bradford ...	7	71	Oldham ...	63	45
Dewsbury ...	8	4	Wakefield ...	38	26

The differences here are mainly due to the non-correspondence between the Registration Districts and the Urban Sanitary Districts. Thus, the Manchester U.S.D. includes part of the R.D. of Prestwich, to which the Registrar-General allots 53 deaths; and the Bradford U.S.D. includes part of the R.D. of North Bierley, to which the Registrar-General allots 117 deaths.

We are indeed as yet very far from being able to obtain such statistics as should underlie an argument worthy to carry conviction. If we could be sure of correct diagnosis in every case, and had in addition unbiassed returns as to patients being vaccinated or not, we should still want better defined districts, distinguishing between urban and rural populations on the principle of density of population. As things are, we are at the mercy of unblushing " *Tendenz-statistik* " for the first part of our information, and of arbitrary and unprincipled boundaries for the latter.

P. 74. *Some Recent Foreign Statistics.*

The unaccountable way in which small-pox epidemics come and go, rising here and falling there, without regard to vaccination laws, or even, in some cases it would seem, to precisely similar sanitary conditions, is illustrated by the following Table, giving the number of deaths from small-pox in 19 foreign towns during the last ten quarters :—

	1893.				1894.				1895.	
	1	2	3	4	1	2	3	4	1	2
Calcutta ...	2	6	3	2	8	199	38	(?)	872	638
Bombay ...	55	106	29	12	176	281	45	27	92	118
Madras ...	1	9	5	3	2	8	—	—	1	1
Paris ...	13	49	82	112	109	53	9	2	7	3
Amsterdam..	—	—	—	—	—	1	2	—	1	2
Rotterdam...	1	—	26	84	121	158	16	19	20	12
Berlin ...	1	—	—	1	1	3	—	2	1	1
Hamburg ...	—	3	—	—	—	—	—	—	1	—
Dresden ...	—	—	—	—	—	—	—	—	1	—
Munich ...	—	—	—	—	—	—	—	—	—	—
Vienna ...	14	15	—	7	9	9	—	—	—	1
Prague ...	77	50	8	6	1	1	1	1	1	—
Buda-Pest ...	—	6	—	—	2	13	30	34	4	5
Trieste ...	23	63	65	52	45	12	1	—	—	—
Rome ...	1	2	1	1	—	1	—	—	—	—
Turin ...	1	1	—	—	—	6	—	—	—	—
Venice ...	57	4	1	1	—	—	—	—	—	—

Here the advocates of compulsory vaccination may undoubtedly claim that the experience of Germany and Italy supports their view; though an opponent, who cared to use small figures in argument, might point out that during the last twelve months there have been four times as many deaths from small-pox at Berlin, where there is compulsory vaccination, as at Vienna, where there is not. But anyhow, it is clear that epidemics die out, as at Paris and the Austrian towns, without recourse to compulsion; while conditions absolutely similar as to compulsory vaccination, and very similar in all other respects, do not prevent a smart epidemic at Rotterdam, though they may seem to prevent one at Amsterdam.* And what, too, about India? In 1810 vaccination was said to have "altogether exterminated" small-pox at Bombay; yet it prevails there still and is raging at Calcutta—naturally enough, one might say, since India is the home of the disease. Yet Madras, meanwhile, is practically free.

P. 83.   *The Bacteriological Proof of the Identity of Cow-pox and Small-pox.*

A further Report on the Etiology of Vaccinia by Dr Klein, whose courtesy towards myself personally I wish to acknowledge, appears in the Medical Officer's "Supplement to the Twenty-third Report of the Local Government Board" (pp. 493-496), which was issued in September this year. The results of his further experiments have been

---

* It must be borne in mind that it is commoner on the Continent than in England for cases of vaccinated and apparently mild small-pox to be styled "varioloid" or "varicella" (chicken-pox); and that, if these cases terminate fatally, they would not appear in the small-pox returns. In England, in 1893, 127 deaths were registered as due to "chicken-pox;" and it is, in fact, impossible to draw a very clear distinction between a mild case of the one and a severe case of the other disease.

purely negative; nor has anything come of experiments in the same field made in Germany by Besser and Buttersack. The Preface to the Report sums up Dr Klein's experiments as follows (p. xxxiii.):—

"In all, his further attempts to grow the bacilli of calf-lymph extended to above 100 culture experiments, but in no single instance did growth result; all his cultures proved sterile. He next sought to cultivate these bacilli in the living subcutaneous tissues of guinea-pigs and of calves. But here again he met with no success; and for the present the question as to the identity of the bacilli found by him alike in vaccine lymph and in small-pox matter must remain undetermined."

We are not likely to hear anything more of the bacteriological proof of the identity of cow-pox and small-pox.

P. 85.   *Vaccination and Nervous Affections.*

An American physician (Allison Hodges, of Richmond, U.S.A.) has recently published a paper on the nervous manifestations of syphilis.   It is referred to in complimentary terms in the *Medical Times and Hospital Gazette*, (Sept. 28, 1895), whence the following particulars are taken.

These nervous manifestations, he says, are more noticeable in the absence of cutaneous symptoms.   They may be developed in each stage of the disease, but are gravest in the tertiary; and these latter are more likely to appear when the secondary symptoms have been slight.   The chief nervous manifestations are headache, insomnia, vertigo, convulsions, tremor, hemiplegia, and erratic distribution of paralysis.   It is exceedingly easy, Dr Hodges points out, to overlook tertiary syphilis in cases where the first and second stages were not noticeable.   In the primary stage no prominent nervous symptoms occur ; while the secondary stages present marked evidences of the implication of the nervous system in neuralgias, nervous dyspepsia, cardiac irregularities, meningitis, etc. ; but it is the tertiary stage in which we meet numberless shades and varieties of nervous affection, due solely to the influence of the specific poison.

Now, if the identification of cow-pox with syphilis be borne in mind, and it be further recognised that the practically universal use of vaccination during this century has thus brought about a mild—though not in every case mild —syphilisation of the whole community, have we not here a reasonable and probable explanation of the general prevalence of nervous affections at the present day ? For it must not be forgotten that, if cow-pox is correctly identified with syphilis, its remote effects may be life-long, and may even be transmitted to children ; indeed, it is on the supposition that the effect of vaccination is life-long, though an effect of a different kind—"a permanently morbid condition of the blood," Sir James Paget styles it—that its use has been so fiercely insisted on.

P. 98.   *Compulsory Vaccination in Switzerland.*

It appears that I had not been correctly informed as to the enforcement of vaccination in Switzerland. The laws are still in force in a few of the Cantons. Details as to the repeal of compulsion in other Cantons will be found above, p. 145.

P. 100.   *The " Times " and the Royal Commission.*

In reviewing my letter to Mr Asquith, the *Times* assured me that I was in error in supposing that their article in February, 1894, on the Fourth Report of the Royal Commission had been written by a medical member of the

Commission. I had concluded that this must be so, because the article appeared a fortnight before the Report was issued to the public. It now appears that a Commissioner, or some official entrusted with a confidential copy, communicated the Report to the *Times*, which was thus enabled to play again its old game of prejudicing public opinion by a premature and partial disclosure of its contents.

P. 109.   *Witnesses who failed to appear before the Royal Commission.*

The medical men who have been urgent in binding the burden of compulsion on the shoulders of a long-suffering people are really very few. I hardly know of any name to add to those of Seaton, Ballard, Simon, Buchanan, Hart, Thorne, and M'Vail. Except the first-named, all of these have been in a position to give evidence before the Royal Commission ; and, if for Dr Seaton we substitute Lord Playfair, who, though not a medical man, has, as Mr Hart's mouthpiece in Parliament, strongly advocated the cause of compulsion, we find that of these seven champions only three were willing to appear as witnesses, though their opportunity extended over four or five years. Sir John Simon indeed gave evidence, but it was brief and formal, and consisted largely in the handing in of a document published in 1857, in which vaccination is spoken of rhetorically as saving so many thousands of lives *per annum*, the evidence for this assertion being merely an inference of the most precarious kind. In cross-examination he cut a very poor figure ; and the same is true of Dr Thorne Thorne, the present head of the medical department at the Local Government Board, who in a most astonishing way confessed over and over again, that he was unable to answer questions of no very abstruse kind relating to vaccination.

M

On Dr M'Vail, of Glasgow, was laid the main burden of defence ; and his evidence has not yet been made public. Mr Hart, to whom I have referred elsewhere, waited until the Commission had ceased to hear witnesses, and then began to beat his drum and to blow his trumpet again in the secure retreat of the columns of the *British Medical Journal.*

But seriously, this failure of the champions of vaccination to appear should be accounted as gravely discrediting their cause. To rule with a rod of iron while they are in power, to retire in due time with titles and pensions, and then, when the public conscience has become a little uneasy on the subject, and an enquiry is ordered, to slink off without a word to say, leaving the cause undefended, is hardly worthy of men who have posed so long as the apostles of Public Health.

P. 109.   *The net Result of the Royal Commission.*

I have perhaps underestimated the value of the work which the Royal Commission will have accomplished when it issues its final Report. If in no other way, by its leisurely procedure it will have achieved one most important— possibly the most important—thing, viz., the advent of the " psychological moment," when the British public will be willing to give a fair consideration to the evidence against the practice of vaccination. For the last forty years sufficient evidence has been in existence ; and since the publication of Mr White's " Story of a Great Delusion," in 1884, anyone who cared to do so could learn how fallacious were the figures on which the fabric of compulsion had been reared ; but only to parents here and there, when vaccination had brought sorrow to their homes, did the " psychological moment " arrive, enabling them to give heed to the evidence available. They who watch the signs of the times can see clearly that such a moment of enlightenment is coming to the British public generally. Perhaps it will come in the course of 1896; and then, when once the evidence is approached with a clear eye and a fair judgment, although the merits of vaccination itself may for many years longer be discussed in medical circles, the controversy as to compulsion will be ended.

The following notes on the work of the Royal Commission up to and including the issue of its Interim Report, may be found serviceable :—

In the House of Commons, on April 5, 1889, Mr J. A. Picton proposed and Dr Farquharson seconded a motion for the appointment of a Royal Commission to enquire into the working of the Vaccination Acts. The motion was technically negatived, after Mr Ritchie, President of the Local Government Board, had announced that the Government intended to appoint such a Commission.

On April 29 it was officially stated that the Commission would be instructed to enquire and report as to :—

1. The effect of vaccination in reducing the prevalence of and the mortality from small-pox.

2. What means, other than vaccination, can be used for diminishing the prevalence of small-pox, and how far such means could be relied on in place of vaccination.

3. The objections made to vaccination on the ground of injurious effects alleged to result therefrom, and the nature and extent of any injurious effects which do in fact so result.

4. Whether any and if so what means should be adopted for preventing or lessening the ill effects, if any, resulting from vaccination, and whether and if so by what means vaccination with animal vaccine should be further facilitated as a part of public vaccination.

5. Whether any alterations should be made in the arrangements and proceedings for securing the performance of vaccination, and in particular in the provisions of the Vaccination Acts with respect to repeated prosecutions for non-compliance with the law.

On May 2 Mr Picton called attention to the word "repeated" in clause 5, as implying that the question of compulsion pure and simple was not to be considered by the Commission. Mr Ritchie admitted the objection, and said that the word had now been struck out, so as not to limit the inquiry in that sense.

On May 3 Mr Bradlaugh enquired whether the history and scientific foundation of vaccination and the justifiability of compulsion would come within the scope of the Commission. Mr Ritchie replied that the Commission itself would decide on these points, but that the Government certainly intended the inquiry to include all aspects of the case.

On May 16 Mr Ritchie announced that Lord Herschell would be Chairman of the Commission, and that the enquiry would not be open to the public and the press. He added that the Commission itself would decide whether the enquiry should include the sources of vaccine lymph, and the pathology of cow-pox.

On May 27 the names of the Commissioners were announced :—

Lord Herschell, *Chairman ;* Sir James Paget, F.R.C.S., Sir Charles Dalrymple, Sir William G. Hunter, F.R.C.P., Sir Edwin H. Galsworthy, Mr Savory, P.R.C.S., Mr Bradlaugh, Dr Bristowe, F.R.C.P., Dr Collins, F.R.C.S., Mr Dugdale, Q.C., Professor Michael Foster, Dr Hutchinson, F.R.C.S., Mr Picton, M.P., Mr Whitbread, M.P., and Mr Meadows White, Q.C.

[Mr Bradlaugh died in 1890, and was replaced by Mr J. A. Bright, M.P. Mr Savory and Dr Bristowe died after the Commission had ceased to receive evidence, and their places were not filled.]

The Commission met eight times in June and July 1889, and examined Sir John Simon, Dr Ogle, Dr Thorne Thorne, and an American, Dr Rauch.

On August 12 it agreed to publish this evidence as its First Report, together with the announcement that, with a view to clearness, it proposed to consider the various questions involved in the following order :—

1. The historical and statistical case in favour of vaccination.
2. The arrangements made for vaccination under the existing law, and the mode in which the law is administered.
3. The case against vaccination, and especially against its continuing to be made compulsory.
4. The reply to these objections.
5. Any substitute that can be suggested in place of vaccination for the purpose of preventing the spread of small-pox.
6. Any improvements that can be suggested in the present law or its administration for the purpose of removing objections to vaccination, or making it more effective.

Between October 9, 1889, and February 19, 1890, the Commission met 20 times, and examined 43 witnesses, including Drs Hopkirk, Gayton, Barry, Farn, Cory, and Creighton.   On May 29 it decided to publish this evidence as its Second Report.

A similar Third Report was agreed to in August the same year, after 21 more meetings, at which 9 witnesses were examined, including Professor Alfred Russel Wallace, Mr Alexander Wheeler, Surgeon Parke, and Mr Tebb.

On July 28, 1891, a similar Fourth Report was agreed to, but it was not issued to the public until the end of Feb-

ruary, 1894. This Report contains a record of 33 meetings
and of the evidence of 53 witnesses, including Professor
Crookshank, Mr Stansfeld, Mr Hopwood, and representa-
tives of the anti-vaccination movement in Leicester, headed
by Mr J. T. Biggs.

A vast mass of other evidence, taken in the latter half of
1891, in 1892, and 1893, and equal in bulk, I am told, to
that contained in the above four volumes (which make up
852 folio pages, closely printed in double columns, besides
voluminous Appendices), still awaits publication, but will, it
is understood, be issued before the Final Report. As the
four volumes already published record more than 18,000
questions asked by the Commissioners, it will be seen that
the enquiry is on an elaborate scale.

Meanwhile, having held 90 meetings and heard 135 witnesses, the Commissioners, on April 21, 1892, agreed to
their Fifth (commonly called their Interim) Report, in
which they dealt exclusively with repeated penalties and
the treatment of persons imprisoned under the Acts :—
"We think that the imposition of repeated penalties in
respect of the non-vaccination of the same child should
no longer be possible. . . . We think they should cease to
be inflicted altogether. We have arrived at this conclusion
quite independently of the question whether vaccination
should continue to be compulsorily enforced. Whatever be
the conclusion which we may have to submit to your
Majesty upon this part of our enquiry, and even if it should
ultimately appear that we are not all able to agree in the same
conclusion, we have had no difficulty in agreeing upon the
recommendation which we now submit." And, in a later
paragraph :—"We have no hesitation in saying that we
think that persons imprisoned under the Vaccination Acts

should no longer be subjected to the same treatment as criminals."

In the forthcoming Final Report of the Royal Commis-sioners the most important point will be, of course, the number of those who recommend the repeal of the com-pulsory law.   But the most interesting point will be the opinion on vaccination itself expressed by Professor Michael Foster.   It has been stated that he accepted the position of a Royal Commissioner with the idea that the evidence would enable him to place vaccination on a scientific basis analogous with that claimed for the methods of Pasteur, Behring, and others.   He is a medical man, but he enjoys a freedom in relation to medicine which the ordinary prac-titioner does not ; his position as Secretary of the Royal Society is sufficient guarantee of his eminence as a man of science ; and he may be trusted not to give to vaccination any testimonial that might seem twenty years hence un-worthy of his great reputation.   If, as a result of this enquiry, he should subscribe to the opinion that vaccination is a specific and trustworthy protection against small-pox, and that its risks are incidental, and can easily be avoided by proper care, I shall hold myself bound to study this question afresh.   But I do not think he will.

INDEX.

PRESS NOTICES OF THE FIRST ISSUE.

" The author argues that the efficacy of this preventive measure is not based on any scientific foundation, as there is no pathological relation between cow-pox and small-pox ; that the statistical evidence is unreliable, as it has been collected under the influence of an erroneous theory, and with perhaps unconscious partiality ; and that there are incidental risks in vaccination which are of sufficient importance to be taken into consideration."—*Morning Post.*

" An interesting attack on the strongholds of compulsory vaccination, which will open the eyes of the ignorant to some of the evils of Jenner's discovery."—*National Observer.*

" Any unbiassed and open-minded reader of Mr Hutton's book will, on a calm and dispassionate review, come to the conclusion that there is a good deal to be said on the other side of the question, and that it deserves an impartial hearing."—*Whitehall Review.*

" While admitting the arguments on the side of use and wont to be strong, and while he states them with the utmost fairness and impartiality, the author marshals a great array of very powerful evidence and objections to the practice. His attack is dialectically a skilful one . . . and his summing up of the arguments *pro* and *con* the point at issue, is worthy of praise for its judicial impartiality and courtesy towards his opponents. For those who wish to ' read up ' the subject no better introduction could be desired than Mr Hutton's *brochure.*"— *The Liberal.*

" However much or however little assent its propositions and reasoning may command, no one interested in the matters of which it treats will read it without profit and instruction."—*The Scotsman.*

" Mr Hutton is an opponent of vaccination, but his treatise will bear perusal, if only for the temperate way in which he states his case : in this respect he is in marked contrast to the common anti-vaccinator of the day. The book should be read by medical men and others, if only to show how a capable mind sees ' the other side.' "—*Glasgow Herald.*

"Mr Hutton discusses the problem with considerable freshness, with much information, and with a calmness which is too seldom displayed by either the apologists or the opponents of vaccination. He ranks himself unmistakably amongst the latter, and his work gives evidence of a careful and thorough study of the various authorities on the subject. . . . His book is able, temperate, and comprehensive."
—*Newcastle Leader.*

"The work is evidently that of a learned and conscientious man, who has laboriously investigated the literature of this important question. He also possesses the enviable accomplishment of a dexterous mastership of English style. He has evidently worked earnestly and laboriously in the examination of the published evidence of the history and the results of vaccination. His judgment is entirely unfavourable to the practice ; and, although experienced medical practitioners will probably be but little influenced by his conclusions, we strongly recommend the perusal of this little work to all those who are interested in one of the most important sanitary questions of the period. The author has said all that can be said against the practice, and has said it well."
—*Dublin Journal of Medical Science.*

"The argument of this little book has for its scientific basis the observations of Creighton and Crookshank as to the identity of cow-pox with syphilis, and in addition considers at length the various statistics of death from small-pox, vaccination, and inoculation. Although nothing of much novelty is presented, the book is written in a style far more temperate than one expects to find in the productions of the 'antis.' As the best presentation of the other side of the question we commend it to our readers, without however expecting that they will find its arguments convincing."—*New York Medical Record.*

UNFAVOURABLE NOTICES.

"This violent polemic against vaccination is not written in a scientific spirit at all. . . . The medical profession is badly treated by Mr Hutton. We gather from this work that the evidence of medical men goes for nothing at all. To begin with, they know very little about vaccination, or small-pox, or anything else apparently ; and in the next place, vaccination has now become a religion with them, or rather, a degrading superstition of harmful—nay, dangerous—character, 'a *damnosa hæreditas*, which the medical profession is now bound to maintain out of respect to its own prestige, quite apart from the pecuniary interest involved.' [See p. 111, for the passage as it actually stands.] A large space is devoted to Jenner, and here we have Dr Creighton's argument reproduced, that vaccination is to be discarded as a delusion, because Jenner happened to choose a particular title for his celebrated pamphlet in 1796 [*sic*]—namely, *Variolæ Vaccinæ.*"—*British Medical Journal.*

"There is now, there always has been, and we suppose there always will be, a curious class of persons who come forward with extraordinary questions, such as—Is it not a fact that the world is a great plane, instead of being round, as some credulous persons believe? Was not Bacon the author of Shakespeare's plays? and so on. With such questions we may class the vaccination question."—*The Sanitary Record.*

"It is a pity, for the sake of humanitarianism, that the Government which adopted such a life-saving policy as vaccination should permit the publication, at the end of a century's marvellous success in that policy, of such an entirely misinformed and misleading book as this. Our country is *too* free in some such respects."—*Health News.*

TURNBULL AND SPEARS, PRINTERS, EDINBURGH.

A LIST OF NEW BOOKS
AND ANNOUNCEMENTS OF
METHUEN AND COMPANY
PUBLISHERS : LONDON
36 ESSEX STREET
W.C.

CONTENTS

SEPTEMBER 1895

SEPTEMBER 1895.

MESSRS. METHUEN'S
ANNOUNCEMENTS

———◆———

Poetry and Belles Lettres

RUDYARD KIPLING

BALLADS. By RUDYARD KIPLING. *Crown 8vo. Buckram. 6s.*
Also 200 copies on hand-made paper. *21s.*
Also 35 copies on Japanese vellum. *42s.*

The exceptional success of '.Barrack-Room Ballads,' with which this volume will be uniform, justifies the hope that the new book too will obtain a wide popularity.

W. E. HENLEY

ENGLISH LYRICS. Selected and Edited by W. E. HENLEY. *Crown 8vo. Buckram. 6s.*
Also 30 copies on hand-made paper *Demy 8vo. 21s.*

Few announcements will be more welcome to lovers of English verse than the one that Mr. Henley is bringing together into one book the finest lyrics in our language. The book will be produced with the same care that made 'Lyra Heroica' delightful to the hand and eye.

ANDREW LANG

THE POEMS OF ROBERT BURNS. Edited, with Introduction, etc., by ANDREW LANG. With Portraits. *Crown 8vo. 6s.*
Also 75 copies on hand-made paper. *Demy 8vo. 21s.*

This edition will contain a carefully collated Text and Notes on the Text, a critical and Biographical Introduction, Introductory Notes to the Poems, and a Glossary.

ROBERT LOUIS STEVENSON

VAILIMA LETTERS. By ROBERT LOUIS STEVENSON. With an Etched Portrait by WILLIAM STRANG, and other Illustrations. *Crown 8vo. Buckram. 7s. 6d.*

Also 125 copies on hand-made paper. *Demy 8vo. 25s.*

A series of long journal letters written from Samoa to Mr. Sidney Colvin during the last five years. They form an autobiography of Mr. Stevenson during this period, giving a full account of his daily life and literary work and ambitions. Mr. Colvin has written a Prologue and Epilogue, and has added numerous notes.

ENGLISH CLASSICS

Edited by W. E. HENLEY.

The books, which are designed and printed by Messrs. Constable, are issued in two editions—(1) A small edition, on the finest Japanese vellum, limited in most cases to 25 copies, demy 8vo, 21s. a volume nett; (2) The popular edition on laid paper, crown 8vo, buckram, 3s. 6d. a volume.

NEW VOLUMES.

THE LIVES OF DONNE, WOTTON, HOOKER, HERBERT, AND SANDERSON. By IZAAK WALTON. With an Introduction by VERNON BLACKBURN, and a Portrait.

THE LIVES OF THE ENGLISH POETS. By SAMUEL JOHNSON, LL.D. With an Introduction by JOHN HEPBURN MILLAR, and a Portrait. *3 vols.*

W. M. DIXON

A PRIMER OF TENNYSON. By W. M. DIXON, M.A., Professor of English Literature at Mason College. *Cr. 8vo. 2s. 6d.*

This book consists of (1) a succinct but complete biography of Lord Tennyson; (2) an account of the volumes published by him in chronological order, dealing with the more important poems separately ; (3) a concise criticism of Tennyson in his various aspects as lyrist, dramatist, and representative poet of his day; (4) a bibliography. Such a complete book on such a subject, and at such a moderate price, should find a host of readers.

Fiction

MARIE CORELLI

THE SORROWS OF SATAN. By MARIE CORELLI, Author of ' Barabbas,' ' A Romance of Two Worlds,' etc. *Crown 8vo. 6s.*

ANTHONY HOPE

THE CHRONICLES OF COUNT ANTONIO. By ANTHONY
HOPE, Author of 'The Prisoner of Zenda,' 'The God in the Car,'
etc. *Crown 8vo.* 6s.

A romance of mediæval Italy.

GILBERT PARKER

AN ADVENTURER OF THE NORTH. By GILBERT
PARKER, Author of ' Pierre and his People,' ' The Translation of a
Savage,' etc. *Crown 8vo.* 6s.

This book consists of more tales of the Far North, and contains the last adventures
of ' Pretty Pierre.' Mr. Parker's first volume of Canadian stories was published
about three years ago, and was received with unanimous praise.

EMILY LAWLESS

HURRISH. By the Honble. EMILY LAWLESS, Author of
' Maelcho,' ' Grania,' etc. *Crown 8vo.* 6s.

A reissue of Miss Lawless' most popular novel.

S. BARING GOULD

NOEMI. By S. BARING GOULD, Author of ' Mehalah,' ' In the
Roar of the Sea,' etc. Illustrated by R. CATON WOODVILLE. *Crown
8vo.* 6s.

A Romance of Old France.

MRS. CLIFFORD

A FLASH OF SUMMER. By MRS. W. K. CLIFFORD,
Author of ' Aunt Anne.' *Crown 8vo.* 6s.

J. MACLAREN COBBAN

THE KING OF ANDAMAN. By J. MACLAREN COBBAN,
Author of 'The Red Sultar,' etc. *Crown 8vo.* 6s.

G. MANVILLE FENN

AN ELECTRIC SPARK. By G. MANVILLE FENN, Author of
'The Vicar's Wife,' ' A Double Knot,' etc. *Crown 8vo.* 6s.

C. PHILLIPS WOOLLEY

THE QUEENSBERRY CUP. A Tale of Adventure. By
CLIVE PHILLIPS WOOLLEY, Author of ' Snap,' Part Author of ' Big
Game Shooting.' Illustrated. *Crown 8vo.* 6s.

This is a story of amateur pugilism and chivalrous adventure, written by an author
whose books on sport are well known.

H. G. WELLS

THE STOLEN BACILLUS, AND OTHER STORIES. By
H. G. WELLS, Author of 'The Time Machine.'   *Crown 8vo.   6s.*

MARY GAUNT

THE MOVING FINGER : chapters from the Romance of
Australian Life. By MARY GAUNT, Author of 'Dave's Sweetheart.'
Crown 8vo.   3s. 6d.

ANGUS EVAN ABBOTT

THE GODS GIVE MY DONKEY WINGS. By ANGUS
EVAN ABBOTT. *Crown 8vo.   3s. 6d.*

Illustrated Books

S. BARING GOULD

OLD ENGLISH FAIRY TALES collected and edited by S.
BARING GOULD. With numerous illustrations by F. D. BEDFORD.
Crown 8vo, 6s.

This volume consists of some of the old English stories which have been lost to
sight, and they are fully illustrated by Mr. Bedford.

A BOOK OF NURSERY SONGS AND RHYMES. Edited
by S. BARING GOULD, and illustrated by the Students of the Birmingham Art School. *Crown 8vo.   6s.*

A collection of old nursery songs and rhymes, including a number which are little
known.   The book contains some charming illustrations, borders, etc., by the
Birmingham students under the superintendence of Mr. Gaskin, and Mr. Baring
Gould has added numerous notes.   This book and the next have been printed in
a special heavy type by Messrs. Constable.

H. C. BEECHING

A BOOK OF CHRISTMAS VERSE.   Edited by H.˙C.
BEECHING, M.A., and Illustrated by WALTER CRANE.   *Crown
8vo.   5s.*

A collection of the best verse inspired by the birth of Christ from the Middle Ages
to the present day.   Mr. Walter Crane has designed several illustrations, and
the cover.   A distinction of the book is the large number of poems it contains
by modern authors, a few of which are here printed for the first time.

JOHN KEBLE

THE CHRISTIAN YEAR. By JOHN KEBLE. With an Intro-
duction and Notes by W. LOCK, M.A., Sub-Warden of Keble College,
Author of 'The Life of John Keble.' Illustrated by R. ANNING
BELL. *Fcap. 8vo.* 3s. 6d.

A new edition of a famous book, illustrated and printed in black and red,
uniform with the 'Imitation of Christ.'

Theology and Philosophy

E. C. GIBSON

THE XXXIX. ARTICLES OF THE CHURCH OF ENG-
LAND. Edited with an Introduction by E. C. GIBSON, M.A.,
Principal of Wells Theological College. *In two volumes. Demy
8vo.* 7s. 6d. each. Vol. I.

This is the first volume of a treatise on the xxxix. Articles, and contains the Introduction and Articles i.-xviii.

R. L. OTTLEY

THE DOCTRINE OF THE INCARNATION. By R. L.
OTTLEY, M.A., late fellow of Magdalen College, Oxon. Principal
of Pusey House. *In two volumes. Demy 8vo.*

This is the first volume of a book intended to be an aid in the study of the doctrine
of the Incarnation. It deals with the leading points in the history of the doctrine,
its content, and its relation to other truths of Christian faith.

F. S. GRANGER

THE WORSHIP OF THE ROMANS. By F. S. GRANGER,
M.A., Litt.D., Professor of Philosophy at University College,
Nottingham. *Crown 8vo.* 6s.

The author has attempted to delineate that group of beliefs which stood in close
connection with the Roman religion, and among the subjects treated are Dreams,
Nature Worship, Roman Magic, Divination, Holy Places, Victims, etc. Thus
the book is, apart from its immediate subject, a contribution to folk-lore and
comparative psychology.

L. T. HOBHOUSE

THE THEORY OF KNOWLEDGE. By L. T. HOBHOUSE,
Fellow and Tutor of Corpus College, Oxford. *Demy 8vo.* 21s.

'The Theory of Knowledge' deals with some of the fundamental problems of
Metaphysics and Logic, by treating them in connection with one another.
PART I. begins with the elementary conditions of knowledge such as Sensation
and Memory, and passes on to Judgment. PART II. deals with Inference in
general, and Induction in particular. PART III. deals with the structural concep-
tions of Knowledge, such as Matter, Substance, and Personality. The main
purpose of the book is constructive, but it is also critical, and various objections
are considered and met.

W. H. FAIRBROTHER

THE PHILOSOPHY OF T. H. GREEN. By W. H. Fair-
brother, M.A., Lecturer at Lincoln College, Oxford. *Crown 8vo.*
5*s.*

This volume is expository, not critical, and is intended for senior students at the
Universities, and others, as a statement of Green's teaching and an introduction
to the study of Idealist Philosophy.

F. W. BUSSELL

THE SCHOOL OF PLATO : its Origin and Revival under
the Roman Empire. By F. W. Bussell, M.A., Fellow and Tutor
of Brasenose College, Oxford. *In two volumes. Demy 8vo. Vol. I.*

In these volumes the author has attempted to reach the central doctrines of Ancient
Philosophy, or the place of man in created things, and his relation to the outer
world of Nature or Society, and to the Divine Being.   The first volume com-
prises a survey of the entire period of a thousand years, and examines the
cardinal notions of the Hellenic, Hellenistic, and Roman ages from this particular
point of view.

In succeeding divisions the works of Latin and Greek writers under the Empire
will be more closely studied, and detailed essays will discuss their various systems,
e.g. Cicero, Manilius, Lucretius, Seneca, Aristides, Appuleius, and the New
Platonists of Alexandria and Athens.

C. J. SHEBBEARE

THE GREEK THEORY OF THE STATE AND THE
NONCONFORMIST CONSCIENCE : a Socialistic Defence of
some Ancient Institutions. By Charles John Shebbeare, B.A.,
Christ Church, Oxford. *Crown 8vo. 2s. 6d.*

History and Biography

EDWARD GIBBON

THE DECLINE AND FALL OF THE ROMAN EMPIRE.
By Edward Gibbon.   A New Edition, edited with Notes,
Appendices, and Maps by J. B. Bury, M.A., Fellow of Trinity
College, Dublin. *In Seven Volumes. Crown 8vo. 6s. each. Vol. I.*

The time seems to have arrived for a new edition of Gibbon's great work—furnished
with such notes and appendices as may bring it up to the standard of recent historical research.   Edited by a scholar who has made this period his special study,
and issued in a convenient form and at a moderate price, this edition should fill
an obvious void.   The volumes will be issued at intervals of a few months.

E. L. S. HORSBURGH

THE CAMPAIGN OF WATERLOO. By E. L. S. HORS-
BURGH, B.A. *With Plans. Crown 8vo.* 5s.

This is a full account of the final struggle of Napoleon, and contains a careful study
from a strategical point of view of the movements of the French and allied armies.

FLINDERS PETRIE

EGYPTIAN DECORATIVE ART. By W. M. FLINDERS
PETRIE, D.C.L. *With 120 Illustrations. Crown 8vo.* 3s. 6d.

A book which deals with a subject which has never yet been seriously treated.

EGYPTIAN TALES. Translated from the Papyri, and edited
with notes by W. M. FLINDERS PETRIE, LL.D., D.C.L. Illustrated by TRISTRAM ELLIS. *Part II. Crown 8vo.* 3s. 6d.

W. H. HUTTON

THE LIFE OF SIR THOMAS MORE. By W. H. HUTTON,
M.A., Author of 'William Laud.' *With Portraits. Crown 8vo.* 5s.

This book contains the result of some research and a considerable amount of information not contained in other Lives. It also contains six Portraits after Holbein
of More and his relations.

R. F. HORTON

JOHN HOWE. By R. F. HORTON, D.D., Author of 'The Bible
and Inspiration,' etc. *With a Portrait. Crown 8vo.* 3s. 6d.
[Leaders of Religion.

F. M'CUNN

THE LIFE OF JOHN KNOX. By F. M'CUNN. With a
Portrait. *Crown 8vo.* 3s. 6d. *[Leaders of Religion.*

General Literature

W. B. WORSFOLD

SOUTH AFRICA: Its History and its Future. By W. BASIL
WORSFOLD, M.A. *With a Map. Crown 8vo.* 6s.

This volume contains a short history of South Africa, and a full account of its
present position, and of its extraordinary capacities.

J. S. SHEDLOCK

THE PIANOFORTE SONATA: Its Origin and Development.
By J. S. SHEDLOCK. *Crown 8vo.* 5s.

This is a practical and not unduly technical account of the Sonata treated historically. It contains several novel features, and an account of various works little
known to the English public.

F. W. THEOBALD

INSECT LIFE. By F. W. THEOBALD, M.A. *Illustrated.*
Crown 8vo. 2s. 6d. [*Univ. Extension Series.*

R. F. BOWMAKER

THE HOUSING OF THE WORKING CLASSES. By F.
BOWMAKER. *Crown 8vo.* 2s. 6d. [*Social Questions Series.*

W. CUNNINGHAM

MODERN CIVILISATION IN SOME OF ITS ECONO-
MIC ASPECTS. By W. CUNNINGHAM, LL.D., Fellow of Trinity
College, Cambridge. *Crown 8vo.* 2s. 6d. [*Social Questions Series.*

M. KAUFMANN.

SOCIALISM AND MODERN THOUGHT. By M. KAUFMANN,
Crown 8vo. 2s. 6d. [*Social Questions Series.*

Classical Translations

NEW VOLUMES

Crown 8vo. Finely printed and bound in blue buckram.

SOPHOCLES—Electra and Ajax. Translated by E. D. A.
MORSHEAD, M.A., late Scholar of New College, Oxford; Assistant
Master at Winchester. 2s. 6d.

CICERO—De Natura Deorum. Translated by F. BROOKS,
M.A. 3s. 6d.

Educational

A. M. M. STEDMAN

STEPS TO GREEK. By A. M. M. STEDMAN, M.A. 18mo.
1s. 6d.

A very easy introduction to Greek, with Greek-English and English-Greek Exercises.

F. D. SWIFT

DEMOSTHENES AGAINST CONON AND CALLICLES.
Edited, with Notes, Appendices, and Vocabulary, by F. DARWIN
SWIFT, M.A., formerly Scholar of Queen's College, Oxford;
Assistant Master at Denstone College. *Fcap. 8vo.* 2s.

A 2

MESSRS. METHUEN'S
PUBLICATIONS

———◆———

Poetry

Rudyard Kipling. BARRACK-ROOM BALLADS; And Other Verses. By RUDYARD KIPLING. *Eighth Edition. Crown 8vo.* 6s.

A Special Presentation Edition, bound in white buckram, with extra gilt ornament. 7s. 6d.

'Mr. Kipling's verse is strong, vivid, full of character. . . . Unmistakable genius rings in every line.'—*Times.*

'The disreputable lingo of Cockayne is henceforth justified before the world; for a man of genius has taken it in hand, and has shown, beyond all cavilling, that in its way it also is a medium for literature. You are grateful, and you say to yourself, half in envy and half in admiration: "Here is a *book*; here, or one is a Dutchman, is one of the books of the year."'—*National Observer.*

'"Barrack-Room Ballads" contains some of the best work that Mr. Kipling has ever done, which is saying a good deal. "Fuzzy-Wuzzy," "Gunga Din," and "Tommy," are, in our opinion, altogether superior to anything of the kind that English literature has hitherto produced.'—*Athenæum.*

'The ballads teem with imagination, they palpitate with emotion. We read them with laughter and tears; the metres throb in our pulses, the cunningly ordered words tingle with life; and if this be not poetry, what is?'—*Pall Mall Gazette.*

Henley. LYRA HEROICA: An Anthology selected from the best English Verse of the 16th, 17th, 18th, and 19th Centuries. By WILLIAM ERNEST HENLEY. *Crown 8vo. Buckram, gilt top.* 6s.

Mr. Henley has brought to the task of selection an instinct alike for poetry and for chivalry which seems to us quite wonderfully, and even unerringly, right.'—*Guardian.*

"Q" THE GOLDEN POMP : A Procession of English Lyrics from Surrey to Shirley, arranged by A. T. QUILLER COUCH. *Crown 8vo. Buckram. 6s.*

Also 40 copies on hand-made paper. *Demy 8vo. £1, 1s.* net. Also 15 copies on Japanese paper. *Demy 8vo. £2, 2s.* net.

'A delightful volume : a really golden " Pomp."'—*Spectator.*
'Of the many anthologies of 'old rhyme' recently made, Mr. Couch's seems the richest in its materials, and the most artistic in its arrangement. Mr. Couch's notes are admirable; and Messrs. Methuen are to be congratulated on the format of the sumptuous volume.'—*Realm.*

"Q." GREEN BAYS : Verses and Parodies. By " Q.," Author of 'Dead Man's Rock,' etc. *Second Edition. Fcap. 8vo. 3s. 6d.*

'The verses display a rare and versatile gift of parody, great command of metre, and a very pretty turn of humour.'—*Times.*

H. C. Beeching. LYRA SACRA : An Anthology of Sacred Verse. Edited by H. C. BEECHING, M.A. *Crown 8vo. Buckram, gilt-top. 6s.*

'An anthology of high excellence.'—*Athenæum.*
'A charming selection, which maintains a lofty standard of excellence.'—*Times.*

Yeats. AN ANTHOLOGY OF IRISH VERSE. Edited by W. B. YEATS. *Crown 8vo. 3s. 6d.*

'An attractive and catholic selection.'—*Times.*
'It is edited by the most original and most accomplished of modern Irish poets, and against his editing but a single objection can be brought, namely, that it excludes from the collection his own delicate lyrics.'—*Saturday Review.*

Mackay. A SONG OF THE SEA : MY LADY OF DREAMS, AND OTHER POEMS. By ERIC MACKAY, Author of 'The Love Letters of a Violinist.' *Second Edition. Fcap. 8vo, gilt top, 5s.*

'Everywhere Mr. Mackay displays himself the master of a style marked by all the characteristics of the best rhetoric. He has a keen sense of rhythm and of general balance ; his verse is excellently sonorous, and would lend itself admirably to elecutionary art. . . . Its main merit is its "long resounding march and energy divine." Mr. Mackay is full of enthusiasm, and for the right things. His new book is as healthful as it is eloquent.'—*Globe.*
'Throughout the book the poetic workmanship is fine.'—*Scotsman.*

Jane Barlow. THE BATTLE OF THE FROGS AND MICE, translated by JANE BARLOW, Author of 'Irish Idylls,' and pictured by F. D. BEDFORD. *Small 4to. 6s. net.*

Ibsen. BRAND. A Drama by HENRIK IBSEN. Translated by WILLIAM WILSON. *Crown 8vo. Second Edition. 3s. 6d.*

'The greatest world-poem of the nineteenth century next to "Faust." "Brand" will have an astonishing interest for Englishmen. It is in the same set with "Agamemnon," with "Lear," with the literature that we now instinctively regard as high and holy.'—*Daily Chronicle.*

"A. G." VERSES TO ORDER. By "A. G." *Cr. 8vo. 2s. 6d. net.*

A small volume of verse by a writer whose initials are well known to Oxford men. 'A capital specimen of light academic poetry. These verses are very bright and engaging, easy and sufficiently witty.'—*St. James's Gazette.*

Hosken. VERSES BY THE WAY. By J. D. HOSKEN. *Crown 8vo. 5s.*

Gale. CRICKET SONGS. By NORMAN GALE. *Crown 8vo. Linen. 2s. 6d.*

Also a limited edition on hand-made paper. *Demy 8vo. 10s. 6d. net.*

'As healthy as they are spirited, and ought to have a great success.'—*Times.*
'Simple, manly, and humorous. Every cricketer should buy the book.'—*Westminster Gazette.*   'Cricket has never known such a singer.'—*Cricket.*

Langbridge. BALLADS OF THE BRAVE: Poems of Chivalry, Enterprise, Courage, and Constancy, from the Earliest Times to the Present Day. Edited, with Notes, by Rev. F. LANGBRIDGE. *Crown 8vo. Buckram 3s. 6d.* School Edition, 2s. 6d.

'A very happy conception happily carried out. These "Ballads of the Brave" are intended to suit the real tastes of boys, and will suit the taste of the great majority. —*Spectator.*   'The book is full of splendid things.'—*World.*

English Classics

Edited by W. E. HENLEY.

Messrs. Methuen are publishing, under this title, a series of the masterpieces of the English tongue, which, while well within the reach of the average buyer, shall be at once an ornament to the shelf of him that owns, and a delight to the eye of him that reads.

The series, of which Mr. William Ernest Henley is the general editor, will confine itself to no single period or department of literature. Poetry, fiction, drama, biography, autobiography, letters, essays—in all these fields is the material of many goodly volumes.

The books, which are designed and printed by Messrs. Constable, are issued in two editions—(1) A small edition, on the finest Japanese vellum, demy 8vo, 21s. a volume net; (2) the popular edition on laid paper, crown 8vo, buckram, 3s. 6d. a volume.

THE LIFE AND OPINIONS OF TRISTRAM SHANDY. By LAWRENCE STERNE. With an Introduction by CHARLES WHIBLEY, and a Portrait. 2 *vols. 7s.*

60 copies on Japanese paper. 42s. *net.*

'Very dainty volumes are these; the paper, type and light green binding are all very agreeable to the eye. "Simplex munditiis" is the phrase that might be applied to them. So far as we know, Sterne's famous work has never appeared in a guise more attractive to the connoisseur than this.'—*Globe.*
'The book is excellently printed by Messrs. Constable on good paper, and being divided into two volumes, is light and handy without lacking the dignity of a classic.'—*Manchester Guardian.*

'This new edition of a great classic might make an honourable appearance in any library in the world. Printed by Constable on laid paper, bound in most artistic and restful-looking fig-green buckram, with a frontispiece portrait and an introduction by Mr. Charles Whibley, the book might well be issued at three times its present price.'—*Irish Independent.*

'Cheap and comely; a very agreeable edition.'—*Saturday Review.*

'A real acquisition to the library.'—*Birmingham Post.*

THE COMEDIES OF WILLIAM CONGREVE. With an Introduction by G. S. STREET, and a Portrait. 2 *vols.* 7*s.*

25 copies on Japanese paper. 42*s. net.*

'The comedies are reprinted in a good text and on a page delightful to look upon. The pieces are rich reading.'—*Scotsman.*

'So long as literature thrives, Congreve must be read with growing zest, in virtue of qualities which were always rare, and which were never rarer than at this moment. All that is best and most representative of Congreve's genius is included in this latest edition, wherein for the first time the chaotic punctuation of its forerunners is reduced to order—a necessary, thankless task on which Mr. Street has manifestly spent much pains. Of his introduction it remains to say that it is an excellent appreciation, notable for catholicity, discretion, and finesse : an admirable piece of work.'—*Pall Mall Gazette.*

'Two volumes of marvellous cheapness.'—*Dublin Herald.*

THE ADVENTURES OF HAJJI BABA OF ISPAHAN. By JAMES MORIER. With an Introduction by E. G. BROWNE, M.A. and a Portrait. 2 *vols.* 7*s.*

25 copies on Japanese paper. 21*s. net.*

History

Flinders Petrie. A HISTORY OF EGYPT, FROM THE EARLIEST TIMES TO THE HYKSOS. By W. M. FLINDERS PETRIE, D.C.L., Professor of Egyptology at University College. *Fully Illustrated. Second Edition. Crown 8vo.* 6*s.*

'An important contribution to scientific study.'—*Scotsman.*

'A history written in the spirit of scientific precision so worthily represented by Dr. Petrie and his school cannot but promote sound and accurate study, and supply a vacant place in the English literature of Egyptology.'—*Times.*

Flinders Petrie. EGYPTIAN TALES. Edited by W. M. FLINDERS PETRIE. Illustrated by TRISTRAM ELLIS. *Crown 8vo.* In two volumes. 3*s.* 6*d. each.*

'A valuable addition to the literature of comparative folk-lore. The drawings are really illustrations in the literal sense of the word.'—*Globe.*

'It has a scientific value to the student of history and archæology.'—*Scotsman*

'Invaluable as a picture of life in Palestine and Egypt.'—*Daily News.*

Clark. THE COLLEGES OF OXFORD: Their History and their Traditions. By Members of the University. Edited by A. CLARK, M.A., Fellow and Tutor of Lincoln College. *8vo. 12s. 6d.*
' A delightful book, learned and lively.'—*Academy.*
'A work which will certainly be appealed to for many years as the standard book on the Colleges of Oxford.'—*Athenæum.*

Perrens. THE HISTORY OF FLORENCE FROM THE TIME OF THE MEDICIS TO THE FALL OF THE REPUBLIC. By F. T. PERRENS. Translated by HANNAH LYNCH. *In Three Volumes. Vol. I. 8vo. 12s. 6d.*
' This is a standard book by an honest and intelligent historian, who has deserved well of all who are interested in Italian history.'—*Manchester Guardian.*

George. BATTLES OF ENGLISH HISTORY. By H. B. GEORGE, M.A., Fellow of New College, Oxford. *With numerous Plans. Second Edition. Crown 8vo. 6s.*
Mr. George has undertaken a very useful task—that of making military affairs intelligible and instructive to non-military readers—and has executed it with laudable intelligence and industry, and with a large measure of success.'—*Times.*
'This book is almost a revelation ; and we heartily congratulate the author on his work and on the prospect of the reward he has well deserved for so much conscientious and sustained labour.'—*Daily Chronicle.*

Browning. GUELPHS AND GHIBELLINES: A Short History of Mediæval Italy, A.D. 1250-1409. By OSCAR BROWNING, Fellow and Tutor of King's College, Cambridge. *Second Edition. Crown 8vo. 5s.*
'A very able book.'—*Westminster Gazette.*
'A vivid picture of mediæval Italy.'—*Standard.*

Browning. THE AGE OF THE CONDOTTIERI: A Short Story of Italy from 1409 to 1530. By OSCAR BROWNING, M.A., Fellow of King's College, Cambridge. *Crown 8vo. 5s.*
This book is a continuation of Mr. Browning's 'Guelphs and Ghibellines,' and the two works form a complete account of Italian history from 1250 to 1530.
'Mr. Browning is to be congratulated on the production of a work of immense labour and learning.'—*Westminster Gazette.*

O'Grady. THE STORY OF IRELAND. By STANDISH O'GRADY, Author of 'Finn and his Companions.' *Cr. 8vo. 2s. 6d.*
' Novel and very fascinating history. Wonderfully alluring.'—*Cork Examiner.*
'Most delightful, most stimulating. Its racy humour, its original imaginings, make it one of the freshest, breeziest volumes.'—*Methodist Times.*
'A survey at once graphic, acute, and quaintly written.'—*Times.*

Malden. ENGLISH RECORDS. A Companion to the History of England. By H. E. MALDEN, M.A. *Crown 8vo. 3s. 6d.*
A book which concentrates information upon dates, genealogy, officials, constitutional documents, etc., which is usually found scattered in different volumes.

Biography

Collingwood. THE LIFE OF JOHN RUSKIN. By W. G.
COLLINGWOOD, M.A., Editor of Mr. Ruskin's Poems. With
numerous Portraits, and 13 Drawings by Mr. Ruskin. *2 vols. 8vo.*
32s. Second Edition.

'No more magnificent volumes have been published for a long time. . . .'—*Times.*
'It is long since we have had a biography with such delights of substance and of
form. Such a book is a pleasure for the day, and a joy for ever.'—*Daily
Chronicle.*
'A noble monument of a noble subject. One of the most beautiful books about one
of the noblest lives of our century.'—*Glasgow Herald.*

Waldstein. JOHN RUSKIN : a Study. By CHARLES WALD-
STEIN, M.A., Fellow of King's College, Cambridge. With a Photo-
gravure Portrait after Professor HERKOMER. *Post 8vo. 5s.*
Also 25 copies on Japanese paper. *Demy 8vo. 21s. net.*

'A thoughtful, impartial, well-written criticism of Ruskin's teaching, intended to
separate what the author regards as valuable and permanent from what is transient
and erroneous in the great master's writing.'—*Daily Chronicle.*

Kaufmann. CHARLES KINGSLEY. By M. KAUFMANN,
M.A. *Crown 8vo. Buckram. 5s.*
A biography of Kingsley, especially dealing with his achievements in social reform.
'The author has certainly gone about his work with conscientiousness and industry.'—
Sheffield Daily Telegraph.

Robbins. THE EARLY LIFE OF WILLIAM EWART
GLADSTONE. By A. F. ROBBINS. *With Portraits. Crown
8vo. 6s.*

'Considerable labour and much skill of presentation have not been unworthily
expended on this interesting work.'—*Times.*
'Not only one of the most meritorious, but one of the most interesting, biographical
works that have appeared on the subject of the ex-Premier. . . . It furnishes a
picture from many points original and striking ; it makes additions of value to the
evidence on which we are entitled to estimate a great public character ; and it
gives the reader's judgment exactly that degree of guidance which is the function
of a calm, restrained, and judicious historian.'—*Birmingham Daily Post.*

Clark. Russell. THE LIFE OF ADMIRAL LORD COL-
LINGWOOD. By W. CLARK RUSSELL, Author of 'The Wreck
of the Grosvenor.' With Illustrations by F. BRANGWYN. *Second
Edition. Crown 8vo. 6s.*

'A really good book.'—*Saturday Review.*
'A most excellent and wholesome book, which we should like to see in the hands of
every boy in the country.'—*St. James's Gazette.*

Southey. ENGLISH SEAMEN (Howard, Clifford, Hawkins, Drake, Cavendish). By ROBERT SOUTHEY. Edited, with an Introduction, by DAVID HANNAY. *Crown 8vo.* 6s.

This is a reprint of some excellent biographies of Elizabethan seamen, written by Southey and never republished. They are practically unknown, and they deserve, and will probably obtain, a wide popularity.

General Literature

Gladstone. THE SPEECHES AND PUBLIC ADDRESSES OF THE RT. HON. W. E. GLADSTONE, M.P. With Notes and Introductions. Edited by A. W. HUTTON, M.A. (Librarian of the Gladstone Library), and H. J. COHEN, M.A. With Portraits. *8vo. Vols. IX. and X.* 12s. 6d. each.

Henley and Whibley. A BOOK OF ENGLISH PROSE. Collected by W. E. HENLEY and CHARLES WHIBLEY. *Cr. 8vo.* 6s.

Also 40 copies on Dutch paper. 21s. net.

Also 15 copies on Japanese paper. 42s. net.

'A unique volume of extracts—an art gallery of early prose.'—*Birmingham Post.*

'An admirable companion to Mr. Henley's "Lyra Heroica."'—*Saturday Review.*

'Quite delightful. The choice made has been excellent, and the volume has been most admirably printed by Messrs. Constable. A greater treat for those not well acquainted with pre-Restoration prose could not be imagined.'—*Athenæum.*

Wells. OXFORD AND OXFORD LIFE. By Members of the University. Edited by J. WELLS, M.A., Fellow and Tutor of Wadham College. *Crown 8vo.* 3s. 6d.

This work contains an account of life at Oxford—intellectual, social, and religious—a careful estimate of necessary expenses, a review of recent changes, a statement of the present position of the University, and chapters on Women's Education, aids to study, and University Extension.

'We congratulate Mr. Wells on the production of a readable and intelligent account of Oxford as it is at the present time, written by persons who are possessed of a close acquaintance with the system and life of the University.'—*Athenæum.*

Ouida. VIEWS AND OPINIONS. By OUIDA. *Crown 8vo.* 6s.

'Her views are always well marked and forcibly expressed, so that even when you most strongly differ from the writer you can always recognise and acknowledge her ability.'—*Globe.*

'Ouida is outspoken, and the reader of this book will not have a dull moment. The book is full of variety, and sparkles with entertaining matter.'—*Speaker.*

Bowden. THE EXAMPLE OF BUDDHA: Being Quotations from Buddhist Literature for each Day in the Year. Compiled by E. M. BOWDEN. With Preface by Sir EDWIN ARNOLD. *Third Edition.* 16mo. 2s. 6d.

Bushill. PROFIT SHARING AND THE LABOUR QUES-
TION. By T. W. BUSHILL, a Profit Sharing Employer. With an
Introduction by SEDLEY TAYLOR, Author of 'Profit Sharing between
Capital and Labour.' *Crown 8vo.* 2s. 6d.

Malden. THE ENGLISH CITIZEN: HIS RIGHTS AND
DUTIES. By H. E. MALDEN, M.A. *Crown 8vo.* 1s. 6d.
A simple account of the privileges and duties of the English citizen.

John Beever. PRACTICAL FLY-FISHING, Founded on
Nature, by JOHN BEEVER, late of the Thwaite House, Coniston. A
New Edition, with a Memoir of the Author by W. G. COLLINGWOOD,
M.A. *Crown 8vo.* 3s. 6d.
A little book on Fly-Fishing by an old friend of Mr. Ruskin.

Science

Freudenreich. DAIRY BACTERIOLOGY. A Short Manual
for the Use of Students in Dairy Schools, Cheesemakers, and
Farmers. By Dr. ED. VON FREUDENREICH. Translated from the
German by J. R. AINSWORTH DAVIS, B.A. (Camb.), F.C.P., Pro-
fessor of Biology and Geology at University College, Aberystwyth.
Crown 8vo. 2s. 6d.

Chalmers Mitchell. OUTLINES OF BIOLOGY. By P.
CHALMERS MITCHELL, M.A., F.Z.S. *Fully Illustrated. Crown
8vo.* 6s.
A text-book designed to cover the new Schedule issued by the Royal College of
Physicians and Surgeons.

Massee. A MONOGRAPH OF THE MYXOGASTRES. By
GEORGE MASSEE. With 12 Coloured Plates. *Royal 8vo.* 18s. net.
'A work much in advance of any book in the language treating of this group of
organisms. It is indispensable to every student of the Myxogastres. The
coloured plates deserve high praise for their accuracy and execution.'—*Nature.*

Theology

Driver. SERMONS ON SUBJECTS CONNECTED WITH
THE OLD TESTAMENT. By S. R. DRIVER, D.D., Canon of
Christ Church, Regius Professor of Hebrew in the University of
Oxford. *Crown 8vo.* 6s.
A welcome companion to the author's famous 'Introduction.' No man can read these
discourses without feeling that Dr. Driver is fully alive to the deeper teaching of
the Old Testament.'—*Guardian.*

Cheyne. FOUNDERS OF OLD TESTAMENT CRITICISM :
Biographical, Descriptive, and Critical Studies. By T. K. CHEYNE,
D.D., Oriel Professor of the Interpretation of Holy Scripture at
Oxford. *Large crown 8vo.* *7s. 6d.*

This important book is a historical sketch of O. T. Criticism in the form of biographi-
cal studies from the days of Eichhorn to those of Driver and Robertson Smith.
It is the only book of its kind in English.
'A very learned and instructive work.'—*Times.*

Prior. CAMBRIDGE SERMONS. Edited by H. C. PRIOR,
M.A., Fellow and Tutor of Pembroke College. *Crown 8vo.* *6s.*

A volume of sermons preached before the University of Cambridge by various
preachers, including the Archbishop of Canterbury and Bishop Westcott. ‛
'A representative collection. Bishop Westcott's is a noble sermon.'—*Guardian.*
'Full of thoughtfulness and dignity.'—*Record.*

Beeching. SERMONS TO SCHOOLBOYS. By H. C.
BEECHING, M.A., Rector of Yattendon, Berks. With a Preface by
Canon SCOTT HOLLAND. *Crown 8vo.* *2s. 6d.*

Seven sermons preached before the boys of Bradfield College.

Layard. RELIGION IN BOYHOOD. Notes on the Religious Training of Boys. With a Preface by J. R. ILLINGWORTH.
By E. B. LAYARD, M.A. *18mo.* *1s.*

Devotional Books.

With Full-page Illustrations.

THE IMITATION OF CHRIST. By THOMAS À KEMPIS.
With an Introduction by ARCHDEACON FARRAR. Illustrated by
C. M. GERE, and printed in black and red. *Fcap. 8vo.* *3s. 6d.*

'We must draw attention to the antique style, quaintness, and typographical excellence of the work, its red-letter "initials" and black letter type, and old-fasnioned
paragraphic arrangement of pages. The antique paper, uncut edges, and illustrations are in accord with the other features of this unique little work.'—*Newsagent.*
'Amongst all the innumerable English editions of the "Imitation," there can have
been few which were prettier than this one, printed in strong and handsome type
by Messrs. Constable, with all the glory of red initials, and the comfort of buckram
binding.'—*Glasgow Herald.*

THE CHRISTIAN YEAR. By JOHN KEBLE. With an Intro-
duction and Notes by W. LOCK, M.A., Sub-Warden of Keble
College, Author of 'The Life of John Keble.' Illustrated by R.
ANNING BELL. *Fcap. 8vo.* *5s.* [*October.*

Leaders of Religion

Edited by H. C. BEECHING, M.A.   *With Portraits, crown 8vo.*

A series of short biographies of the most prominent leaders
of religious life and thought of all ages and countries.   3/6
The following are ready—

CARDINAL NEWMAN. By R. H. HUTTON.
JOHN WESLEY. By J. H. OVERTON, M.A.
BISHOP WILBERFORCE. By G. W. DANIEL, M.A.
CARDINAL MANNING. By A. W. HUTTON, M.A.
CHARLES SIMEON. By H. C. G. MOULE, M.A.
JOHN KEBLE. By WALTER LOCK, M.A.
THOMAS CHALMERS. By Mrs. OLIPHANT.
LANCELOT ANDREWES. By R. L. OTTLEY, M.A.
AUGUSTINE OF CANTERBURY. By E. L. CUTTS, D.D.
WILLIAM LAUD. By W. H. HUTTON, M.A.

Other volumes will be announced in due course.

Works by S. Baring Gould

OLD COUNTRY LIFE. With Sixty-seven Illustrations by
W. PARKINSON, F. D. BEDFORD, and F. MASEY. *Large Crown
8vo, cloth super extra, top edge gilt,* 10s. 6d. *Fifth and Cheaper
Edition.* 6s.

'"Old Country Life," as healthy wholesome reading, full of breezy life and movement, full of quaint stories vigorously told, will not be excelled by any book to be
published throughout the year. Sound, hearty, and English to the core.'—*World.*

HISTORIC ODDITIES AND STRANGE EVENTS. *Third
Edition. Crown* 8vo. 6s.

'A collection of exciting and entertaining chapters. The whole volume is delightful
reading.'—*Times.*

FREAKS OF FANATICISM. *Third Edition. Crown* 8vo. 6s.

'Mr. Baring Gould has a keen eye for colour and effect, and the subjects he has
chosen give ample scope to his descriptive and analytic faculties. A perfectly
fascinating book.'—*Scottish Leader.*

A GARLAND OF COUNTRY SONG : English Folk Songs
with their traditional melodies. Collected and arranged by S.
BARING GOULD and H. FLEETWOOD SHEPPARD. *Demy 4to.* 6s.

SONGS OF THE WEST: Traditional Ballads and Songs of the West of England, with their Traditional Melodies. Collected by S. BARING GOULD, M.A., and H. FLEETWOOD SHEPPARD, M.A. Arranged for Voice and Piano. In 4 Parts (containing 25 Songs each), *Parts I., II., III.*, 3s. each. *Part IV.*, 5s. *In one Vol.*, *French morocco*, 15s.

'A rich collection of humour, pathos, grace, and poetic fancy.'—*Saturday Review.*

A BOOK OF FAIRY TALES retold by S. BARING GOULD. With numerous illustrations and initial letters by ARTHUR J. GASKIN. *Crown 8vo. Buckram. 6s.*

'Mr. Baring Gould has done a good deed, and is deserving of gratitude, in re-writing in honest, simple style the old stories that delighted the childhood of "our fathers and grandfathers." We do not think he has omitted any of our favourite stories, the stories that are commonly regarded as merely "old fashioned." As to the form of the book, and the printing, which is by Messrs. Constable, it were difficult to commend overmuch.'—*Saturday Review.*

YORKSHIRE ODDITIES AND STRANGE EVENTS *Fourth Edition. Crown 8vo. 6s.*

STRANGE SURVIVALS AND SUPERSTITIONS. With Illustrations. By S. BARING GOULD. *Crown 8vo. Second Edition. 6s.*

'We have read Mr. Baring Gould's book from beginning to end. It is full of quaint and various information, and there is not a dull page in it.'—*Notes and Queries.*

THE TRAGEDY OF THE CAESARS: The Emperors of the Julian and Claudian Lines. With numerous Illustrations from Busts, Gems, Cameos, etc. By S. BARING GOULD, Author of 'Mehalah,' etc. *Third Edition. Royal 8vo. 15s.*

'A most splendid and fascinating book on a subject of undying interest. The great feature of the book is the use the author has made of the existing portraits of the Caesars, and the admirable critical subtlety he has exhibited in dealing with this line of research. It is brilliantly written, and the illustrations are supplied on a scale of profuse magnificence.'—*Daily Chronicle.*

'The volumes will in no sense disappoint the general reader. Indeed, in their way, there is nothing in any sense so good in English. . . . Mr. Baring Gould has presented his narrative in such a way as not to make one dull page.'—*Athenæum.*

THE DESERTS OF SOUTHERN FRANCE. By S. BARING GOULD. With numerous Illustrations by F. D. BEDFORD, S. HUTTON, etc. *2 vols. Demy 8vo. 32s.*

This book is the first serious attempt to describe the great barren tableland that extends to the south of Limousin in the Department of Aveyron, Lot, etc., a country of dolomite cliffs, and cañons, and subterranean rivers. The region is full of prehistoric and historic interest, relics of cave-dwellers, of mediæval robbers, and of the English domination and the Hundred Years' War.

'His two richly-illustrated volumes are full of matter of interest to the geologist, the archæologist, and the student of history and manners.'—*Scotsman.*

'It deals with its subject in a manner which rarely fails to arrest attention.'—*Times.*

Fiction

SIX SHILLING NOVELS

Marie Corelli. BARABBAS : A DREAM OF THE WORLD'S TRAGEDY. By MARIE CORELLI, Author of 'A Romance of Two Worlds,' 'Vendetta,' etc. *Seventeenth Edition. Crown 8vo. 6s.*

'The tender reverence of the treatment and the imaginative beauty of the writing have reconciled us to the daring of the conception, and the conviction is forced on us that even so exalted a subject cannot be made too familiar to us, provided it be presented in the true spirit of Christian faith. The amplifications of the Scripture narrative are often conceived with high poetic insight, and this "Dream of the World's Tragedy" is, despite some trifling incongruities, a lofty and not inade-quate paraphrase of the supreme climax of the inspired narrative.'—*Dublin Review.*

Anthony Hope. THE GOD IN THE CAR. By ANTHONY HOPE, Author of 'A Change of Air,' etc. *Sixth Edition. Crown 8vo. 6s.*

'Ruston is drawn with extraordinary skill, and Maggie Dennison with many subtle strokes. The minor characters are clear cut. In short the book is a brilliant one. "The God in the Car" is one of the most remarkable works in a year that has given us the handiwork of nearly all our best living novelists.'—*Standard.*

'A very remarkable book, deserving of critical analysis impossible within our limit ; brilliant, but not superficial ; well considered, but not elaborated ; constructed with the proverbial art that conceals, but yet allows itself to be enjoyed by readers to whom fine literary method is a keen pleasure ; true without cynicism, subtle without affectation, humorous without strain, witty without offence, inevitably sad, with an unmorose simplicity.'— *The World.*

Anthony Hope. A CHANGE OF AIR. By ANTHONY HOPE, Author of 'The Prisoner of Zenda,' etc. *Second Edition. Crown 8vo. 6s.*

'A graceful, vivacious comedy, true to human nature. The characters are traced with a masterly hand.'—*Times.*

Anthony Hope. A MAN OF MARK. By ANTHONY HOPE, Author of 'The Prisoner of Zenda,' 'The God in the Car,' etc. *Second Edition. Crown 8vo. 6s.*

'A bright, entertaining, unusually able book, quite worthy of its brilliant author.'—*Queen.*

'Of all Mr. Hope's books, "A Man of Mark" is the one which best compares with "The Prisoner of Zenda." The two romances are unmistakably the work of the same writer, and he possesses a style of narrative peculiarly seductive, piquant, comprehensive, and—his own.'—*National Observer.*

Conan Doyle. ROUND THE RED LAMP. By A. CONAN DOYLE, Author of 'The White Company,' 'The Adventures of Sherlock Holmes,' etc. *Fourth Edition. Crown 8vo. 6s.*

'The book is, indeed, composed of leaves from life, and is far and away the best view that has been vouchsafed us behind the scenes of the consulting-room. It is very superior to "The Diary of a late Physician."'—*Illustrated London News.*

'Dr. Doyle wields a cunning pen, as all the world now knows. His deft touch is seen to perfection in these short sketches—these "facts and fancies of medical life," as he calls them. Every page reveals the literary artist, the keen observer, the trained delineator of human nature, its weal and its woe.'—*Freeman's Journal.*
'These tales are skilful, attractive, and eminently suited to give relief to the mind of a reader in quest of distraction.'—*Athenæum.*

Stanley Weyman. UNDER THE RED ROBE. By STANLEY WEYMAN, Author of 'A Gentleman of France.' With Twelve Illustrations by R. Caton Woodville. *Seventh Edition. Crown 8vo. 6s.*

A cheaper edition of a book which won instant popularity. No unfavourable review occurred, and most critics spoke in terms of enthusiastic admiration. The 'Westminster Gazette' called it '*a book of which we have read every word for the sheer pleasure of reading, and which we put down with a pang that we cannot forget it all and start again.*' The 'Daily Chronicle' said that '*every one who reads books at all must read this thrilling romance, from the first page of which to the last the breathless reader is haled along.*' It also called the book '*an inspiration of manliness and courage.*' The 'Globe' called it '*a delightful tale of chivalry and adventure, vivid and dramatic, with a wholesome modesty and reverence for the highest.*'

Emily Lawless. MAELCHO : a Sixteenth Century Romance. By the Hon. EMILY LAWLESS, Author of 'Grania,' 'Hurrish,' etc. *Second Edition. Crown 8vo. 6s.*

'A striking and delightful book. A task something akin to Scott's may lie before Miss Lawless. If she carries forward this series of historical pictures with the same brilliancy and truth she has already shown, and with the increasing self-control one may expect from the genuine artist, she may do more for her country than many a politician. Throughout this fascinating book, Miss Lawless has produced something which is not strictly history and is not strictly fiction, but nevertheless possesses both imaginative value and historical insight in a high degree.'—*Times.*
'A really great book.'—*Spectator.*
'There is no keener pleasure in life than the recognition of genius. Good work is commoner than it used to be, but the best is as rare as ever. All the more gladly, therefore, do we welcome in "Maelcho" a piece of work of the first order, which we do not hesitate to describe as one of the most remarkable literary achievements of this generation. Miss Lawless is possessed of the very essence of historical genius.'—*Manchester Guardian.*

E. F. Benson. DODO : A DETAIL OF THE DAY. By E. F. BENSON. *Crown 8vo. Sixteenth Edition. 6s.*

A story of society which attracted by its brilliance universal attention. The best critics were cordial in their praise. The 'Guardian' spoke of 'Dodo' as '*unusually clever and interesting*'; the 'Spectator' called it '*a delightfully witty sketch of society*;' the 'Speaker' said the dialogue was '*a perpetual feast of epigram and paradox*'; the 'Athenæum' spoke of the author as '*a writer of quite exceptional ability*' ; the 'Academy' praised his '*amazing cleverness*;' the 'World' said the book was '*brilliantly written*'; and half-a-dozen papers declared there was '*not a dull page in the book.*'

E. F Benson. THE RUBICON. By E. F. BENSON, Author of 'Dodo.' *Fourth Edition. Crown 8vo. 6s.*

Of Mr. Benson's second novel the 'Birmingham Post' says it is '*well written, stimulating, unconventional, and, in a word, characteristic*': the 'National Observer' congratulates Mr. Benson upon '*an exceptional achievement,*' and calls the book '*a notable advance on his previous work.*'

M. M. Dowie. GALLIA. By MÉNIE MURIEL DOWIE, Author of 'A Girl in the Carpathians.' *Second Edition. Crown 8vo. 6s.*

'The style is generally admirable, the dialogue not seldom brilliant, the situations surprising in their freshness and originality, while the subsidiary as well as the principal characters live and move, and the story itself is readable from title-page to colophon.'—*Saturday Review.*

'A very notable book; a very sympathetically, at times delightfully written book.' —*Daily Graphic.*

MR. BARING GOULD'S NOVELS

'To say that a book is by the author of "Mehalah" is to imply that it contains a story cast on strong lines, containing dramatic possibilities, vivid and sympathetic descriptions of Nature, and a wealth of ingenious imagery.'—*Speaker.*

'That whatever Mr. Baring Gould writes is well worth reading, is a conclusion that may be very generally accepted. His views of life are fresh and vigorous, his language pointed and characteristic, the incidents of which he makes use are striking and original, his characters are life-like, and though somewhat exceptional people, are drawn and coloured with artistic force. Add to this that his descriptions of scenes and scenery are painted with the loving eyes and skilled hands of a master of his art, that he is always fresh and never dull, and under such conditions it is no wonder that readers have gained confidence both in his power of amusing and satisfying them, and that year by year his popularity widens.'—*Court Circular.*

Baring Gould. URITH: A Story of Dartmoor. By S. BARING GOULD. *Third Edition. Crown 8vo. 6s.*

'The author is at his best.'—*Times.*

'He has nearly reached the high water-mark of "Mehalah."'—*National Observer.*

Baring Gould. IN THE ROAR OF THE SEA: A Tale of the Cornish Coast. By S. BARING GOULD. *Fifth Edition. 6s.*

Baring Gould. MRS. CURGENVEN OF CURGENVEN. By S. BARING GOULD. *Fourth Edition. 6s.*

A story of Devon life. The 'Graphic' speaks of it as '*a novel of vigorous humour and sustained power*'; the 'Sussex Daily News' says that '*the swing of the narrative is splendid*'; and the 'Speaker' mentions its '*bright imaginative power.*'

Baring Gould. CHEAP JACK ZITA. By S. BARING GOULD. *Third Edition. Crown 8vo. 6s.*

A Romance of the Ely Fen District in 1815, which the 'Westminster Gazette' calls '*a powerful drama of human passion*'; and the 'National Observer' '*a story worthy the author.*'

Baring Gould. THE QUEEN OF LOVE. By S. BARING GOULD. *Third Edition. Crown 8vo. 6s.*

The 'Glasgow Herald' says that '*the scenery is admirable, and the dramatic incidents are most striking.*' The 'Westminster Gazette' calls the book '*strong, interesting, and clever.*' 'Punch' says that '*you cannot put it down until you have finished it.*' 'The Sussex Daily News' says the it '*can be heartily recommended to all who care for cleanly, energetic, and interesting fiction.*'

Baring Gould. KITTY ALONE. By S. BARING GOULD, Author of 'Mehalah,' 'Cheap Jack Zita,' etc. *Fourth Edition. Crown 8vo. 6s.*

'A strong and original story, teeming with graphic description, stirring incident, and, above all, with vivid and enthralling human interest.'—*Daily Telegraph.*
'Brisk, clever, keen, healthy, humorous, and interesting.'—*National Observer.*
'Full of quaint and delightful studies of character.'—*Bristol Mercury.*

Mrs. Oliphant. SIR ROBERT'S FORTUNE. By MRS. OLIPHANT. *Crown 8vo. 6s.*

'Full of her own peculiar charm of style and simple, subtle character-painting comes her new gift, the delightful story before us. The scene mostly lies in the moors, and at the touch of the authoress a Scotch moor becomes a living thing, strong, tender, beautiful, and changeful. The book will take rank among the best of Mrs. Oliphant's good stories.'—*Pall Mall Gazette.*

W. E. Norris. MATTHEW AUSTIN. By W. E. NORRIS, Author of 'Mademoiselle de Mersac,' etc. *Third Edition. Crown 8vo. 6s.*

'"Matthew Austin" may safely be pronounced one of the most intellectually satisfactory and morally bracing novels of the current year.'—*Daily Telegraph.*
'Mr. W. E. Norris is always happy in his delineation of every-day experiences, but rarely has he been brighter or breezier than in "Matthew Austin." The pictures are in Mr. Norris's pleasantest vein, while running through the entire story is a felicity of style and wholesomeness of tone which one is accustomed to find in the novels of this favourite author.'—*Scotsman.*

W. E. Norris. HIS GRACE. By W. E. NORRIS, Author of 'Mademoiselle de Mersac.' *Third Edition. Crown 8vo. 6s.*

'Mr. Norris has drawn a really fine character in the Duke of Hurstbourne, at once unconventional and very true to the conventionalities of life, weak and strong in a breath, capable of inane follies and heroic decisions, yet not so definitely portrayed as to relieve a reader of the necessity of study on his own behalf.'—*Athenæum.*

W. E. Norris. THE DESPOTIC LADY AND OTHERS. By W. E. NORRIS, Author of 'Mademoiselle de Mersac.' *Crown 8vo. 6s.*

'A delightfully humorous tale of a converted and rehabilitated rope-dancer.'—*Glasgow Herald.*
'The ingenuity of the idea, the skill with which it is worked out, and the sustained humour of its situations, make it after its own manner a veritable little masterpiece.'—*Westminster Gazette.*
'A budget of good fiction of which no one will tire.'—*Scotsman.*
'An extremely entertaining volume—the sprightliest of holiday companions.'—*Daily Telegraph.*

Gilbert Parker. MRS. FALCHION. By GILBERT PARKER, Author of 'Pierre and His People.' *Second Edition. Crown 8vo. 6s.*

Mr. Parker's second book has received a warm welcome. The 'Athenæum' called it '*a splendid study of character*'; the 'Pall Mall Gazette' spoke of the writing as '*but little behind anything that has been done by any writer of our time*'; the 'St. James's' called it '*a very striking and admirable novel*'; and the 'Westminster Gazette' applied to it the epithet of '*distinguished.*'

Gilbert Parker. PIERRE AND HIS PEOPLE. By GILBERT PARKER. *Second Edition. Crown 8vo. 6s.*

'Stories happily conceived and finely executed. There is strength and genius in Mr. Parker's style.'—*Daily Telegraph.*

Gilbert Parker. THE TRANSLATION OF A SAVAGE. By GILBERT PARKER, Author of 'Pierre and His People,' 'Mrs. Falchion,' etc. *Crown 8vo. 6s.*

'The plot is original and one difficult to work out; but Mr. Parker has done it with great skill and delicacy. The reader who is not interested in this original, fresh, and well-told tale must be a dull person indeed.'—*Daily Chronicle.*

'A strong and successful piece of workmanship. The portrait of Lali, strong, dignified, and pure, is exceptionally well drawn.'—*Manchester Guardian.*

'A very pretty and interesting story, and Mr. Parker tells it with much skill. The story is one to be read.'—*St. James's Gazette.*

Gilbert Parker. THE TRAIL OF THE SWORD. By GILBERT PARKER, Author of 'Pierre and his People,' etc. *Third Edition. Crown 8vo. 6s.*

'Everybody with a soul for romance will thoroughly enjoy "The Trail of the Sword."'—*St. James's Gazette.*

'A rousing and dramatic tale. A book like this, in which swords flash, great surprises are undertaken, and daring deeds done, in which men and women live and love in the old straightforward passionate way, is a joy inexpressible to the reviewer, brain-weary of the domestic tragedies and psychological puzzles of everyday fiction; and we cannot but believe that to the reader it will bring refreshment as welcome and as keen.'—*Daily Chronicle.*

Gilbert Parker. WHEN VALMOND CAME TO PONTIAC: The Story of a Lost Napoleon. By GILBERT PARKER. *Second Edition. Crown 8vo. 6s.*

'Here we find romance—real, breathing, living romance, but it runs flush with our own times, level with our own feelings. Not here can we complain of lack of inevitableness or homogeneity. The character of Valmond is drawn unerringly; his career, brief as it is, is placed before us as convincingly as history itself. The book must be read, we may say re-read, for any one thoroughly to appreciate Mr. Parker's delicate touch and innate sympathy with humanity.'—*Pall Mall Gazette.*

Arthur Morrison. TALES OF MEAN STREETS. By ARTHUR MORRISON. *Third Edition. Crown 8vo. 6s.*

'Told with consummate art and extraordinary detail. He tells a plain, unvarnished tale, and the very truth of it makes for beauty. In the true humanity of the book lies its justification, the permanence of its interest, and its indubitable triumph.'—*Athenæum.*

'A great book. The author's method is amazingly effective, and produces a thrilling sense of reality. The writer lays upon us a master hand. The book is simply appalling and irresistible in its interest. It is humorous also; without humour it would not make the mark it is certain to make.'—*World.*

Julian Corbett. A BUSINESS IN GREAT WATERS. By JULIAN CORBETT, Author of 'For God and Gold,' 'Kophetua XIIIth.,' etc. *Crown 8vo. 6s.*

'There is plenty of incident and movement in this romance. It is interesting as a novel framed in an historical setting, and it is all the more worthy of attention from the lover of romance as being absolutely free from the morbid, the frivolous, and the ultra-sexual.'—*Athenæum.*

'A stirring tale of naval adventure during the Great French War. The book is full of picturesque and attractive characters.'—*Glasgow Herald.*

Robert Barr. IN THE MIDST OF ALARMS. By ROBERT BARR, Author of 'From Whose Bourne,' etc. *Second Edition. Crown 8vo. 6s.*

'A book which has abundantly satisfied us by its capital humour.'—*Daily Chronicle.*
'Mr. Barr has achieved a triumph whereof he has every reason to be proud.'—*Pall Mall Gazette.*
'There is a quaint thought or a good joke on nearly every page. The studies of character are carefully finished, and linger in the memory.'—*Black and White.*
'Distinguished for kindly feeling, genuine humour, and really graphic portraiture.' —*Sussex Daily News.*
'A delightful romance, with experiences strange and exciting. The dialogue is always bright and witty; the scenes are depicted briefly and effectively; and there is no incident from first to last that one would wish to have omitted.'— *Scotsman.*

Mrs. Pinsent. CHILDREN OF THIS WORLD. By ELLEN F. PINSENT, Author of 'Jenny's Case.' *Crown 8vo. 6s.*

'There is much clever writing in this book. The story is told in a workmanlike manner, and the characters conduct themselves like average human beings.'— *Daily News.*
'Full of interest, and, with a large measure of present excellence, gives ample promise of splendid work.'—*Birmingham Gazette.*
'Mrs. Pinsent's new novel has plenty of vigour, variety, and good writing. There are certainty of purpose, strength of touch, and clearness of vision.'—*Athenæum.*

Clark Russell. MY DANISH SWEETHEART. By W. CLARK RUSSELL, Author of 'The Wreck of the Grosvenor,' etc. *Illustrated. Third Edition. Crown 8vo. 6s.*

Pryce. TIME AND THE WOMAN. By RICHARD PRYCE, Author of 'Miss Maxwell's Affections,' 'The Quiet Mrs. Fleming,' etc. *Second Edition. Crown 8vo. 6s.*

'Mr. Pryce's work recalls the style of Octave Feuillet, by its clearness, conciseness, its literary reserve.'—*Athenæum.*

Mrs. Watson. THIS MAN'S DOMINION. By the Author of 'A High Little World.' *Second Edition. Crown 8vo. 6s.*

'It is not a book to be read and forgotten on a railway journey, but it is rather a study of the perplexing problems of life, to which the reflecting mind will frequently return, even though the reader does not accept the solutions which the author suggests. In these days, when the output of merely amusing novels is so overpowering, this is no slight praise. There is an underlying depth in the story which reminds one, in a lesser degree, of the profundity of George Eliot, and "This Man's Dominion" is by no means a novel to be thrust aside as exhausted at one perusal.'—*Dundee Advertiser.*

Marriott Watson. DIOGENES OF LONDON and other Sketches. By H. B. MARRIOTT WATSON, Author of 'The Web of the Spider.' *Crown 8vo. Buckram. 6s.*

'By all those who delight in the uses of words, who rate the exercise of prose above the exercise of verse, who rejoice in all proofs of its delicacy and its strength, who believe that English prose is chief among the moulds of thought, by these Mr. Marriott Watson's book will be welcomed.'—*National Observer.*

Gilchrist. THE STONE DRAGON. By MURRAY GILCHRIST.
Crown 8vo. Buckram. 6s.
'The author's faults are atoned for by certain positive and admirable merits. The
romances have not their counterpart in modern literature, and to read them is a
unique experience.'—*National Observer.*

THREE-AND-SIXPENNY NOVELS

Edna Lyall. DERRICK VAUGHAN, NOVELIST. By
EDNA LYALL, Author of 'Donovan,' etc. *Forty-first Thousand.*
Crown 8vo. 3s. 6d.

Baring Gould. ARMINELL: A Social Romance. By S.
BARING GOULD. *New Edition. Crown 8vo. 3s. 6d.*

Baring Gould. MARGERY OF QUETHER, and other Stories.
By S. BARING GOULD. *Crown 8vo. 3s. 6d.*

Baring Gould. JACQUETTA, and other Stories. By S. BARING
GOULD. *Crown 8vo. 3s. 6d.*

Miss Benson. SUBJECT TO VANITY. By MARGARET
BENSON. *With numerous Illustrations. Second Edition. Crown
8vo. 3s. 6d.*
'A charming little book about household pets by a daughter of the Archbishop of
Canterbury.'—*Speaker.*
'A delightful collection of studies of animal nature. It is very seldom that we get
anything so perfect in its kind. . . . The illustrations are clever, and the whole
book a singularly delightful one.'—*Guardian.*
'Humorous and sentimental by turns, Miss Benson always manages to interest us
in her pets, and all who love animals will appreciate her book, not only for their
sake, but quite as much for its own.'—*Times.*
'All lovers of animals should read Miss Benson's book. For sympathetic understanding, humorous criticism, and appreciative observation she certainly has not
her equal.'—*Manchester Guardian.*

Gray. ELSA. A Novel. By E. M'QUEEN GRAY. *Crown 8vo.
3s. 6d.*
'A charming novel. The characters are not only powerful sketches, but minutely
and carefully finished portraits.'—*Guardian.*

J. H. Pearce. JACO TRELOAR. By J. H. PEARCE, Author of
'Esther Pentreath.' *New Edition. Crown 8vo. 3s. 6d.*
The 'Spectator' speaks of Mr. Pearce as '*a writer of exceptional power*'; the 'Daily
Telegraph' calls the book '*powerful and picturesque*'; the 'Birmingham Post'
asserts that it is '*a novel of high quality.*'

X. L. AUT DIABOLUS AUT NIHIL, and Other Stories.
By X. L. *Crown 8vo. 3s. 6d.*
'Distinctly original and in the highest degree imaginative. The conception is almost
as lofty as Milton's.'—*Spectator.*
'Original to a degree of originality that may be called primitive—a kind of passion-
ate directness that absolutely absorbs us.'—*Saturday Review.*
'Of powerful interest. There is something startlingly original in the treatment of the
themes. The terrible realism leaves no doubt of the author's power.'—*Athenæum.*

O'Grady. THE COMING OF CUCULAIN. A Romance of the Heroic Age of Ireland. By STANDISH O'GRADY, Author of 'Finn and his Companions,' etc. Illustrated by MURRAY SMITH. *Crown 8vo. 3s. 6d.*

'The suggestions of mystery, the rapid and exciting action, are superb poetic effects.' —*Speaker.*

'For light and colour it resembles nothing so much as a Swiss dawn.'—*Manchester Guardian.*

'A romance extremely fascinating and admirably well knit.'—*Saturday Review.*

Constance Smith. A CUMBERER OF THE GROUND. By CONSTANCE SMITH, Author of 'The Repentance of Paul Wentworth,' etc. *New Edition. Crown 8vo. 3s. 6d.*

Author of 'Vera.' THE DANCE OF THE HOURS. By the Author of 'Vera.' *Crown 8vo. 3s. 6d.*

Esmè Stuart. A WOMAN OF FORTY. By ESMÈ STUART, Author of 'Muriel's Marriage,' 'Virginié's Husband,' etc. *New Edition. Crown 8vo. 3s. 6d.*

'The story is well written, and some of the scenes show great dramatic power.'— *Daily Chronicle.*

Fenn. THE STAR GAZERS. By G. MANVILLE FENN, Author of 'Eli's Children,' etc. *New Edition. Cr. 8vo. 3s. 6d.*

'A stirring romance.'—*Western Morning News.*

'Told with all the dramatic power for which Mr. Fenn is conspicuous.'—*Bradford Observer.*

Dickinson. A VICAR'S WIFE. By EVELYN DICKINSON. *Crown 8vo. 3s. 6d.*

Prowse. THE POISON OF ASPS. By R. ORTON PROWSE. *Crown 8vo. 3s. 6d.*

Grey. THE STORY OF CHRIS. By ROWLAND GREY. *Crown 8vo. 5s.*

Lynn Linton. THE TRUE HISTORY OF JOSHUA DAVIDSON, Christian and Communist. By E. LYNN LINTON. *Eleventh Edition. Post 8vo. 1s.*

HALF-CROWN NOVELS

A Series of Novels by popular Authors.

2/6

1. THE PLAN OF CAMPAIGN. By F. MABEL ROBINSON.
2. DISENCHANTMENT. By F. MABEL ROBINSON.
3. MR. BUTLER'S WARD. By F. MABEL ROBINSON.
4. HOVENDEN, V.C. By F. MABEL ROBINSON.
5. ELI'S CHILDREN. By G. MANVILLE FENN.
6. A DOUBLE KNOT. By G. MANVILLE FENN.
7. DISARMED. By M. BETHAM EDWARDS.

8. A LOST ILLUSION. By LESLIE KEITH.
9. A MARRIAGE AT SEA. By W. CLARK RUSSELL.
10. IN TENT AND BUNGALOW. By the Author of 'Indian Idylls.'
11. MY STEWARDSHIP. By E. M'QUEEN GRAY.
12. A REVEREND GENTLEMAN. By J. M. COBBAN.
13. A DEPLORABLE AFFAIR. By W. E. NORRIS.
14. JACK'S FATHER. By W. E. NORRIS.
15. A CAVALIER'S LADYE. By Mrs. DICKER.
16. JIM B.

Books for Boys and Girls

A Series of Books by well-known Authors, well illustrated.
Crown 8vo.

3|6

1. THE ICELANDER'S SWORD. By S. BARING GOULD.
2. TWO LITTLE CHILDREN AND CHING. By EDITH E. CUTHELL.
3. TODDLEBEN'S HERO. By M. M. BLAKE.
4. ONLY A GUARD-ROOM DOG. By EDITH E. CUTHELL.
5. THE DOCTOR OF THE JULIET. By HARRY COLLING-WOOD.
6. MASTER ROCKAFELLAR'S VOYAGE. By W. CLARK RUSSELL.
7. SYD BELTON : Or, The Boy who would not go to Sea. By G. MANVILLE FENN.

The Peacock Library

A Series of Books for Girls by well-known Authors,
handsomely bound in blue and silver, and well illustrated.
Crown 8vo.

3|6

1. A PINCH OF EXPERIENCE. By L. B. WALFORD.
2. THE RED GRANGE. By Mrs. MOLESWORTH.
3. THE SECRET OF MADAME DE MONLUC. By the Author of 'Mdle Mori.'
4. DUMPS. By Mrs. PARR, Author of 'Adam and Eve.'
5. OUT OF THE FASHION. By L. T. MEADE.
6. A GIRL OF THE PEOPLE. By L. T. MEADE.
7. HEPSY GIPSY. By L. T. MEADE. 2s. 6d.
8. THE HONOURABLE MISS. By L. T. MEADE.
9. MY LAND OF BEULAH. By Mrs. LEITH ADAMS.

University Extension Series

A series of books on historical, literary, and scientific subjects, suitable for extension students and home reading circles. Each volume is complete in itself, and the subjects are treated by competent writers in a broad and philosophic spirit.

Edited by J. E. SYMES, M.A.,

Principal of University College, Nottingham.

Crown 8vo. Price (with some exceptions) 2s. 6d.

The following volumes are ready :—

THE INDUSTRIAL HISTORY OF ENGLAND. By H. DE B. GIBBINS, M.A., late Scholar of Wadham College, Oxon., Cobden Prizeman. *Fourth Edition. With Maps and Plans.* 3s.

'A compact and clear story of our industrial development. A study of this concise but luminous book cannot fail to give the reader a clear insight into the principal phenomena of our industrial history. The editor and publishers are to be congratulated on this first volume of their venture, and we shall look with expectant interest for the succeeding volumes of the series. —*University Extension Journal.*

A HISTORY OF ENGLISH POLITICAL ECONOMY. By L. L. PRICE, M.A., Fellow of Oriel College, Oxon.

PROBLEMS OF POVERTY: An Inquiry into the Industrial Conditions of the Poor. By J. A. HOBSON, M.A. *Second Edition.*

VICTORIAN POETS. By A. SHARP.

THE FRENCH REVOLUTION. By J. E. SYMES, M.A.

PSYCHOLOGY. By F. S. GRANGER, M.A., Lecturer in Philosophy at University College, Nottingham.

THE EVOLUTION OF PLANT LIFE: Lower Forms. By G. MASSEE, Kew Gardens. *With Illustrations.*

AIR AND WATER. Professor V. B. LEWES, M.A. *Illustrated.*

THE CHEMISTRY OF LIFE AND HEALTH. By C. W. KIMMINS, M.A. Camb. *Illustrated.*

THE MECHANICS OF DAILY LIFE. By V. P. SELLS, M.A. *Illustrated.*

ENGLISH SOCIAL REFORMERS. H. DE B. GIBBINS, M.A.

ENGLISH TRADE AND FINANCE IN THE SEVEN-TEENTH CENTURY. By W. A. S. HEWINS, B.A.

THE CHEMISTRY OF FIRE. The Elementary Principles of Chemistry. By M. M. PATTISON MUIR, M.A. *Illustrated.*

A TEXT-BOOK OF AGRICULTURAL BOTANY. By M. C. POTTER, M.A., F.L.S. *Illustrated.* 3s. 6d.

THE VAULT OF HEAVEN. A Popular Introduction to Astronomy. By R. A. GREGORY. *With numerous Illustrations.*

METEOROLOGY. The Elements of Weather and Climate. By H. N. DICKSON, F.R.S.E., F.R. Met. Soc. *Illustrated.*

A MANUAL OF ELECTRICAL SCIENCE. By GEORGE J. BURCH, M.A. *With numerous Illustrations.* 3s.

THE EARTH. An Introduction to Physiography. By EVAN SMALL, M.A. *Illustrated.*

INSECT LIFE. By F. W. THEOBALD, M.A. *Illustrated.*

ENGLISH POETRY FROM BLAKE TO BROWNING. By W. M. DIXON, M.A.

ENGLISH LOCAL GOVERNMENT. By E JENKS, M.A., Professor of Law at University College, Liverpool.

Social Questions of To-day

Edited by H. DE B. GIBBINS, M.A.

Crown 8vo. 2s. 6d.

2/6

A series of volumes upon those topics of social, economic, and industrial interest that are at the present moment foremost in the public mind. Each volume of the series is written by an author who is an acknowledged authority upon the subject with which he deals.

The following Volumes of the Series are ready :—

TRADE UNIONISM—NEW AND OLD. By G. HOWELL, Author of ' The Conflicts of Capital and Labour.' *Second Edition.*

THE CO-OPERATIVE MOVEMENT TO-DAY. By G. J. HOLYOAKE, Author of ' The History of Co-operation.'

MUTUAL THRIFT. By Rev. J. FROME WILKINSON, M.A., Author of ' The Friendly Society Movement.'

PROBLEMS OF POVERTY : An Inquiry into the Industrial Conditions of the Poor. By J. A. HOBSON, M.A. *Second Edition.*

THE COMMERCE OF NATIONS. By C. F. BASTABLE, M.A., Professor of Economics at Trinity College, Dublin.

THE ALIEN INVASION. By W. H. WILKINS, B.A., Secretary to the Society for Preventing the Immigration of Destitute Aliens.

THE RURAL EXODUS. By P. ANDERSON GRAHAM.

LAND NATIONALIZATION. By HAROLD COX, B.A.

A SHORTER WORKING DAY. By H. DE B. GIBBINS and R. A. HADFIELD, of the Hecla Works, Sheffield.

BACK TO THE LAND: An Inquiry into the Cure for Rural Depopulation. By H. E. MOORE.

TRUSTS, POOLS AND CORNERS: As affecting Commerce and Industry. By J. STEPHEN JEANS, M.R.I., F.S.S.

THE FACTORY SYSTEM. By R. COOKE TAYLOR.

THE STATE AND ITS CHILDREN. By GERTRUDE TUCKWELL.

WOMEN'S WORK. By LADY DILKE, MISS BULLEY, and MISS WHITLEY.

MUNICIPALITIES AT WORK. The Municipal Policy of Six Great Towns, and its Influence on their Social Welfare. By FREDERICK DOLMAN. With an Introduction by Sir JOHN HUTTON, late Chairman of the London County Council. *Crown 8vo. Cloth. 2s. 6d.*

Classical Translations

Edited by H. F. FOX, M.A., Fellow and Tutor of Brasenose College, Oxford.

Messrs. Methuen propose to issue a New Series of Translations from the Greek and Latin Classics. They have enlisted the services of some of the best Oxford and Cambridge Scholars, and it is their intention that the Series shall be distinguished by literary excellence as well as by scholarly accuracy.

Crown 8vo. Finely printed and bound in blue buckram.

CICERO—De Oratore I. Translated by E. N. P. MOOR, M.A., Assistant Master at Clifton. *3s. 6d.*

ÆSCHYLUS—Agamemnon, Chöephoroe, Eumenides. Translated by LEWIS CAMPBELL, LL.D., late Professor of Greek at St. Andrews. *5s.*

LUCIAN—Six Dialogues (Nigrinus, Icaro-Menippus, The Cock, The Ship, The Parasite, The Lover of Falsehood). Translated by S. T. IRWIN, M.A., Assistant Master at Clifton; late Scholar of Exeter College, Oxford. *3s. 6d.*

SOPHOCLES—Electra and Ajax. Translated by E. D. A. MORSHEAD, M.A., late Scholar of New College, Oxford; Assistant Master at Winchester. *2s. 6d.*

TACITUS—Agricola and Germania. Translated by R. B. TOWNSHEND, late Scholar of Trinity College, Cambridge. *2s. 6d.*

CICERO—Select Orations (Pro Milone, Pro Murena, Philippic II., In Catilinam). Translated by H. E. D. BLAKISTON, M.A., Fellow and Tutor of Trinity College, Oxford. *5s.*